MY LADY

"Detective Beaumont has been trying to find you since yesterday," social worker Alice Fields said. "Something terrible has happened, LeAnn. Your husband is dead."

For several long seconds, we sat there quietly.

"You're kidding," LeAnn said at last. She turned to me. "Is it true?" she asked.

"Yes, Mrs. Nielsen," I answered. "I'm afraid it is. He was murdered in his office."

Tears sprang to her eyes. She put one hand to her mouth to stifle a sob, but the wail that escaped her lips wasn't a cry so much as it was a laugh, a strangled, hyenalike, hysterical laugh.

The very sound of it made my blood run cold.

J. P. Beaumont Mysteries by
J. A. Jance

UNTIL PROVEN GUILTY
INJUSTICE FOR ALL
TRIAL BY FURY
TAKING THE FIFTH
A MORE PERFECT UNION
DISMISSED WITH PREJUDICE
MINOR IN POSSESSION
PAYMENT IN KIND
WITHOUT DUE PROCESS
FAILURE TO APPEAR
LYING IN WAIT
NAME WITHHELD

Joanna Brady Mysteries by
J. A. Jance

DESERT HEAT
TOMBSTONE COURAGE
SHOOT/DON'T SHOOT
DEAD TO RIGHTS
SKELETON CANYON

and

HOUR OF THE HUNTER

And in Hardcover

RATTLESNAKE CROSSING

J.A. JANCE

IMPROBABLE CAUSE

AVON BOOKS NEW YORK

This is a work of fiction. Names, characters, places, and incidents either are the product of the author's imagination or are used fictitiously. Any resemblance to actual events, locales, organizations, or persons, living or dead, is entirely coincidental and beyond the intent of either the author or the publisher.

AVON BOOKS, INC.
1350 Avenue of the Americas
New York, New York 10019

Inside cover author photo by Jerry Bauer
Published by arrangement with the author
Visit our website at **www.AvonBooks.com**
Library of Congress Catalog Card Number: 87-91701
ISBN: 0-380-75412-6

First Avon Books Printing: February 1988

AVON TRADEMARK REG. U.S. PAT. OFF. AND IN OTHER COUNTRIES, MARCA REGISTRADA, HECHO EN U.S.A.

Printed in the U.S.A.

WCD 20

This book could not have been written
without the help of many different people,
but it is dedicated to three of them:

To Gary,
the finest of Seattle's Finest,
To Carol,
a criminalist who is not a criminologist,
and
To Andrea,
the only real live Woodland Park docent I know.

CHAPTER 1

"What we've got here this morning," Dr. Howard Baker announced somewhat pompously to the crowd of reporters assembled in the small dental office's waiting room, "what we've got here is one dead dentist."

Doc Baker, King County's medical examiner, is a political type who likes to be quotable, no matter what. And Seattle's eager newshounds, packed like so many note-taking sardines in the impeccably decorated reception area, were only too happy to oblige. They responded with an enthusiastic clicking and whirring of various audio and video recording devices.

As I pushed my way into the room, the news-gathering sounds annoyed me. I can't help it. My name is J. P. Beaumont. As a detective with the Seattle Police Department Homicide Squad, I resent it when reporters manage to beat detectives to a crime scene.

Doc Baker was holding forth and waxing eloquent. He's an irascible old bear of a man with a full head of white hair who enjoys seizing the limelight. He towered over the rowdy group of reporters milling around him. Eventually, though, he caught sight of me standing on the edge of the crowd along with my partner, Detective Allen Lindstrom—Big Al, as he's known around homicide on the fifth floor of Seattle's Public Safety Building.

"The homicide detectives are here now," Baker informed the reporters. "You'll have to excuse us." With that, he turned on his heel and disappeared through a door that led to a short hallway, imperiously motioning for us to follow. Doc Baker can be somewhat overbearing on occasion.

There was a short silence after Baker left the room, a silence punctuated by the sound of a woman crying. The muffled noise originated from behind a closed door just to the right of the receptionist's desk. There was no time to check it out, however. Doc Baker didn't give us that much slack.

"Hey, Beaumont, Lindstrom," he bellowed back down that hall. "Are you coming or not?"

Big Al started moving, his physical bulk mowing a pathway through the crush of reporters. I hurried along in his wake before the narrow opening closed behind him.

The moment we entered the hallway, I knew it was going to be bad. I recognized the faint, telltale stench of decaying flesh only too well.

The waiting room had smelled distinctly of fresh paint and new carpet overlaid with the suffocating scent of some female reporter's exotic, pungent perfume. But the hallway held a different odor, one that became stronger as we neared one of two swinging doors at the end of it. When Al pushed it open, a blast of gagging odor hit us full in the face.

My years on the force have taught me to prefer my murder victims fresh—the fresher the better. This one wasn't. The body had been left unattended for far too long in the muggy summer heat of an unusually warm July.

I stepped through the swinging door only to be blinded by a sudden flash of light. When I could see again, I saw Nancy Gresham, a fairly new police photographer, snapping pictures of someone seated in a laid back, futuristic-looking dental examination chair.

Big Al Lindstrom got far enough around the chair to see what was in it. He stopped short. "Jesus!" he muttered.

I was right behind him. I guess I've seen

worse, but I don't remember when.

It was every kid's worst nightmare of what might happen once you wind up in a dentist's chair. The man's eyes were open and his mouth agape. He looked like a terrified patient waiting for some crazed dentist to start drilling and blasting. But below the open mouth, below the slack chin, was a second opening, a small, round, ugly wound through which the man's lifeblood had drained away.

And there was a surprisingly large amount of it. Blood had soaked down through his clothing and dripped off both sides of the chair, where a dark brown stain etched the outline of the chair's contours into plush, snowy white carpet. Blurred, bloody footprints led back and forth across the rug.

"Why the hell would anyone bother to put a white carpet in a dentist's office?" Big Al demanded. "Seems pretty stupid to me."

"Stupid or not, he never had a chance to enjoy it," Doc Baker said. "Looks like he croaked before whoever was installing the carpet managed to finish the job."

"Excuse me, Detective Beaumont," Nancy Gresham said, coming up behind me and moving a little to one side. "I need a little more room."

She knelt on one shapely knee directly where I had been standing and aimed her camera up at the dead man's sagging face. Once more the camera flashed. I noted with some dismay that Nancy Gresham no longer turned green at the prospect of taking grisly pictures. It was too bad. I had liked her better before she toughened up.

I glanced around the room. A plastic garbage can was tipped on its side. A stainless steel tray with an assortment of dental tools beneath and around it lay on the floor. A large plant in a blue and white crock had been knocked off a counter. The crock had broken into three large pieces, and muddy dirt lay scattered on the floor. My professional assessment was that a hell of a fight had taken place in that room. Mentally I took in all the visual information, but I returned to Doc Baker's comment.

"What makes you say the carpeting job wasn't finished?" I asked.

He raised one bushy eyebrow. "Look," he answered, pointing toward a corner of the room. "The molding's still loose."

I followed his pointing finger. Sure enough, there in the corner several long pieces of oak molding leaned upright against the wall.

"Knee-kicker's there too," Baker added.

Carefully avoiding the bloody footprints, I stepped over to the corner. On the floor beside the molding lay a carpet kicker—a wickedly toothed, five-pound metal tool with a leather cushion on one end. I had seen one like it a few months earlier when carpet installers had laid the carpet in my new condominium. I had watched them shove the sharp metal teeth deep into the carpet's pile; then they pounded their knees against the leather cushion to stretch the rug taut and attach it to the tack strips that lined the room. One of the installers told me that in his business the knees are the first to go.

Without touching it, I bent down to examine the kicker. A dozen or more inch-and-a-half-long metal teeth stuck out of the business end of the kicker. Three of them—the ones on the upper left-hand corner—were covered with something brown, something that looked suspiciously like blood.

"Hey, Al," I said, straightening up. "Come look at this."

It was then I noticed several long curving parallel gouges in the freshly painted finish on the wallboard, scratches that ended only inches from the sharp teeth of the kicker.

Big Al and Doc Baker both came to see what I had found.

"Murder weapon maybe?" Al asked.

"No way," Baker answered. "The hole in his throat is from a single sharp implement. That thing would have turned his throat into a goddamned computer punch card."

"I'm finished," Nancy Gresham announced.

Baker turned to her and nodded. "Good. Wait outside just in case I need anything else."

"I heard you telling the reporters this guy was a dentist. How do you know that?" I asked.

"His receptionist identified him. She found him about nine this morning when she came in to work."

"That's who's crying in the office down the hall? The receptionist?" I asked. "We heard her as we came past."

Again Baker nodded. "I told her to go in there and wait, that you'd need to talk to her when you got here."

"What's the dentist's name?" Al had taken out a notebook and stood waiting with his pencil poised to write.

"Nielsen," the medical examiner replied. "Dr. Frederick Nielsen. He's been dead a day or two, from the looks of things."

"And the smell," Al added. "What about this receptionist? Who's she?"

"Rush. Said her name is Debi Rush." Doc Baker spelled out the receptionist's first name. Al and I both wrote it down.

Just then a pair of crime-scene investigators bustled into the room. Bill Foster tackled

Baker. "Hey, Doc, are you guys just about done so we can get started?"

"You bet. Give us a couple of minutes to get him packed up and out of here. Then the place is all yours."

Baker summoned two of his waiting technicians to remove the body. I didn't envy them their odious task. I motioned to Al. "What say we get out of here and go talk to the receptionist?"

Big Al Lindstrom leaped at my suggestion. He was just as anxious as I was to get away from the gagging stench. Grateful to breathe fresh air again, we retreated through the swinging door and hurried back down the hallway.

A uniformed police officer had pulled the plug and drained the reporters out of the waiting room. Arms crossed, he had taken up a position in front of the door. Except for the patrolman and Nancy Gresham, busily stowing her gear, the reception area was empty.

There was no longer any sound coming from beyond the closed door. I walked up to it and knocked.

"Who is it?" The woman's answering voice sounded strained and weak.

"Detectives Beaumont and Lindstrom with the Seattle Police Department, Miss Rush," I replied. "May we come in?"

The door opened slowly, tentatively. A buxom young brunette in a rumpled white uniform stood before us. Her eyes and nose were red from weeping. Streaks of makeup muddied her pale cheeks.

"Who are you?" she asked.

"Homicide detectives," I answered. "We're going to have to ask you a few questions. Do you mind?"

Debi Rush swayed dangerously like a tree buffeted by a strong wind. She clutched desperately at the doorknob for support. I caught her and helped her into a chair beside a pristine rosewood desk. For a few moments, she sat there with her face buried in her hands while violent shudders shook her entire body.

"It's all my fault," she whispered.

"I beg your pardon?"

"It's my fault," she repeated. "I never should have left them alone."

"Who?"

"Dr. Nielsen and that carpet installer. They were arguing when I left."

"About what?"

"He was late."

"Who was late?"

"The installer was. He was supposed to be here by the time our last patient left at ten-thirty Saturday morning, but he wasn't. Dr. Fred hated to be kept waiting. He was furious.

When the installer still didn't show by twelve, I offered to stay late, but Dr. Fred wouldn't hear of it. He said no, that I should go on home and he would wait. The guy came then, just as I was packing up to leave."

"This carpet installer," Big Al interjected. "What was his name?"

"Larry Martin. I wrote it down in the appointment book. He's from Damm Fine Carpets over on the other side of Queen Anne Hill. Down by the Fremont Bridge."

I nodded. "I know where that is," I said. "Go on."

"Dr. Fred lit into him. Said he had things to do, appointments to keep, that he couldn't afford to be kept waiting. He said he was going to call the carpet store and see to it that the installer was fired. And all the while the installer kept apologizing. He claimed that his first job that morning had run him late and that he was sorry." Debi Rush broke off abruptly.

"Go on," I urged.

"That's all," she said.

"What do you mean, that's all?"

"That's all I heard. I left after that."

"Where did you go?" I asked.

"Home," she answered dully.

But something in her manner had changed, ever so slightly, enough so that it caught my attention. Her answer had come just a hair too quickly.

"Where's home?" I asked.

"Over on Eastlake," she said, giving us the address. "It's cheap," she continued. "But it's the best we can do on my salary."

"We?"

"My husband and I. Tom's in the dental school at the University of Washington. Just two more years and he'll be done. Then he'll work and I'll stay home."

"You're helping him through school?"

Debi Rush smiled wanly and nodded. "Getting my PHT," she said. "Putting Hubby Through."

The tenor of her answer bothered me. It was pat and meant to be cute, but it was out of place on the lips of someone who had just been crying the way Debi Rush had been. And it bugged me that she felt obliged to explain it to us. It's an old joke, one that's been around longer than I have.

"So you're actually *Mrs*. Rush, then?"

She nodded.

"What happened this morning, Mrs. Rush?"

Faint color had crept back into her cheeks, but now it faded suddenly. "It was awful," she answered.

"Tell us about it. When did you get here?"

"Five to eight. The time I always do unless

the bus runs late. That was one of the things Dr. Fred insisted on. Be here on time or early. Don't be late."

"The office opened at eight?"

"Yes, although we usually didn't start booking patients until eight-thirty. The lights were on when I got here, but the door was locked. I assumed Dr. Fred must have come in and then gone back out for some reason."

"You didn't look in the back room?"

"No. I had plenty of work to do out here."

"And you didn't go down the hall?"

Debi Rush shook her head. "I started calling to confirm today's appointments. Then, just before the first patient was due, I went in to set up the tray."

"What time was that?"

"Twenty-five after eight. Around then, I guess."

"And that's when you found him?"

"God, it was awful! All that blood! I couldn't believe it. I mean, he was so alive the last time I saw him."

"What did you do?" I asked.

"I called 911."

"Right then?"

"I don't remember. It must have been right then."

"Our records show that the call came in at five to nine a half hour later."

Debi Rush looked at me in seeming disbelief. "A half hour? Really? Maybe I was in shock," she offered. "Or maybe I fainted or something. I don't remember. The first thing I do remember is the aid car showing up."

A two-toned bell chimed, telling us someone had entered the outer office. A moment later the uniformed officer knocked on the door. "Mrs. Rush, your husband is here."

"I asked him to come pick me up," Debi Rush told us. "I couldn't stand riding home on the bus, not today. Not after what's happened. Are we almost finished?"

I looked at Al Lindstrom, who was leaning casually against the wall near the door, his thick arms crossed. He shrugged. "Not quite," he answered.

She glanced at me. "We'll need a few more minutes," I told her.

Debi Rush got up and hurried out of the room. I glanced back at Big Al.

"She's lying," I said.

He nodded. "That's what I thought, too. Now all we've got to do is find out why."

That's really what this homicide job is all about. If we can figure out who's lying and why, we can usually find out who the killer is.

At least, that's how it's supposed to work.

CHAPTER 2

Anyone who's seen my desk will understand that I'm a longtime subscriber to the old adage that a clean desk is a sign of an cluttered mind. While Debi Rush was out of the room, I grabbed the opportunity to examine Dr. Frederick Nielsen's gleaming rosewood desk. It was remarkably clean. Disturbingly clean.

No absentminded doodle or marauding paper clip marred the unblemished green felt of Dr. Fred's ink blotter. The wooden surface was polished to a high gloss, and no speck of dust or smudge of fingerprint appeared on the shiny brass pen holder or the heavy marble ashtray which sat, side by side, at the top of the immaculate desk.

Six file folders with their name labels clearly visible lay in a deliberately cantilevered stack on the leather-framed blotter. On top of the files sat a neatly typed listing of the day's scheduled appointments, a detailed inventory of the patients and people Dr. Fred would have seen in the course of that Monday. If he hadn't died first.

So Dr. Frederick Nielsen had been a neat freak—either that, or downright compulsive. Behind the gleaming desk sat a matching rosewood credenza. On it were two wooden baskets marked IN and OUT. A stack of unopened envelopes waited in the IN basket while three additional file folders rested in the OUT. On top of those folders was another piece of paper, lying facedown. Using the tip of my pencil, I flipped the paper over. It proved to be an additional typed schedule, this one labeled Saturday, July 14.

Studying the schedule, I quickly jotted down the list of names and times into my notebook: 8:30 A.M., Grace Simmons, root canal. 9:00 A.M., Don Nuberg, two fillings. 10:00 A.M., Reece Bowers, cleaning. Beneath the patients' names were two more notations, one typed and the other handwritten. The typed one said, "10:30, Larry Martin, Damm Fine Carpets." The second, carefully printed in black ink, said nothing but "LeAnn."

As far as Dr. Nielsen was concerned, LeAnn evidently needed no last name to identify her.

It was safe to assume she wasn't a patient. Her name wasn't listed on any of the Saturday file folders in the OUT basket. According to the schedule, LeAnn had been due in the office at twelve, well after the carpet installer was supposed to have finished with the carpet, and after Debi Rush should have gone home.

Beneath LeAnn's name were several more notations, all in the same precise printing: shoes, groceries, tickets, flowers. Dr. Nielsen had evidently used the written schedule as a personal "to do" list as well as a tool for keeping track of his daily appointments.

Big Al stopped prowling around the desk long enough to peer over my shoulder and examine the list himself.

"What about this LeAnn?" I asked, tapping the name with the tip of my pencil. "A girl friend maybe?"

Al nodded. "Like as not. This guy was so organized he probably couldn't get it up if it wasn't written on the schedule."

That made me laugh. Big Al and I had been thrown together and packaged as a temporary team right after my other partner, Detective Ron Peters, was injured. We had worked together now for several months. I was learning to enjoy the big Norwegian's square-headed sense of humor, as well as to ignore his sometimes surly attitudes.

Debi returned to the small office, bringing with her a lanky, loose-jointed young man who looked a whole lot more like a beardless high school basketball player than someone only two years away from being a real, live, grown-up dentist. College kids seem to look younger with every passing year.

It's one of the hazards of growing older.

"This is my husband Tom Rush," Debi said to me, urging the reluctant young man forward. "These are the two detectives I was telling you about."

I held out my hand. "J. P. Beaumont," I said. "And this is my partner, Allen Lindstrom."

Tom Rush nodded politely to each of us, but the hand he extended was cold and clammy. It was like shaking hands with a long dead mackerel.

"I can't believe he's dead," Tom Rush said, shuddering with dismay. "I just can't believe it. And like this, too. Murdered."

"I'm sure it's a shock to you. Murder is always a shock," I told him. "We've been asking your wife some questions, and we're not finished. Would you mind waiting outside for a few more minutes?"

Tom Rush put it in reverse and backed toward the door. "No problem," he answered quickly. "I don't mind at all. I'll be right out here, if that's okay."

He stumbled all over himself escaping the small office. It struck me that Tom Rush was either incredibly shy or terribly nervous. I couldn't tell which.

As soon as the door closed behind her husband, I turned back to Debi Rush. "Who's LeAnn?" I asked.

She paused for a moment. "His wife, I guess," she said.

"You guess? You mean you don't know? You must be fairly new here if you don't know his wife's name."

"I mean I guess they're still married," she added quickly. "They were separated. I don't know if the divorce was final yet."

"As far as you know, then, his wife would still be the next of kin?"

Debi Rush nodded.

"Any idea where we can find her?"

"No."

"Did you see her at all on Saturday before you left?"

"No. Why would I?"

"She was due here at noon."

"She was?" Debi Rush seemed surprised.

"And she didn't get here before you went home?" I asked.

Debi shook her head. "No, I didn't even know she was . . ."

"But that's what it says on the schedule."

Debi stopped abruptly and took a deep breath. A slight flush colored her pale cheeks. "Then Dr. Fred must have written it down himself," she answered firmly. "I know I didn't put it on the schedule, and she wasn't here when I left."

"You said they were separated. Is she still living in the family home?"

Debi shook her head. "No, she took the kids and moved out."

"Kids?"

"Two of them. A boy and a girl. Seven and eight."

"So where are they staying?"

"In one of those shelters someplace."

"What kind of shelter?"

"You know, one of those places for battered women."

"A domestic violence shelter? Was LeAnn Nielsen a battered woman?"

"You mean, did Dr. Fred beat her?" Debi Rush's eyes struck sparks of anger. "Never. He wouldn't have done that. He said her lawyer probably suggested it in hopes she'd get a better settlement."

"Do you know which shelter? We're going to have to locate her to tell her what's happened."

Debi shook her head. "I don't have any idea. Dr. Fred didn't either. I know he tried to find her when she first took off, but they keep the location of those places a secret."

"Right," I said. "Is there anyone else, any other relatives that you know of, who might be able to help us locate her?"

Debi shrugged. "His mother, maybe."

"His mother? What's her name?"

"Dorothy, I believe that's her first name. She always called herself Mrs. Nielsen whenever she called here and talked to me."

"And where does she live?"

"With Dr. Fred. She's lived with them for several years now."

"What's the address?"

"Green Lake Way North, 6610. It's one of those big old houses facing the lake."

"You haven't made any effort to contact her, have you?"

"No," Debi answered.

"Do you think she'd be at home?"

Debi shook her head. "Maybe. I haven't tried to call. One of the officers told me not to, not until someone had notified her in person."

"Right," I said. "Detective Lindstrom and I will be taking care of that just as soon as we finish here. Now, let's go back to Saturday morning for a minute. What happened after the last patient left?" I glanced at my list. "Reece Bowers, I think his name was. Cleaning only."

For some reason Debi Rush looked down at her hands and smoothed the front of her skirt. "Nothing," she said. "Like I told you, after he left, we just waited for the installer to get here."

"We. You mean you and Dr. Fred. Did you talk while you were waiting?"

She shrugged. "I guess," she said, "but I don't remember what about."

There it was again, some tiny alarm inside me, sounding a warning, telling me that Debi Rush was lying through her teeth. But why? What was she covering up? Who was she protecting?

"Where did you wait?" I insisted, pressing for more detail. "In here? Out by your desk?"

"Here," she answered quickly, nodding toward a short couch that sat opposite the desk. "I remember now. He dictated a couple of letters, and then we talked."

"About?"

"Things," she answered evasively. "He wanted to know how Tom was doing in school, stuff like that. But then as it got later and the installer still wasn't here, he started getting more and more upset."

"Did that seem unusual to you, for him to be disturbed because someone was late?"

"That's just the way he was," she said.

"Was anything out of place at the time you

left? For instance, what about the plant in that one examining room. Was it broken?"

"No. It was fine. I put it up on the counter just before I left to keep it out of the installer's way, but it wasn't broken."

"What about this morning when you came into the office. Was there anything out of place when you came to work?"

"No," she replied. "Not out here. Everything seemed to be fine until I went down the hall."

"What about the door from outside, was it still locked?"

"As far as I know, both of them were."

"Both?"

"There's another door that you may not have seen. It leads from the second examining room and goes directly out into the parking garage. That's the way Dr. Fred usually came into the office."

"But you didn't use that door?"

She shook her head. "I ride the bus, so I don't use the garage. My key is to the front door."

"When you came in this morning, didn't you notice the smell?" Al asked. There was a thinly veiled tone of sarcasm in his voice. I noticed it. Debi Rush didn't. She shook her head.

"My allergies have been acting up for the

last two months. I haven't been able to smell anything for days."

"All right," I said. "One more time. Tell us once more what you did when you got here today."

"Like I said before, I called today's list of patients to confirm their appointments, then I came in here and dusted, the way I always do. I always tried to have the dusting done before Dr. Fred got here. And I put the schedule and today's files on his desk. Dr. Fred liked everything orderly."

"You dusted?" I focused on that. In this day and age dusting didn't sound like something that would still be in any self-respecting dental assistant's job description.

Debi continued. "Every morning. In here, at least. And I polished his desk, too. The whole thing. That's one of the reasons I got along so well with Dr. Fred. I was always on time, and I was willing to do whatever he wanted."

"So much for fingerprints," Big Al grunted under his breath, but I went on with the questions.

"What about the patient files from Saturday?"

"What about them?"

"Shouldn't they have been refiled? They're still here in the OUT basket."

"I was going to put them away just as soon

as I set up Dr. Fred's tray. That's when I found him, and I—" She broke off suddenly, too overcome by emotion to continue.

I glanced at Big Al, who looked disgusted. He doesn't have a very high tolerance for tears. "Anything else you want to know at the moment?" I asked him.

Al shook his head. "Not that I can think of right now. Maybe later."

"All right then, Debi," I said. "You can go for the time being, but will you be home in case we need to get back in touch with you?"

She nodded slowly. "Sure, I'll be there," she said. "There's no sense in staying here."

We found Bill Foster on his hands and knees in the gore-spattered examination room, cutting out the section of blood-soaked carpeting from beneath the examining chair. Big squares where the footprints had been were already missing.

"Finding anything?" I asked, walking up behind him.

Foster looked up at me and shrugged. "Who knows? We've raised latent prints all over the place, but I'd lay odds none of them are going to belong to the killer."

"Why not?"

He nodded in the direction of a Formica counter next to the chair. On it sat an open cardboard dispenser of disposable rubber gloves.

"With that sitting right there? I'd bet money he put on gloves. I sure as hell would."

"If he had time," I said.

"Doc Baker and I got talking after you left. He thinks somebody coldcocked the sucker, hit him over the head with something, then finished him off while he was out cold."

"Hit him with something, like that carpet kicker for instance?" I asked. "It looked like blood on those teeth to me."

He shrugged. "You're right about the blood, Beau, but that's not what clobbered the dentist, at least not the sharp part. There's no matching wound. Somebody else must be wearing the bite from that set of teeth. In the meantime, I think we may have found the murder weapon."

"What? Where?"

"A single dental pick. It was in the autoclave."

"Sterilized?" I asked.

"You bet."

"What makes you think that? This is a dentist's office for Christ's sake! The place must be crawling with dental picks."

"Maybe so, but what dental assistant in her right mind would sterilize only one dental pick at a time?"

"A dental pick!" Big Al repeated the words, shaking his head. "Come on now, Bill, you'd have to be at pretty close quarters to use one of those things, wouldn't you? And who's going to take time to clean it afterward?"

Bill Foster nodded. "You'd have to be a cool customer, all right, but according to Doc Baker, the killer wasn't the least bit squeamish. He went straight for the jugular."

I glanced at Big Al, wondering what he was thinking. It wasn't long before he let me know, sighing as if dismissing some theory that had been growing in his head. "Debi Rush may be lying," he reasoned, "but she definitely strikes me as the squeamish type. Besides, I didn't notice any scratches on her, either."

"At least none we could see," I added.

"So why's she lying to us?" Big Al asked with a frown.

"Beats the hell out of me," I told him.

We left the criminalist to do his painstaking work and made our way out of the office, a plush ground floor space in a building called Cedar Heights at the corner of Second and Cedar. It's only a block or so from my own building, Belltown Terrace, at Second and Broad.

Both buildings are located at the northern end of the Denny Regrade, a man-made flat area in an otherwise hilly Seattle. The streets are broad and straight, lined with a duke's mixture of buildings, from high-rise, pricey condominium/office buildings to rat-infested hovels months away from a close encounter with a wrecking ball.

The Regrade is a neighborhood of contrasts. Gay bars and trendy restaurants exist side by side with small appliance repair shops. Flash-in-the-pan delis spring up periodically. During their brief lifetimes they serve the varied collection of longtime, thriving insurance agencies and short-term, faddish specialty shops. Directly across Second Avenue from where we stood, a deserted hot tub company had gone the way of hula hoops and Howdy Doody.

It was still and warm on the sidewalk as we walked out and looked up at a glaringly blue sky. It would be hot later in the day, the kind of hot that many of Seattle's older buildings are hard pressed to handle.

Big Al and I stood on the sidewalk for a moment, conferring, trying to decide on a next step. "So why'd the carpet installer leave without finishing the job?" I asked. "And how come he took off without his tools?"

Al shrugged. "He must have left in a hurry. So maybe now we've got two suspects, Debi Rush and the carpet installer. What if they're in it together?"

"Stranger things have happened," I said.

"What now? Notify the family or go looking

for that carpet installer?" Al asked.

"We don't have a choice," I told him. "Family comes first. We'll have to find the installer later."

While we talked, an older man wearing a pair of bright orange coveralls had ambled slowly around the corner of the building. Dragging a plastic garbage container behind him and picking up trash as he went, he gradually edged his way over to where we were standing.

Stopping a few feet away, he removed a frayed toothpick from his mouth and tossed it into the trash can. "Had some excitement around here this morning, I guess," he said casually. "You fellows wouldn't happen to be reporters or something, would you?"

"Police detectives," I said. "I take it you work around here?"

He let go of the handle on the trash can and fumbled in a pocket of the coveralls until he located a hanky, which he used to wipe his hands before holding one out to me. "Name's Henry," he said. "Henry Calloway. I'm the resident manager here at Cedar Heights."

"I'm J. P. Beaumont," I replied. "And this is my partner, Allen Lindstrom." Calloway nodded briefly when I showed him my badge.

"It's too bad about the doc," he said. "He was a good tenant. A bit fussy now and again,

I suppose, but he usually paid his rent right on time."

When you're a homicide cop, you get paid to look for discrepancies, and the word *usually* offered the promise of something out of the ordinary.

"You mean he didn't always pay on time," I said.

Henry Calloway shook his head. "Oh, there was just that once. One of the neighborhood bums spent the night camped out on the steps here and took a piss in the doorway before he left. The doc claimed I hadn't cleaned it up good enough. Held up the rent until it passed inspection. That was the only time."

Unfortunately, it wasn't a discrepancy at all. It seemed totally in character, considering what we had learned so far about Dr. Frederick Nielsen.

Calloway wasn't about to let us leave. "Heard someone say he's been dead in there over the weekend," he went on. "That's too bad. When will I be able to get inside to clean up?"

"You won't," I answered shortly. "Bill Foster's still in there, gathering evidence. When he leaves, he'll put up crime-scene tape. No one goes in or out until the tape comes down."

"I see," Calloway said, sounding disappointed.

I know the type. I meet at least one on every case. These turkeys thrive on morbid curiosity. They like to view crime scenes for themselves, preferably while the smell of spilled blood still hangs heavy in the air. Having a murder committed in his building would give Henry Calloway a lifetime's worth of grist for barstool conversations.

I suppressed a shudder. I don't like the Henry Calloways of the world, but occasionally they prove useful. Big Al was the one who gave Calloway his chance to shine.

"By the way," he put in casually, "you didn't happen to see anything unusual over the weekend, did you?"

Calloway straightened his shoulders, puffed out his chest, and drew himself to full attention. "Can't say that I did, except maybe this morning."

"This morning?" I asked. "What about this morning?"

"Well, sir, when I saw that little receptionist of his go racing into the office a little before nine, I says to my wife, I says, 'Jody, there's going to be hell to pay. You mark my words.' Dr. Nielsen didn't hold with people being late, you know. But then, I guess he won't be firing her on that account, now will he?"

"No," I agreed. "I suppose not. Did you notice anything else unusual, anything at all?"

"Not that I remember."

"What about your wife? Does she work here, too?"

"She does, and you're welcome to ask her," he said, "but I doubt she saw anything else."

We took his name and phone number. Henry Calloway wandered away, no longer making even the slightest pretense of picking up the trash.

"That lying little wench," Big Al growled, as soon as Calloway was out of earshot. "She told us she was here at eight o'clock. What the hell do you think she's up to?"

"I don't know," I answered, "but we're by God going to find out. First, though, we'd better go tell his wife."

CHAPTER 3

Green Lake is a former swamp that was dredged and landscaped during the thirties and forties. The lake and surrounding park constitute an urban Mecca for the city's physical-fitness sorts, making it one of the most congested parks in the city.

Every day crowds of people run, jog, skate, walk, bike, and, on occasion, even ski around its three-mile perimeter, jostling for position on the complicated set of lines and symbols that specify who can do what where on the narrow asphalt pathways.

Legend has it that the name Green Lake comes from the brilliant coat of algae that formed on the swamp's stagnating water, after development diverted cleansing contributory streams and creeks into sewers. I sometimes wonder if those modern health freaks out for their daily constitutional realize they're doing today's running on a foundation of yesterday's garbage. Probably not. I'm sure it would offend their tender environmental sensibilities.

The houses that front on the lake itself are mostly well-constructed older homes. Built high above massive stone retaining walls, they sit like unassailable fortresses guarding the street.

Sixty-six ten Green Lake Avenue North was true to type. From a distance, we could see that it was large and white and gabled, with a windowed front porch and two full stories. But from directly below, only the latticed top of a gazebo was visible in one front corner. Steep steps led up through the rock retaining wall to a decorative wrought-iron gate.

That Monday morning Green Lake teemed with summer-crazed Seattlites who had gobbled up every bit of on-street parking for blocks. Al pulled over to the side of the street and paused in a bike lane long enough for me to get out of the car and climb up the stairs to the gate. It was locked from the inside.

Through the narrow bars I saw an immaculately tended front yard that instantly reminded me of Dr. Frederick Nielsen's desk.

The yard was bordered by a series of scrupulously trimmed miniature trees that looked like they'd been pruned by a surgeon wielding a scalpel. The grass was mowed within an inch of its life. No forgotten toys or tricycles or wagons lingered in that well-ordered, manicured yard. They wouldn't have dared. There was no indication that children had come within miles of the place, to say nothing of ever having lived there.

I felt a sudden, surprising wave of sympathy for Dr. Frederick Nielsen's children, for that nameless seven- and eight-year-old boy and girl. Not because their father was dead, but because he had been their father.

I turned and walked back down to the car. "The gate's locked," I told Al. "Let's go around back and try the alley."

Finding the alley was easier said than done. Instead of running parallel to Green Lake as we expected, the alley was perpendicular to it. The entrance looked more like a driveway than a legitimate alley. When we finally attempted to enter it, however, we discovered it was totally blocked by a U-Haul trailer.

Sitting with its end gates wide open, the trailer was parked beside a shaky pile of assorted household goods and boxes. A wooden rocking chair, moving slightly with every hint of breeze, sat next to the trailer's open end, while nearby two women struggled to load an unwieldy four-poster bed-frame canopy into the trailer. They hadn't bothered to take it all the way apart.

"Looks to me like Mrs. Nielsen is bailing out and taking all her worldly possessions with her," Big Al commented as he parked our vehicle as close as he could to the mountain of household goods.

He switched on our yellow hazard lights, and we both climbed out of the car. We had moved only a step or two toward the end of the trailer when a voice exploded from the shadowy interior of the trailer.

"Freeze, sucker!"

The reflex is automatic. We froze, but only for a moment. Clutching desperately for the loaded Smith and Wesson in my shoulder holster, I dove for cover. On the other side of the car Big Al dodged behind the front wheel, groping for his own weapon as he too hit the ground.

"Buddy!" a woman's voice scolded sharply. "You knock that off right this minute! Do you hear me?"

"Buddy's a bad boy, Buddy's a bad boy," replied a suddenly artificial, singsong voice.

One woman entered the trailer and emerged with a huge multicolored parrot perched jauntily on one shoulder. With his yellow head cocked to one side, he regarded Big Al and me with what seemed to be a lively interest.

The woman, a silver-haired lady in her sixties or seventies, clambered down from the trailer and hurried over to me. She recoiled a full foot when she encountered my drawn .38.

"Goodness gracious! Buddy's just a harmless bird. You're not going to shoot him, are you?" she demanded.

Police officers live and die by the unexpected. Response to danger, real or imagined, is reflexive, instantaneous, decisive. Hesitating a moment too long can be crucial. And deadly.

But now as the sudden burst of adrenaline dissipated uselessly in my system, I fumbled sheepishly with my gun. My hand trembled violently. That silver-haired little old lady with her loudmouthed bird had come very close to dying in a hail of bullets. It would have been hell explaining that to a shooting review board.

"No," I managed with some difficulty. "I'm not going to shoot him. We're police officers." I finally succeeded in shoving my Smith and Wesson back into its holster and pulled my identification from my pocket.

I glanced at Big Al, who was also struggling to his feet, his face gray and ashen. It had scared him as badly as it had me. For all the same reasons.

"See what you did, Buddy?" the woman said crossly, turning back to the offending bird. "You caused these nice men all kinds of trouble."

"Buddy's a bad boy, Buddy's a bad boy," the parrot agreed cheerfully, nodding his head up and down.

A second woman, almost a carbon copy of the first, appeared at the open end of the trailer. Both women wore their hair cut short, with a thin fringe of straight bangs across the forehead—Mamie Eisenhower bangs in my book. Both wore gold wire-rimmed glasses and stood ramrod straight.

"What's going on, Rachel?" the second one asked briskly, smoothing her gray skirt and stepping to the ground in one easy movement. She was a spry old dame wearing what my mother always called sensible shoes.

"Oh, nothing," Rachel replied. "Buddy's up to his old tricks again. He scared these two nice men half out of their wits, but there's no harm done."

The second woman shook her head and clicked her tongue. "That bird never did have a lick of sense," she said.

Rachel turned back to me. "You'll have to forgive him. Buddy spent his formative years sitting in a living room with his cage next to a television set. He grew up on 'Police Story' and 'Starsky and Hutch.' "

Big Al, getting a grip on himself, made a

stab at polite conversation. "How old is he?" he asked.

"Watch it, buster," warned the bird. "Don't come any closer." Al stopped dead in his tracks.

One look at Al's face as he backed away from that parrot, and it was all I could do to keep from laughing. For two cents I think he would cheerfully have wrung that parrot's cocky neck.

"Buddy!" Rachel exclaimed, handing the bird over to the other woman, who had come to stand beside her. The three of them made quite a picture, the twin old ladies with the wise-ass bird between them. I surmised the women must be sisters.

"Put him in the car, would you please, Daisy?" Rachel asked.

Without a word, Daisy took the parrot and placed him in the back seat of an old two-toned brown and beige Buick Electra that was hooked to the trailer. As soon as the door slammed shut behind him, Buddy hopped up to the back window and sat there, hunched over, glaring out at us.

I managed, with some difficulty, to stifle my laughter, but I was having a hell of a time thinking of anything useful to say. That didn't matter much since Rachel was more than capable of keeping the conversation afloat single-handedly.

"Buddy's sixteen now," she continued. "Parrots can live as long as forty or fifty years. Jake, the man who owned him first, was a neighbor of ours. He was in a wheelchair, housebound you know. For years it was just the two of them. All they did was eat and watch television together. Finally, Jake's kids had to put him in a nursing home, and Buddy couldn't go along. That's when Daisy and I inherited him. He was so fat the first thing we had to do was put him on a diet."

I was still standing there holding out my ID, waiting for her to look at it. I felt a little silly. Eventually Rachel stopped for breath long enough to give my ID a cursory glance. I took the opportunity to get a word in edgewise.

"I'm Detective Beaumont, and this is my partner, Allen Lindstrom. We're with the Seattle Police Department. We're trying to locate either Dorothy or LeAnn Nielsen."

The second woman, the one named Daisy, returned from the car. She stopped briefly beside her sister. "They're not here," Daisy answered curtly in response to my question. "Neither one of them."

Abruptly, Daisy turned toward the stack of boxes beside the trailer. Something seemed to have offended her, and I wasn't sure what it was. I watched her tackle the stack of boxes. She wasn't a particularly stout woman, but she was evidently quite strong. With a groan, she hefted a trunk-sized box from the swaying stack in the alley and dropped it with a thump onto the floor of the trailer. The U-Haul bounced on its springs.

Daisy turned back to her sister. "Come on, Rachel. Let's get busy. We haven't got all day. I have to be at the zoo before long."

"Do you have any idea where either one of those people could be found?" I insisted, directing my question at Rachel now, trying to steer the conversation back to the dead man's wife and mother. "It's important that we reach one or the other of them this afternoon at the latest."

Daisy stopped where she was and stood with both hands on her hips. "What do you want 'em for?" she demanded.

"I'm not at liberty to say."

"Well, stick it out your ear then," Daisy said sharply. She turned away and grabbed another box.

Daisy may have been her name, but a sweet little wild flower she wasn't.

Rachel looked shocked. "You're almost as bad as Buddy, Daisy," she scolded. "There's no need to be rude."

Her comment made me wonder which of

them was older. It sounded like someone older and wiser chastising someone much younger. I would have thought those roles and distinctions would disappear with age, and these two were obviously well into retirement. But what would I know about that? I grew up as an only child.

Rachel turned back to me.

"Dotty's in the hospital," she said.

"Dotty?" I asked.

"Dotty. Dorothy, our sister—the one you asked about. She's recovering from an accident, Mr. Beaumar," Rachel explained.

I didn't attempt to correct her pronunciation of my name. There was no percentage in it. "Could you tell us which hospital?" I asked. "It's urgent that we be in touch with her."

"Why? Is something wrong?"

"We really must speak directly to her."

Rachel shook her head doubtfully. "I don't know. She's supposed to be released tomorrow, but there's no one here to take care of her. I don't know where that no-good, worthless son of hers is. We haven't been able to reach him in days. We're bringing her home with us. We just came by to pick up some of her things."

From that comment I gleaned at least one important scrap of information—there was no love lost between this zany pair of aunties with their outspoken bird and their precise, well-ordered, and recently deceased nephew. I'm sure he would have been shocked at the haphazard manner with which his mother's prized possessions, including the four-poster canopy bed, were being crammed into the trailer. These ladies may have been quick movers, but careful they weren't.

"Ma'am, this happens to be police business," I argued gently. "Of course we wouldn't want to trouble your sister if she's too ill to see us. Instead, maybe you could tell us how to contact LeAnn Nielsen, then. It's about your nephew, Dr. Frederick Nielsen."

Rachel turned back to her sister, just as Daisy heaved another loaded box into the trailer. "What do you think, Daze?" she asked. "Should we tell him or not?"

Daisy shrugged. "I already told him what I think. Nothing he's said has changed my mind one whit." Daisy went right on loading boxes with a vengeance.

Meanwhile, Rachel was taking her sister's opposition into consideration. She put one finger to her lips as if lost in thought. "I just don't know what to say. I don't think we should let you bother Dotty, not in her condition. This has been terribly hard on her, you know."

I had almost decided to take the bull by the horns and tell them. Those two stubborn old bats weren't going to give us an inch unless we gave them a damn good reason to do so. Evidently, Big Al had reached the same conclusion a little sooner than I did. He beat me to the punch.

"Look," he said patiently. "Like Detective Beaumont told you, we're from the Seattle P.D. With homicide. There's been a murder."

Rachel's jaw dropped. Daisy swung away from the stack of boxes, her sharp eyes riveted on Big Al's face. "A what?" she demanded.

"A murder," he repeated. "We've tentatively identified the victim as your nephew. Our first responsibility is to notify his next of kin. Out of common courtesy, we try to do that in person. If you could put us in touch with either your sister or your nephew's wife, LeAnn, it would be a big help."

"My land!" Rachel exclaimed. "Daisy, did you hear that?"

"I heard," Daisy answered grimly.

Behind us a raucous horn sounded as a huge blue garbage truck rumbled into the alley behind our unmarked patrol car. The driver of the truck leaned out the window and shook his fist at our offending vehicles. "Hey, you guys. You gotta clear outa my way. I got work to do."

Which is how Big Al Lindstrom and J. P. Beaumont, detectives with Seattle's homicide squad, ended up helping two white-haired little old ladies load the last of Dorothy Nielsen's personal possessions into a U-Haul trailer.

When it was all loaded, with the rocking chair settled in the last bit of open space, the end result looked none too stable to me, but Rachel assured us that they weren't going far. She stood to one side while Daisy pulled the trailer's doors shut, bolted them, and headed for the driver's side of the Buick.

Rachel paused uncertainly with us as the old crate's engine coughed and sputtered when Daisy turned the key and gunned the engine.

"Why don't you follow us?" Rachel offered tentatively. "We'll try to decide what to do on our way to the house. Maybe you two could join us for a bite of lunch. That would be nice, wouldn't it?"

I walked her to the car and held open the door while she slid onto lumpy, clear plastic seat covers that had stiffened and yellowed with age to an opaque beige.

"Why, thank you," she said graciously.

With a squawk, Buddy flapped his way from the back window to the front seat. There he settled comfortably on Rachel's shoulder.

"Freeze, sucker!" he ordered again, glaring sideways up at me, waiting for a reaction. This time neither Al nor I gave him the satisfaction.

I closed the door and the Buick lurched away, belching a cloud of thick exhaust smoke.

The driver of the garbage truck laid on his horn again. We were still in his way. Hurrying into our car, we started after them. By then, the U-Haul was already around the corner and nearly out of sight.

"We're not really going to have lunch with those two old battle-axes, are we?" Big Al asked plaintively.

"We're going to do whatever it takes to worm some information out of them, including having lunch," I told him.

Al shook his head dolefully. "If that means being in the same room with that son of a bitch of a bird, we ought to ask for hazardous duty pay."

I laughed. "I've heard of guard dogs before," I told him. "But this is the first time I ever met an attack parrot."

That's one nice thing about this job. I learn something new every day.

CHAPTER

4

I suppose I had seen the Edinburgh Arms on occasion before in the course of my travels around Seattle, but it had never registered. The complex was situated in the 4800 block of Fremont Avenue, but its brick row house construction made it look like it had been plucked straight out of Merrie Old England. Scotland, actually, as Rachel was happy to explain to us during lunch.

Built as apartments but now converted to cozy condos, the Edinburgh Arms is a clone of another building, a project built in Edinburgh in the late 1920s. The Seattle contractor used the exact same specifications and plans. Now, some sixty years later, the weathered red brick, the squat chimneys to each unit's fireplace, and the formal English garden courtyard gave the place a quaint, settled charm. Even the fat-cheeked, concrete cherub, peeing in the red brick fountain, seemed totally at home.

Al pulled up and stopped behind the Buick and the U-Haul, which were parked near an open doorway. The end gates were still closed and locked, however. Rachel and Daisy must have decided to eat lunch first and unload later.

"I shoulda figured those two dippy broads would live in a place like this," Al grumbled, looking around.

"Why? What's wrong with it?" I asked.

"It looks just like 'em," he answered.

Rachel came to the door to let us in. A newly built plywood wheelchair ramp covered the two short steps leading up to the doorway.

"Daisy's upstairs changing," Rachel explained. "Come on in and have a seat. Lunch will be ready in a moment."

The living room had an old-fashioned high ceiling with an amber-colored light fixture hanging from a brass chain in the middle of the room. It could have been a spacious, roomy place, but the furniture had been shoved together to make room for a hospital bed that had been set up in the far corner next to the fireplace. It was unmade. A stack of sickroom rental supply linens sat on a piece of plain brown paper on top of the bare mattress ticking.

Rachel saw me look at it. "They just delivered the bed this morning," she explained. "We're not quite organized yet. We had a hard time fitting it in here, but of course, Dotty would never be able to manage the stairs to get up and down to a bedroom."

"What seems to be the matter with your sister?" I asked.

Rachel stopped in the doorway and looked at me before she answered. Reticence and hesitation weren't her style.

"She broke her hip," she said finally, decisively, then turned on her heel and disappeared through the dining room into the kitchen. Moments later we heard the banging of pots and pans as Rachel bustled about making lunch.

Buddy, confined to a large cage in the corner of the dining room, had been quiet when we first entered the house. Now, with Rachel out of the room, he piped up again. "What's your name?" he asked, not once but several times.

We ignored him. There's something undignified about being trapped into a conversation with a parrot.

The living room was light and airy, but filled with the motley collection of cheap knickknacks and trinkets—"tack" my mother would have called it—that had been gathered over two separate lifetimes and then somehow blended together.

In the corner next to the front door sat a papier-mâché elephant's foot jammed full of umbrellas. Above it, an antique wood and brass hat rack held two yellow rain slickers with matching hats, two bright red motorcycle helmets, and two identical khaki-colored pith helmets. The two sets of helmets puzzled me. Neither Daisy nor Rachel looked much like the motorcycle or jungle safari type.

I wandered over to the fireplace to examine the marble mantel. On it sat a miniature zoo, complete with tiny, inch-to inch-and-a-half-tall animals, cheaply but recognizably made. There must have been a hundred of them in all. For a fastidious housekeeper, it would have created a dusting problem of mammoth proportions. From the layer of dust visible on each of the animals, however, fastidious housekeeping didn't seem to be part of Rachel and Daisy's program.

Rachel came into the dining room carrying a stack of dishes, stopped by the table, and looked over at me. "Those belong to Daisy," she announced when she saw I was examining the animals. "The salt and pepper shakers are mine," she added.

The built-in bookshelves on either side of

the fireplace were loaded with equally dusty salt and pepper shakers of all sizes and descriptions, many of them imprinted with gaudy letters that proclaimed the item's geographic origin. Matching headstones came from Tombstone, Arizona. A set of bears were emblazoned with Yellowstone National Park. A smiling senor and senorita had Tijuana printed on their shoes.

"Where are you from?" Rachel asked, walking up to stand beside me.

"I've lived in Seattle all my life," I answered.

She bent down, reached unerringly to the back of the bottom shelf, and retrieved two tiny replicas of the Space Needle. "I got these from the World's Fair in 1962," she told me proudly, rubbing off a dusty film with the hem of her apron. "I keep them all loaded. That way I can always put something appropriate on the table whenever we have company. It's less expensive than ordering flowers."

She took the two mini-Space Needles to the dining room and placed them in the middle of the table with a genuine flourish.

"What's your name?" Buddy asked her.

"You be quiet or I'll cover you up," she warned. Buddy shut up and ducked his head under a wing.

Daisy came down the steps just then. She

was wearing a pair of light khaki trousers and a matching khaki shirt with a giraffe symbol sewn above the breast pocket and a series of silver and gold pins attached to the top of the pocket itself. On her feet were a pair of rubber-soled yellow and gray duck-hunting shoes straight out of an L. L. Bean catalog.

She spoke to Rachel, who was busily setting the table. "It'll still be light by the time I get home. We can unpack the trailer then."

Walking over to the hat rack, she peered critically into a mirror while she settled one of the two khaki pith helmets on her head. I took back everything I'd thought about her not being the safari type. She looked the part to a T.

"You're not planning to leave without eating lunch, are you, Daze?" Rachel asked. "It's almost ready."

I think Daisy would have left without lunch if she could have gotten away with it. She sighed, put the helmet back on the rack, and led us to the dining room table.

I would have left, too, if I'd only known what was coming. The table was set with what had once been state-of-the-art Melmac, now scratched and worn with too many years of hard use. The orange wild flowers that bordered the edge of the plates had long since faded to a shadow of their former glory.

Daisy directed Al and me to chairs while

Rachel began serving soup into mercifully shallow plastic soup dishes. The moment she ladled some into my dish, I knew I was in deep trouble. It was as though my mother had returned from the grave to haunt me.

It was soup all right, tomato soup, but not the thick, dark-colored, good kind. This was a thin, faded pink, made with milk and tomato juice. Small darker pink sunrises of curdling tomato floated here and there on the pale, milky surface.

The soup was exactly the kind my mother used to make when I was a child. I had been able to choke it down only if I could fill the bowl so full of crushed soda crackers that I couldn't see the color of the soup anymore—or the curdles. Unfortunately, there wasn't a soda cracker in sight, only a platter of what later turned out to be tofu sandwiches that proved to be tougher to choke down than the soup.

"We're both vegetarians," Rachel explained lightly as she passed me the platter of sandwiches. "I don't know what we're going to do about Dotty."

Dotty evidently wasn't.

Al managed to down the meal with every evidence of gusto. Daisy finished her soup, gulped half a sandwich, and left the table, taking both a pith helmet and a motorcycle helmet with her as she rushed out the door.

Rachel glanced at her watch. "She's supposed to be there by two, but she's always early. That's the way she is."

When Rachel disappeared into the kitchen to serve the coffee, I stuffed the remainder of my tofu sandwich in my jacket pocket. Al caught me in the act and gave me a quick wink just as our hostess returned.

"What's so funny?" she demanded.

"Nothing," Big Al said. "I got something in my eye." Telling fibs comes naturally to Detective Allen Lindstrom.

During lunch I had deliberately delayed our questioning in hopes of dealing with Rachel alone. I had a hunch she'd be far more communicative once Daisy was out of the way. Now, over strong coffee and stale cookies, I opened the discussion.

"You don't seem to be very curious about what happened to your nephew."

"Curious?" she demanded, with bright sparks lighting up her pale blue eyes. "Why should I be curious about him? Whatever happened to him, it was probably better than he deserved."

So much for auntlike decorum and sorrow.

"Oh, I'm sure Dotty will be wild with grief," she continued. "She always doted on him so, even though he never deserved it, not for a minute. He was just like his father, you know."

"How's that?"

Rachel looked at me carefully, appraisingly. "Don't you go trying to trick me into talking to you," she cautioned. "Our mama always told us that the Beasons don't wash their dirty laundry in public. I married into the Millers, but I'm still a Beason at heart."

"Tell me about your sister," I said.

"Which one, Dorothy or Daisy?"

"Dorothy, the one who's in the hospital. Which hospital is she in?"

"I told you, she's in no condition to talk to you. If I tell you where she is, you'll go straight there and bother her with all this. It'll be better if she doesn't find out about it until tomorrow when she's home here with us."

"Rachel," I said reasonably, "the department does its best to notify the next of kin personally. We don't release the victim's name to the media until we're sure the family has been properly notified. In this case, however, someone else may very well let something slip to a reporter. It's possible your sister will hear the news over the radio or television when she's by herself with no one there to help her, to be with her."

I watched Rachel's face as I spoke. My argument made some headway, but she still wasn't ready to capitulate.

"Eventually we'll be able to find her with or without your help," I went on, "but it would be nice if we didn't have to fight our way through official channels. It would save us a lot of time."

"I'll have to think about that," Rachel Miller said.

"How long has Dotty been in the hospital?" I pressed.

"Four weeks yesterday. It's been dreadful. They're only letting her come home now because there'll be two of us here to take care of her. The doctor wanted to put her in a nursing home, you see."

I took a long, deliberate sip of coffee as I tried to understand her reticence. I wondered if maybe she thought Dorothy Nielsen was a suspect in her son's murder. That was easy enough to put to rest, so I set about doing just that.

"Since your nephew died on Saturday, and since your sister didn't get out of the hospital until today, we could hardly consider her a suspect, now, could we."

Rachel appeared shocked that I should even mention such a thing. "Certainly not," she snapped. "That idea never even crossed my mind."

"So why are you so reluctant to tell us where she is?"

Rachel sighed. "It's been awful for her, such an ordeal, that even now she gets confused. I'm afraid to add one more burden."

"She'll have to find out sooner or later," Big Al offered. "Wouldn't it be better if you had some control over how and when she was told?"

Just then the doorbell rang and Rachel hurried to answer it. Outside I could see an elderly gentleman also dressed in khaki and wearing the same kind of pith helmet, which he removed as soon as she opened the door.

"I saw your car was still loaded," he said. "I thought I'd offer to unload for a while before I go to the zoo."

"I'm busy right now, George," Rachel told him. "I have people here, but if you want to come back later, that's fine. Daisy's already gone. She's working on the Jungle Party this afternoon, but we could use some help later, after she gets back."

George seemed disappointed. "Are you sure you can't use me right now?"

"No, really. I've got company, George." At that, he peered in through the door as though trying to identify exactly who Rachel's "company" might be. He made no move to leave.

"Come back around suppertime," Rachel

added firmly. "We'll have some nice macaroni and cheese. You can help us unload."

He nodded grudgingly. "All right," he said. "I'll be here at six."

Rachel returned to the table smiling. "He's my gentleman caller," she explained. "He's been hanging around here for months, ever since his wife died. I like him well enough, but only as a friend, you understand."

It was none of my business, but I nodded anyway, just to be polite. "Look," I said, "if you won't give us any information regarding your sister, what about your nephew's wife?"

"What about her? It took a lot of gumption for LeAnn to do what she did," Rachel said. "I'm proud of her."

"To do what?"

"To pack up those two kids and leave, just like that, without saying anything to anyone." There was undisguised admiration in Rachel's voice.

"She didn't tell her mother-in-law?" I asked.

"Nope. Not anybody. Not a word."

"Why did she do it?"

"She had to."

There was no point in circling the question any longer.

"Did your nephew beat his wife?" I asked the question bluntly, letting the words fall heavily in the quiet room. I saw the slight hesitation before Rachel Miller raised her eyes to meet mine.

"That's LeAnn's business, not mine. If she wants to tell people about what all went on, that's up to her."

"Do you have any idea where she is?" I asked. "As I told you before, we're obligated to notify the next of kin. If you think it's a bad idea for us to talk to your sister, then maybe we should speak to LeAnn instead."

That's what I said. I left unsaid the domestic violence statistics, particularly the murder ones, that show how often an abused spouse finally hits the end of her rope and turns on her tormentor. It was more than slightly possible that LeAnn Nielsen herself would turn up among our prime suspects.

"No, I don't know where she is," Rachel replied. "Besides, I wouldn't tell you if I did."

In my book white-haired little old ladies (LOLs for short) are due a certain amount of respect, just on the basis of longevity, if nothing else, but I was fast losing patience with this one. Rachel Miller had information that would make Big Al's and my work infinitely easier.

"Look," I said, "we're involved in a homicide investigation. Are you aware that deliberately withholding evidence in a case like this is a crime? It's called obstructing justice. You could wind up going to jail."

Without blinking, Rachel Miller looked from my face to Al's and then back to me. "All right," she said, nodding slowly. "If that's the way it is, just let me put the food away. We can go as soon as I clear up the dishes and leave a note for Daisy."

Rachel Miller got up swiftly and marched through the swinging doors into the kitchen, carrying a stack of dirty dishes with her.

"She's calling your bluff," Al whispered under his breath. "What are you going to do now, dummy?"

All I could do was give him a helpless shrug. "Beats me," I said.

Ask anyone from my college fraternity. Ask anyone from the department. J. P. Beaumont never was and never will be much of a poker player. Besides, although I didn't know it yet, Rachel Miller had me totally outclassed in the bluff, raise, and call department.

Al and I moved back to the living room couch to wait while Rachel carried dirty dishes and leftovers from the dining room into the kitchen.

While we sat there waiting for her to finish, I kept wondering how I'd paint my way back out of the obstruction-of-justice corner I was in. I envisioned Gray Panthers coming out of the woodwork to protest and make my life miserable once they got wind that I'd so much as threatened to lock her up. Not only that, I know from experience that Seattle Police Department brass listen with a very attentive ear when senior citizens start protesting. Pissing off the elderly, particularly the vocal elderly, is bad for public relations. Every reporter in Seattle would have a field day.

Several minutes passed. Several long minutes. Eventually, it registered in my brain that although water was still running in the kitchen, I was no longer hearing the accompanying clatter of rinsing plates and silverware. I got up and hurried to the kitchen with Big Al right on my heels.

The kitchen was empty. The faucet was running full blast, but Rachel Miller was long gone. She had slipped out the open back door with the noise of the water masking her movements.

We went outside, dashed up the grassy lawn to Fremont Avenue, and looked in both directions. Rachel Miller was nowhere in sight.

"I'll be a son of a bitch!" Big Al muttered.

Those were my sentiments exactly.

CHAPTER

5

Rachel Miller got us good. Al and I had been snookered, plain and simple. Without exchanging a word, we walked back to our car, got in, and drove away. It wasn't something either one of us wanted to discuss or write down in a report or even remember. It was the oldest trick in the book, and a couple of homicide squad veterans had no excuse for being taken in by it.

"I guess you don't want to call Sergeant Watkins and put out an APB on the lady." Big Al's comment was laced with sarcasm.

"We'll just let it pass," I said.

"We sure as hell will," he agreed.

If word of the incident leaked out, I knew we'd be the laughingstock of the department, enduring weeks of pointed ribbing from all the other detectives on the fifth floor of the Public Safety Building. Neither one of us was tough enough for that. No way José!

We drove up and down the streets of the neighborhood, trying to spot Rachel Miller, but there was no sign of her. She had vanished completely, totally, although the Buick and the U-Haul remained parked exactly where Daisy had left them. Knowing that Rachel had not only ditched us but that she'd done it on foot rubbed salt into the wound.

We stopped at the stop sign at Forty-eighth and Fremont and waited for the break in traffic. "Why do you think she took off like that?" I asked. "It doesn't make sense."

"It does to me," Al grumbled.

"What do you mean?"

"It's exactly what you'd expect from a dame kooky enough to love that stupid bird." Al was still packing a grudge against Buddy. He wasn't any too happy with me, either.

"So what do you want to do now?" he asked. "Try getting a line on the wife, go back to Cedar Heights and talk to the neighbors, or track down the carpet installer?"

It was an impressive list of possibilities. Multiple choice. I picked one.

"Let's stop by the carpet company on the way back downtown. I remember seeing it down by the Fremont Bridge. It's on our way."

Behind us a car honked impatiently for us to move. We were blocking traffic. Al glowered at the driver in his rearview mirror, but he turned left and got back on Fremont going south.

I could remember back when the Damm Fine Carpets building used to house a fire extinguisher company, although I had forgotten the exact name. I had driven past it for years, and I remembered hearing stories that the place had originally served as a Model T Ford assembly plant.

Now, though, all trace of both Model T's and fire extinguishers had been obliterated. The place sported a brand-new coat of brilliant yellow paint, and the company's name, emblazoned in six-foot-tall block letters, ran the entire length of the building. The only reminder that the shell was a relic from a bygone era was the old-fashioned metal grillwork in each of the small glass windows.

We parked in a "customer only" parking place and went inside the compact showroom. It was ten to three when an eager salesman zeroed in on us. We must have looked like live ones. "Can I interest you in some carpet today?" he asked, rubbing his hands together.

I shook my head. "Actually, we're here looking for the owner. Is he in?"

The man shrugged and glanced down at his

watch. "Mr. Damm isn't available right now, not for ten minutes or so." He pointed toward one side of the room, where we saw a counter with a woman sitting behind it. "That's Mr. Damm's secretary. You'll have to talk to her."

We walked over to the counter. The secretary was a reasonably attractive sweet young thing in her early twenties. She had that funny, nerve-wracking blink of people who have yet to master the art of comfortably wearing their contact lenses. The most noticeable thing about her, however, were her fingernails. They were at least two inches long. Each. It crossed my mind that typing couldn't be a major part of her job description. A brass plate on the counter told us her name was Cindy.

"We're here to see Mr. Damm," I said when she looked up at me and blinked.

"Was he expecting you?" she asked.

"No, we're here on police business." I held out my ID. She took it, holding it close to her face to read it. Even with the contacts, she must have been terrifically nearsighted.

"He'll be out in about . . ." She held her watch up to her face. "In about five minutes now. You can talk to him then. If you'd like to have a chair . . ."

She motioned us into two blue side chairs across from the counter, and we settled down to wait. It wasn't long before a tiny alarm on the secretary's watch went off. She got up and hurried to a door halfway down a short hallway behind her. I had known there was a doorway there, and from the outside it looked ordinary enough. When she opened it, however, I could tell it was anything but ordinary.

The inside of the door was covered with fur. Fake white fur. The kind you'd expect to find on a soft, stuffed Easter bunny in some little kid's Easter basket. The secretary disappeared into a room, closing the door behind her.

I nudged Al. "Did you get a load of that?"

He rolled his eyes and shook his head. "This must be our lucky day," he said.

Moments later the secretary reappeared. "Mr. Damm will see you now," she announced. "In his office. This way, please." Since she stood holding the fur-lined door open and motioning for us to enter, that had to be the place. We got up and walked inside.

Outside the door, the interior of Damm Fine Carpets looked like any other fluorescent-lit, modern storefront and warehouse, but walking through the door into Richard Damm's office was like entering another world. I had never seen an office anything like it. It was dark for one thing, the heavy, oppressive darkness of a dim bar or darkened theater when you first come in from outside and your eyes haven't adjusted to the light.

Big Al and I stopped long enough to get our bearings while the door swished shut behind us. The better part of the wall to the right of the door was made up of a huge, dimly lit fish tank complete with a wide variety of colorful fish. Beside the aquarium, in one corner of the room was a small fountain where beads of water cascaded down in a circle around a statuette of a naked lady.

At the far end of the room was a seating area—a conversation pit I think they call them—facing a complex home entertainment center. The back of a man's head was barely visible over the top of the couch. He was seated directly in front of a color television set that was playing the credits to some afternoon program. On either side of the set were a series of four VCRs, all of them with red lights glowing.

By now, our eyes had adjusted to the light enough so that details of the room gradually became clearer. The secretary had called it an office, but there was no sign of a desk or a file cabinet. Directly across from us was a fully equipped, well-stocked bar, and to our left was a tiny efficiency kitchen. The place didn't look like an office at all. It was a home away from home.

There were no windows in the room. The carpeting, plush white, not only covered the floor, but ran halfway up the walls wherever walls were visible. It reminded me of a padded cell. For all I know, it was a padded cell.

Richard Damm didn't bother to get up. "Come on in," he called. "I always watch 'General Hospital' during lunch, but it's over now."

He was fiddling with a remote control. The program credits disappeared and a movie came on. He had evidently stopped a video in midstream, because the action was already well in progress.

It was one of those Debbie-Does-Dallas kinds of porno flicks, one the first amendment never should have protected in the first place. I thought Big Al's eyes were going to pop right out of his head when he saw what was happening on the screen.

I suppose I shouldn't make fun of Al. I wasn't exactly immune myself. When the sound track got too graphic, Damm finally turned off the volume, but not the machine. Without bothering to take his eyes from the movie, he motioned for us to sit down. "I'm Richard Damm," he said shortly. "What can I do for you?"

The owner of Damm Fine Carpets was your basic low-brow voyeur with all the class and style of a K-Mart blue-light special. He was probably in his mid to late fifties with a luxurious headful of wavy silver hair and a matching mustache. A closer examination revealed that the mustache was his. The hair wasn't.

He was definitely not a staid, three-piece-suit, coat-and-tie man. He was wearing a gaudy blue-and-white Hawaiian shirt with white slacks and turquoise boat shoes. The top three buttons on his palm-tree-covered shirt were unbuttoned, exposing far too much of a totally hairless chest. He wore not one but three long gold chains and lots of sickly sweet froufrou water. I figured the chains were as phony as the hair. The bony remains of a Kentucky Fried Chicken lunch sat on the coffee table in front of him.

"Help yourself to a drink," he suggested.

"No thanks," I said. "We're on duty."

"Coffee, then? It's already made."

"No thank you. Nothing. We're in a hurry." I was trying my best to keep the questions on track, to keep my mind from wandering away from the point of our visit, but Debbie and her antics with the men from Dallas were interfering with my train of thought.

"We're looking for one of your employees," I said.

For the first time, Richard Damm glanced away from the writhing living-color bodies on his television screen. He seemed mildly interested. "Which one?" he asked.

Al and I sat down side by side on the couch. "Larry Martin," I answered.

Richard Damm sighed, punched his remote control, and froze a mass of naked, nubile bodies in midscrew. "That little shit," he said. "I'm looking for him, too."

"He didn't come to work today?"

"That's right. He left a note saying that he was taking this week off. The whole goddamned week, when I've got twenty-three installations scheduled. He can take the rest of his life off, for all I care. If he shows his face around here again, I'll fire his ass."

Damm got up, walked to the kitchen, and came striding back with a stack of Styrofoam cups and a coffeepot. "A hell of a lot of thanks a guy gets for trying to help."

In his agitation, Damm must have forgotten I had told him we didn't want coffee. Truth be known, he probably hadn't been listening. He poured coffee into three cups, passed one each to Al and me, then flopped back down on the couch with his own. He punched a button on the remote control and the bodies on the screen resumed their impossible contortions.

"What do you mean, 'thanks'?" I asked.

Richard Damm shook his head. "Larry's been straight for five years, give or take. I figured he had his act together, that I could trust him. But now this."

He lit a cigarette and pulled a brimming ashtray within easy reach.

"Straight?" I asked. "I don't understand."

"Me either. It's guys like him who make it tough on everybody else."

"You'd better tell us about it," I suggested.

"Like I said, I hired him about five years ago, fresh out of the slammer. I let him work in my warehouse. It was like my civic duty, know what I mean? One of those work-release arrangements. It looked to me like it was working out fine."

"He's worked for you the whole time, then?"

Richard Damm nodded. "He handled the warehouse job for a couple of years, and then asked if he could start doing installations. He could make a lot more money doing that. I figured what the hell. He was a good enough worker. Turned out I was right. At least it looked that way at the time. He was a little slow at first, but he caught on."

"What did he get sent up for?" Al asked.

"Vehicular manslaughter. DWI. He came out of the joint sober and went straight to AA. Hasn't had a drop since, as far as I know."

"How about lately? Any unexplained absences before this morning?"

Damm shook his head. "Not so as you'd notice. But he screwed up a truck over the weekend. My mechanic is pissed as hell about that, and I've been waiting all morning to hear whether or not he got that dentist's office finished before he took off."

"Dr. Nielsen's office?" I asked.

Richard Damm seemed surprised. "That's right. How'd you know about that? Nielsen's a son of a bitch to work for. I call him 'Mister Got Bucks.' He's just like an old woman—fussy as hell. If Larry took off without completing that job, Nielsen'll have my ass. I tried calling his office a couple of minutes ago. No answer."

And there isn't going to be, I thought. I said, "What makes you think Martin didn't complete the job?"

"You wanna know what I really think?" Richard Damm demanded.

"Yes."

"I think he went out on the town Friday night, fell off the wagon, and got himself in some kind of hassle. Maybe even skipped town. If he did, he took off with enough of my tools to be able to get himself another job wherever the hell he ends up."

I happened to know that most of Larry Martin's tools, minus the kicker that was down at the crime lab, were still in Dr. Frederick Nielsen's office, but I didn't tell Richard Damm that. I wasn't about to tell him anything I didn't have to. For some reason—maybe the phony hair, maybe the phony smile—Richard Damm rubbed me the wrong way.

"You always jump to these kinds of conclusions when one of your employees doesn't show up for work on a Monday morning?" I asked.

Richard Damm's whole manner changed abruptly. "I'm not stupid," he said. "I had one of my guys drive by to check on him. His car wasn't there, and nobody answered the door. That's all I know."

"You said something about him screwing up one of your trucks," Al mentioned. "Tell us about that."

"One of my installation vans. It's a mess."

"What about it?"

"He musta gotten in some kind of fight, that's what we figure, or maybe an accident. All I know is there was blood all over the place, and one of the doors is bashed in. I guess I should be grateful, though. At least he didn't steal it."

"You say there was blood in the van?"

"You deaf or what? All over the seat, all over the floor."

"We'd better have a look at it," Big Al said,

getting up and starting toward the door. "Where is it?"

"Nick took it down to Westlake to have it cleaned up and detailed. He's probably back by now. It had been sitting out in the sun for a day and a half at least. Those stains really set up good. Nick says he doesn't know if they can save the upholstery or not. He may have to tear it all out."

"Who's Nick?"

"Nick Wallace, my mechanic. We've got a whole fleet of vans. He's in charge of keeping them all on the road."

"And where is he?"

"Out back, in the garage. That's usually where he is, him and his trucks—his babies he calls 'em. He couldn't treat 'em better if they all belonged to him personally, know what I mean?"

I got up and followed Al toward the fur-lined door. "So where's the garage?"

"Straight through the warehouse. You'll have to ring the bell for him to let you in."

I stopped in the doorway door and turned back toward the room. The movie had returned to life on the television screen with all the moanings and pantings turned back up to full volume.

"Do you know Larry Martin's address?"

Enthralled once more, Damm didn't bother

to look up. "Not off the top of my head. Get it from Cindy, my secretary. Tell her I said she should give it to you."

"We may be back," I added.

"Sure thing. I'll be right here."

Cindy gave us Larry Martin's address and phone number up in Lake City, then she directed us through the warehouse to the garage at the far end of the building. She assured us that was where we'd find Nick Wallace.

"Do you believe that little shit?" Big Al asked as we made our way through canyons of carpet rolls. "Damm must not be getting any, or he wouldn't have to watch that crap on TV."

I certainly wasn't getting any at the moment. The X-rated action on Richard Damm's television set had made me painfully aware of my own particular lack.

"Probably not," I said, and let it go at that.

Big Al is forever telling me that I need to get hooked up with some nice, warm-blooded Swedish girl like his Molly.

He could very well be right.

CHAPTER 6

Just as Richard Damm had warned us, we had to ring a bell to gain admittance to Nick Wallace's garage. The door was locked from the inside. He came to open it himself. Nick was an older man, somewhere in his late sixties I'd say, with a ruddy complexion and thinning gray hair. He was wearing a pair of bright blue coveralls with a greasy towel hanging from one back pocket.

He opened the door, all right, but just a crack, enough for him to see us but not enough for us to step inside.

"Yeah?" he said gruffly. "Whadya want?"

Al, leading the way, held out his ID. "Detectives Lindstrom and Beaumont. We're with Seattle P.D. Homicide," he explained. "We'd like to talk to you about one of your vans."

Nick Wallace's watery blue eyes narrowed slightly behind his thick wire-rimmed glasses. "Which one?"

"The one Larry Martin was driving Saturday," Al said. "The one with the bloodstains."

"Oh, that one," Nick said. He opened the door a little wider then and allowed us to come inside, reluctantly admitting us to his sanctum sanctorum.

And that's exactly what it was. I suspect Nick Wallace of being an original, card-carrying member of *Zen and the Art of Motorcycle Maintenance*. Entering his small shop in the back of Damm Fine Carpets was nothing short of a religious experience. He had every tool imaginable, from small milling lathes to complex electronic testing equipment. It was one of those workrooms that had a place for everything and everything in its place.

I'm the kind of messy mechanic who hates to work on cars. I do it only when absolutely necessary, and I never have the right tool for the right job. Oh, I may have it, but I can never lay my hands on it when I need it.

Through the years I've counted my lack of mechanical aptitude as a real character flaw, chalking it up to laziness and sloth as well as growing up with no mechanically inclined father living in the house. At the time of my divorce, it was one of the reasons Karen gave for throwing me over for the chicken conglomerate accountant from Cucamonga. She said she was tired of having to do her own oil changes.

Now I've got that Guard Red Porsche. I've looked under the hood of my 928, but I've never had guts enough to tackle anything I've found there. At this point, I'd a whole lot rather pay somebody who knows what he's doing than screw up something by attempting to do it myself.

Besides, there's no place to work on a car in the basement parking area of a downtown condo.

Considering all this, I was somewhat envious of the shipshape conditions in Nick Wallace's private domain. He could have given Rachel Miller and her sister lessons in housekeeping. There wasn't as much dust visible in all of Nick's garage as there had been on Rachel's collection of salt and pepper shakers. The shiny concrete floor had no telltale grease spots. For that matter, the place didn't even smell like a garage. There was only the mildly pungent odor of some kind of cleaning solvent.

At the moment, there were just two vans in the shop. One of them was obviously in for a tune-up. Its hood stood open, and a new set of spark plugs lay on the rolling mechanic's chest nearby. The other van sat in the far corner with both front doors wide open.

Nick Wallace went back to the one van and stopped dead in front of the open hood. "Whoever designed this sucker never planned on changing the plugs." It was a complaint aimed at the universe in general, not at us in particular. Once he had voiced it, however, Nick resolutely bent over and began resetting the plugs.

"What is it you want to know?" he asked without looking up.

"Which van is it?" I returned.

He jerked his head in the direction of the van with the open doors. "That one," he said. "I'm still trying to dry it out."

I've seen a few carpet installation vans in my time. They're usually dented and dinged. Mostly they look neglected, like they're lucky if somebody bothers to feed them gas and oil occasionally. That, however, was not the case with the Damm Fine Carpets fleet of vans. Not if the two currently parked in Nick Wallace's garage were any indication.

They were several years old, but they still looked brand new. The outside paint was waxed and polished to a high gloss. If they had ever been dented or scratched, the damage had been carefully rubbed out and repainted. On my way to the one van, I walked past the other and managed to catch a glimpse of what was under the hood. The engine had been steam-cleaned. It could have come fresh from the factory that very day.

When we reached Larry Martin's van, the one with the open doors, we found that the cleaning solvent smell was emanating from there. It was industrial-strength carpet and upholstery cleaner.

The entire interior of the van had been custom carpeted. I guess that shouldn't have surprised me. After all, it was a carpet company's vehicle. The outside of the van looked perfect until I walked around to the other side and discovered that the door on the rider's side had been badly smashed.

"What do you think happened here?" I asked.

Nick Wallace poked his head out from under the hood of the other van. "You talkin' to me?" he asked.

"Yes. I said what do you think happened here?"

"Looks to me like he ran it into a post of some kind. Not only that, the stupid son of a bitch bled all over it like a stuck hog without ever bothering to try to clean it up. He just parked it out there on the lot and took off. It was hotter'n hell around here yesterday. The sun cooked it up real good. It was a real mess when I opened her up this morning."

"Did you clean it up yourself?"

"Some. But there's a detail place down on Westlake that's got a steam-cleaning process that's better on floor mats and upholstery than anything I can do by hand. I took it down there first thing."

"Did anyone tell you to do it?" I asked.

"Tell me? You mean like order me to get it cleaned up?"

I nodded.

"Look," he said. "When it comes to the trucks, I'm the boss, see? I got it cleaned up, and I'll straighten out the door, too, when I get half a chance."

"Didn't it cross your mind that with all that blood maybe you should report it to the police?" I asked.

Wallace left what he was doing and walked over to us, wiping his hands on the towel dangling from his hip pocket. "Why should I?" he asked.

"Why not? If one of your vehicles shows up covered with blood, it seems reasonable to me that you might think it would be of interest to us."

Al nodded his head in agreement.

"Look, fellas," Nick Wallace said, drawing himself erect. "I got myself a fine job here, understand? Mr. Damm pays me a fair amount of money to keep all his trucks running and looking good. He don't pay me to butt my nose into other people's business, no-sir-ee. The trucks come in broke down, I fix 'em. They come in dirty, I clean 'em up. I don't ask no questions, I don't hassle nobody, and I get a paycheck every single Friday."

That speech probably comprised more words than Nick Wallace had ever strung together at one time in his whole life. There was no point in antagonizing the man. We needed him. Since both the exterior and the interior of the van had been washed, and since we couldn't see the bloodstains in the van for ourselves, we would have to depend on Nick Wallace's recollections and goodwill for details about the condition of Larry Martin's truck when it was found that morning.

"Would you mind telling us a little more about it, then?" I asked, in my most conciliatory manner. "Detective Lindstrom and I are here investigating a homicide. We have reason to believe that this truck was somehow involved."

"There was blood all over the seat," Wallace answered.

"Both sides?"

He nodded. "Both sides, driver's and rider's."

"What about the door handles?"

"Both of them were bloody, too. Beats me how he managed to make that much of a mess without ending up dead himself."

I looked at Big Al. "Maybe there were two people in the van," I suggested.

"Could be," he agreed.

I turned back to Wallace. "After Larry Martin brought the truck back here, how did he leave?"

"In his car, I guess," Nick answered. "I mean, it ain't here this morning."

"What kind of car?"

"A VW bug, '68 or '69 probably. Runs real good for as old as it is."

"A bug? What color?"

"Red. Bright red. I helped him repaint it just a few months ago."

"You wouldn't happen to remember the license number, would you?" It was a hopeless question. I knew it when I asked. Nick Wallace shook his head in reply.

"Got enough trouble remembering my own," he said.

"Was there anything unusual in the van when you opened it up?" I asked. "Anything out of place, or anything there that shouldn't have been?"

"Well, the tools were missing. I went straight in and reported that to Mr. Damm. I figured he ought to know about that right away."

"Anything else?"

Wallace shifted uneasily from foot to foot as though fighting some private interior battle.

"I don't suppose it matters none," he said at last. "Even if Larry shows back up here, Mr. Damm's sure to fire his ass."

"What doesn't matter?" I asked.

"It's against the rules to have anybody who doesn't work for us riding in a company truck," he said.

"And you think somebody who didn't belong there was in Larry Martin's truck?"

"You said so yourself."

"But I didn't say it was someone who wasn't authorized," I countered. "You're the one who said that."

Nick turned and walked away from us, picked up something from his workbench, and then came back, holding a small brown object in his hands. He gave it to me.

It was a plastic card case, the freebie kind they give you with business-card orders. Under the clear plastic laminate inside the cover was a Washington state driver's license with a woman's picture on it. I didn't recognize the picture, but I recognized the name—LeAnn Patricia Nielsen.

Without a word, I passed the license to Al.

"Where'd this come from?" he demanded.

Nick Wallace looked down at his feet. "I found it in the van. Under the front seat. On the driver's side."

Nick Wallace's terse words put a whole new light on the case. If LeAnn Nielsen had been in the bloodied van, there was a good chance that she and Larry Martin were somehow involved together. Maybe together the two of them had plotted to get rid of her husband. Permanently.

I turned back to Nick. "We'll take this," I told him, pocketing the case.

He nodded. "You bet. I sure as hell don't need it."

"Tell us once more exactly what happened when you found the van this morning."

"Like I told you, it was parked outside in the sun, right next to the building. I was gonna bring it inside and gas it up when I saw the mess on the front seat. I opened the windows to air it out a little while I got the other vans on the road. Then, as soon as I got caught up, I cleaned up what I could and took it down to the detail place, the one down on Westlake."

"You cleaned it yourself initially? What with?"

Wallace shrugged. "Rags," he said. "And paper towels too. I used up practically a whole roll."

"Where are they?"

"Where's what?"

"The rags you used. The paper towels."

"The paper's over there in the trash. It don't go out until tonight some time. And the towels are on the bottom of the laundry basket."

"Could you get them for us?"

He paused, looking at us for a long moment. "Homicide, huh?" he said, musing to himself. At last he nodded his head as though he'd made up his mind. "I guess," he said. "Whadya want 'em in? Another laundry bag be okay?"

"That'll be fine," I told him.

So we stood there and waited while Nick Wallace rummaged through first a laundry cart and then a fifty-gallon trash container. He stuffed his findings into a canvas laundry bag. When he was finished, he pulled the rope drawstring shut and brought the bag over to us.

He handed it over, then led us to the garage doors, opening one of them with an electrical switch on the wall just inside. Nick Wallace wasn't about to be disturbed by unannounced visitors coming and going at will. He was sole keeper of the doors, both front and back.

I turned back to him, once Big Al and I were standing outside in the lot. "Thanks for all your help," I told him, "but there's one more thing."

Nick was already shutting the door behind us. He had to reverse the procedure and open the door again high enough so we could see him. He looked impatient.

"What now?" he asked.

"Where does Larry Martin usually park his car?"

He pointed. "Over there, under the billboard."

The billboard was one of those new state-of-the-art ones, an ad for some kind of fresh ground coffee that included a huge cup with what looked like steam rolling off it. One of my drinking buddies down at the Doghouse works for Ackerly Communications. He told me the steam is really a chemical reaction caused by dropping something called voodoo juice into a powder. It makes an interesting billboard, though, if you like that sort of thing. Under this particular one sat several parked cars.

By the time I turned back to Wallace to ask him another question, the garage door was all the way shut and Damm Fine Carpets' resident mechanic had disappeared, locked safely away in self-imposed solitary confinement.

Al took the bag from my hand. "I'll lock this

stuff in the trunk before we go take a look at Martin's parking place."

That's what we did. With the laundry bag safely stowed in our car, we went back to the steaming billboard and prowled around under it. There were six cars parked there in all, but no red VW bug.

"This must be the Damm Fine Carpets employee parking lot," Al observed.

We scrambled around in the hot dusty gravel for ten or fifteen minutes, but found nothing that seemed out of place, nothing that appeared to have anything to do with Dr. Frederick Nielsen's murder.

"Do you think Nielsen's wife set him up?" Al asked finally as we abandoned our search of the parking lot.

"Could be," I said, "but how?"

"Let's go back inside and ask around."

So we walked back in the front door of Damm Fine Carpets. The same eager salesman started toward us but quickly backed off when he recognized us. We went straight to Cindy at the counter.

"Can you tell us who Dr. Frederick Nielsen ordered his carpet from?" I asked.

"I guess," she said. "Do you know the invoice number?"

"No. It was supposed to be installed on Saturday."

She hefted a huge three-ring binder from a shelf under the counter and leafed through several dozen pages of yellow carbon copies. She had to lean over the counter to read what was written on the papers.

"Here it is," she said at last, pointing with one of her crimson talons. "It was a special phone-in order. Mr. Damm took it himself."

"I see," I said. "One more thing. Can you tell us anything at all about Larry Martin. Did he have a girl friend, that you know of?"

Cindy shrugged. "I wouldn't know about that," she said.

"Maybe we'd better go talk to Damm about the order," Al suggested.

"Oh no," Cindy objected. "Not right now. He's in conference. He's not to be disturbed."

"Have him call us when he's done," I said, scribbling my home phone number on one of my cards and handing it to her. "We need to ask him a few more questions."

We left then. Big Al Lindstrom was fuming by the time we got to the car.

"Conference my ass!" he exclaimed. "That SOB's probably sitting in there watching dirty movies and jacking off."

"It's no skin off our teeth," I reminded him. "It isn't illegal you know. They now have definite clinical proof that masturbation doesn't cause blindness."

Al glowered at me as if my sense of humor was wearing thin on his straitlaced, Scandinavian sensibilities.

"Isn't it almost time to go home?" he asked plaintively.

"Almost," I told him. "Just as soon as we get a line on LeAnn Nielsen."

CHAPTER 7

We stopped by the crime lab to drop off our bag of bloody towels. Janice Morraine took it from me, glanced inside, then closed it back up.

"Thanks," she said, wrinkling her nose in distaste at the smell. "Where'd this come from, a dry cleaners?"

"A Damm Fine Carpets van," I replied.

"You don't need to get pissed off about it, Beau."

People in the crime lab tend to be somewhat defensive at times. "I'm not pissed," I explained. "It's Damm Fine Carpets. D-A-M-M. The owner's name is Richard Damm. It's part of the Nielsen case."

"Oh," she said.

I filled out the lab request and handed it to

her. Jan signed the bottom of the form.

"What are we looking for?" she asked.

"Blood," I answered. "Can you type blood even if it's been diluted with cleaning solution?"

"That depends," she said.

"See if it matches up with what came in on that carpet kicker from the crime scene on Second Avenue, will you?"

She nodded. "Knowing you, I suppose you want it yesterday, right?"

"You got it."

Al and I walked up the three flights of stairs between the crime lab and the fifth floor. There, in our cubicle, he took charge of the paperwork while I got on the horn to Sergeant Bob Daniels at the Community Services Section over at Eighteenth and Yesler.

Daniels is the commander of the twenty or so community service officers, that strange branch of Seattle P.D. that's neither fish nor fowl. Daniels told us we'd need to come to talk to the nighttime supervisor of the CSOs.

The concept of CSOs is fairly new on the scene. They've only been around for the last few years, and I'm one of the die-hard oldtimers who resisted the idea tooth and nail when they first talked about instituting it. In my book, cops are cops and social workers are social workers and never the twain shall meet.

But CSOs turn out to be a little of both without quite being either. They aren't sworn police officers. According to the procedures manual, they're supposed to relieve street cops of a lot of the landlord disputes, juvenile runaways, utility turnoff problems, domestic violence, and other noncriminal crap that eat up law enforcement time without taking any hardened criminals—routine killers, drug dealers, and other professional bad guys—off the streets.

Don't get me wrong. I'm not saying that domestic violence isn't a crime. And I'm not implying that there's that much more of it now than there used to be. Like child abuse, it's finally being reported more these days. And DV cases take time, lots of it.

As the number of reported incidents increases, some of the old domestic violence myths are gradually biting the dust. DV doesn't happen only in blue-collar families on payday Saturday nights. Rachel Miller hadn't said as much in so many words, and Debi Rush had flat-out denied it, but I suspected LeAnn and Frederick Nielsen's big gracious house on Green Lake had been the setting of some ugly scenes most people prefer to relegate to the wrong side of the tracks.

But to get back to the community service officers. They are called to reported cases of domestic violence, the ones where someone—usually a woman—has had the crap beaten out of her. The CSOs take over where street cops leave off. Once the initial police report has been taken, they provide moral support for the victims, as well as transportation to a local safe house.

I was vaguely aware that safe houses existed in Seattle, three of them by actual count, but this was my first experience at trying to find someone who was staying in one. I was surprised to find myself running smack into a brick wall, a petite red-haired brick wall whose name was Marilyn McDougal.

There are always rumors downtown of street cops and detectives running afoul of the CSOs, but this was the first time I had tangled with one. It turned out that all those rumors were fact, not fiction.

If I had seen Marilyn McDougal on the street, I might have thought her cute, but I'd hate to think what would have happened to anyone dumb enough to call her that to her face. They wouldn't do it twice, that's for damn sure. She was like a little bull terrier, all growl and teeth and determined as hell.

She sat there, dwarfed by the bulk of her regulation-sized desk. Her brown, lightweight summer uniform was open at the collar. With horn-rimmed glasses pushed up into curly red hair like some offbeat crown, she regarded me with a kind of regal disdain.

"Of course we don't give out that information," she said archly in answer to my question about the location of the various shelters in Seattle.

"What do you mean you don't give it out?" I demanded. "Not even to fellow cops? Aren't we playing on the same team?"

She smiled a chilly smile. "Let me remind you that we're not all cops, Detective Beaumont. There happen to be a few cops who beat their wives, too, you know," she added.

"I'm not one of them," I snapped back. "I'm not even married."

Unruffled, Marilyn McDougal looked meaningfully from me to the wide gold band on Big Al Lindstrom's ring finger. "He is," she said, "but it doesn't matter if you are or aren't. We don't divulge the shelters' locations to anyone. That's a closely guarded secret. Besides," she added, "you haven't said why you want to know."

No, I hadn't said why, deliberately hadn't said why, and wasn't going to if I could help it. After all, if Marilyn McDougal was reluctant to talk to us then, how much more reluctant would she be once she knew we were working a homicide investigation, once she figured out that one of her little safe-house chicks, LeAnn Nielsen, was a prime suspect.

"But CSOs do deliver the women to these safe houses, don't they? Isn't that your job?" Al tried attacking the problem from the flank.

Unperturbed, Marilyn McDougal nodded. "Right. About eighty percent of the time we're the ones who take them. But not directly."

"What does that mean? Either you do or you don't."

Marilyn McDougal shook her head impatiently. "Look," she said. "The women who work in these shelters put their lives on the line every single day. They're not cops. They don't carry weapons. The husbands are frantic to find their wives, want to get them back no matter what. The CSOs take the women to a drop point, some public place near the shelter. One of the shelter workers meets them there, picks the woman up, and takes her the rest of the way."

I could hardly fault the cloak-and-dagger mentality. After all, we were investigating a homicide. Frederick Nielsen was dead and his abused wife was under suspicion.

"So how would we go about getting in touch with someone in one of the shelters? What would you suggest?"

Marilyn shrugged. "You could call and leave a message. They won't tell you whether or not she's there, but they'll post a message on the bulletin board. She can call you back or not. The choice is up to her."

"What do you suppose the chances are that she'd actually return the call?"

"Not very good."

"That's about what I figured." The brick wall wasn't giving an inch. I got up to leave. "Come on, Al, let's get going. We're wasting time."

Al eased his bulky frame out of the chair while Marilyn McDougal leaned back in hers, a sharpened yellow pencil balanced deftly between two opposing index fingers. She regarded me seriously over the top of the pencil.

"Are you going to stop playing games and tell me what this is all about, Detective Beaumont?"

The brick wall won. I sat back down. So did Big Al.

"It's a homicide," I said. If sneaking around hadn't worked with Marilyn McDougal, maybe honesty was the best policy after all. It couldn't hurt to try.

"I figured as much. Whose?" she asked.

"A man by the name of Nielsen—Dr. Frederick Nielsen. He's a dentist with a house on Green Lake and a swish office up in the Denny Regrade."

"And the woman?"

"LeAnn Nielsen, his wife."

"Why are you trying to find her—notification of next of kin or is she a suspect?'

"Both," I said simply.

Marilyn dropped the pencil onto her desk, got up, and walked to the door of her office. "Wait right here," she said. It was an order, not an invitation.

"Now what?" Al asked.

"Beats me," I replied. I've long since given up trying to understand how women think. It's too complicated. Besides, Marilyn McDougal was in a league by herself. She came back a few minutes later. "I checked our records. We didn't transport her," she announced firmly. "Which means, if she's actually there, that she checked in on her own. What makes you think she is?"

"The husband's secretary told us. So did his aunt."

"I see. Are there children?"

"Two. A boy and a girl as I understand it. Seven and eight."

"When did this happen?"

"Saturday. The body wasn't found until this morning. We're worried someone will slip the name to the media before we have a chance to notify the wife."

"If she didn't do it," Marilyn added.

"That's right."

She sat back down at her desk. "It happens over and over. We see it all the time. They stay too long, until they feel totally trapped and can't see any other way to break the cycle. They end up trying to fight fire with fire and somebody gets hurt or killed."

She didn't seem to be talking to us. With a sudden, decisive movement, she spun the Rolodex on her desk, picked up the discarded pencil, and jotted a series of names and telephone numbers onto a piece of paper. When she finished, she handed the paper to me.

"Those are the numbers of each of the three shelters. The women on that list are the executive directors. When you call them, tell them I gave you their names. I don't know exactly what the reaction will be, but I expect they'll want to be sure the wife is properly notified so the family isn't traumatized more than they already are."

"What made you change you mind?" I asked.

Marilyn shook her head again. "It's got to stop," she said. "The violence must stop somewhere. Killing the sons of bitches isn't the answer."

On that score, we were in total agreement.

"I'd try Phoenix House first," Marilyn added. "The last one. It's fairly new. It has better facilities for women with children."

"Thanks," I told her. "We'll do that."

Once outside the door I noticed Al was shaking his head. "We may do it all right," he said, "but not today. It's past quitting time. We're having company for dinner. Molly'll have my ears if I get home much later than this. I'm already in deep shit."

We drove back to the Public Safety Building. Al took off from the parking garage without bothering to come upstairs. I was in no particular rush to get home, however, so I stopped by our cubicle long enough to try calling the three numbers Marilyn McDougal had given us. Shelter directors must keep bankers hours because at ten to five not one of the three was in her office. I left messages with my name and both telephone numbers and headed home.

A man's home is his castle, right? It's supposed to be a haven of tranquility where he can recover from the slings and arrows that the world and his job throw at him, right? And since I live in the penthouse of one of Seattle's newest condominiums, it should have been true. But when I got off the elevator and saw the two distinct puddles dripped on the carpet outside my front door, I knew there was trouble afoot.

Ron Peters, my partner until March when he was badly injured, was still confined to the rehabilitation floor at Harborview Hospital. His dippy ex-wife had disappeared into thin air while on a religious mission to South America. As far as his kids were concerned, that left things pretty much up to me.

I had moved Peters' two young daughters, Heather and Tracie, as well as their live-in baby-sitter, Mrs. Edwards, into a vacant unit several floors below mine. It was a hell of a lot easier for me to pay the extra rent than it was to run back and forth across Lake Washington to their house in Kirkland. Mrs. Edwards is by and large a fine baby-sitter, but during Mrs. Edwards' occasional naps, the girls tend to get into mischief.

I'm sure the mischief is mostly inadvertent on their part. In fact, when they left the swimming pool with Mrs. Edwards sound asleep in a deck chair, the plan was simply to raid my refrigerator for the sodas they knew I keep there as special treats.

But the sodas had somehow evolved into ice cream floats that had overflowed and slopped all over my kitchen floor. They were both down on their hands and knees trying to mop up the mess when they heard my key in the lock. One of them jumped and the remains of her float disappeared entirely under the drip tray of my refrigerator.

If it had been ten years earlier, if it had been

my own kids, Kelly and Scott, I probably would have raised hell. I've evidently mellowed with age. I helped clean up the mess, fixed the tearful Heather a replacement float, and went in search of the still slumbering Mrs. Edwards.

"Oh dear," she said when I shook her awake. "I must have dozed off. They didn't get into any trouble, did they?"

"No trouble at all," I said. Did I say mellow? Soft in the head is more like it. I didn't even chew Mrs. Edwards out for sleeping on the job. She looked worn out. Besides, both Heather and Tracie swim like fish.

I left the girls with Mrs. Edwards on the sixth floor and went back up to my apartment. I dialed Ron Peters' number at Harborview. He answered on his speaker-phone.

"How's it going?" I asked.

"Can't complain," he replied. "How about you?"

"Big Al and I got sent out on that murder in the Regrade today, the one in the dentist's office."

"What does it look like?"

"Domestic violence probably. The husband was a first-class shit. We think maybe the wife hooked up with a carpet installer to do him in."

"Same old story. We've heard it dozens of

times," Peters said. "Anything I can do to help?"

During the months of confinement, Peters had functioned behind the scenes as the third man on Al's and my team, using the telephone to track down leads we didn't have time to pursue ourselves. It was a way of letting him keep his hand in.

"As a matter of fact there is," I told him. "You can check around with the local emergency rooms and see if someone came in Saturday or Sunday with some bad scratches. Deep cuts, probably, made with the teeth of a carpet kicker."

"Ouch," Peters said. "I've seen those before. They're wicked."

"You've got that right," I said. "The van the guy was driving had blood all over it, but he's disappeared. Maybe you can help us get a line on him."

"I'll do my best. By the way, how are the girls?"

"They're fine. They were here just a while ago. I invited them up for an ice cream float. We all had a good time. I probably spoiled their dinners."

There was a pause. "Thanks," Peters said. He sounded about half choked up.

"Don't make a big deal out of it, Peters," I told him. "It's just like taking the girls to see *Bambi*. I needed an excuse so I could have a float, too."

CHAPTER 8

The bachelor life doesn't have a lot to recommend it, especially if you're a lousy cook. One exception, however, is the ability to kick off your shoes in the middle of the living room and take a nap right after work, without anyone telling you that you need to mow the lawn or haul the garbage cans out to the street.

I'm what's known as a world-class sleeper. If left undisturbed, these afternoon naps of mine can sometimes last right on through to morning. Unless the phone rings, which it did. Right at nine o'clock.

"Detective Beaumont, please," a woman's voice said. It was a crisp, businesslike voice I didn't recognize.

"Yes," I mumbled, trying not to sound as groggy as I felt.

"My name is Alice Fields. I'm the executive director of Phoenix House. You left a message for me to call you. I was going to wait until morning, but then I had another call tonight from Marilyn McDougal."

My stupefied brain cells finally woke up and snapped to attention. "Oh yes, Miss Fields. Thanks for returning my call."

"*Mrs.* Fields," she corrected firmly. She spoke with a sharp Midwestern twang that made her sound as though she had just stepped off the train from Minneapolis-Saint Paul.

"I understand you're looking for a woman who may possibly be a resident in our shelter."

J. P. Beaumont wasn't much of a poker player, but neither was Alice Fields. I was bright enough to figure out that she wouldn't be calling me four hours after quitting time if she didn't know LeAnn Nielsen from a hole in the wall, if she didn't give a damn.

"Might be a resident" like hell! That's what I thought, but I didn't say it aloud. "Did Marilyn tell you that LeAnn Nielsen's husband is dead?" I asked.

There was a sigh, a long weary sigh. "Yes, she told me. She also said that you're in charge of the murder investigation. What I want to know is this: is his wife under suspicion or not?"

"At this stage, the whole world is under suspicion." It was half truth, half quip. It met with icy rejection.

"In that case, Detective Beaumont, I don't believe we have anything further to discuss."

"No, wait. Right now we need to reach LeAnn for two reasons, the most important of which is to tell her of her husband's death. We've held off releasing his name pending notification of next of kin, but that doesn't mean one of the television or radio stations might not get it from another source and put it on the air."

"What's the other reason?" Alice Fields asked.

"We'll need to ask her some questions, to see if she can shed any light on the case."

"Which is another way of saying she is a suspect."

I wasn't making much of a dent in Alice Fields' suit of armor. "We know she was expected at her husband's office shortly before he died. She may have seen or overheard something that would be of help to us in solving the case."

There was dead silence on the other end of the phone. It lasted so long that I began to wonder if Alice Fields had hung up on me.

"Do you know where the Hi-Spot Cafe is?" she asked at last. "It's in the Madrona district, at Thirty-fourth and Union."

"I don't know it, but I'm sure I can find it."

"Meet me there tomorrow morning at nine," Alice Fields said decisively.

"How will I know you?" I asked. I'm a veteran of enough missed connections that I've finally learned to ask important questions *before* I go looking for someone I don't know at a place I don't know either.

"I'm short, white hair, glasses—" she began, then she stopped. "I have a better idea. Tell them you want to sit at the round table. That room's far enough off the beaten path that we'll have some privacy, especially on a Tuesday morning."

She hung up without bothering to wait for me to say yes or no and without saying goodbye, either. I realized later that I hadn't asked her if she'd be bringing LeAnn Nielsen along to the Hi-Spot Cafe. It was just as well. She wouldn't have told me anyway.

My ice cream float was long gone. I was starving. I padded out to the kitchen in hopes of finding food, but before I could lay hands on the refrigerator door handle, the phone rang again.

"Hi there, Beau." It was Ron Peters, speaking to me from the echoing distance of his handless speaker-phone. "I didn't wake you, did I?"

"Don't worry about it. You're not the first. I had another call a minute ago. That's the one that woke me up."

"What are you doing sleeping at this time of night? It's not that late. Besides, I thought you'd want to know what I found out."

"Who found out?" I recognized Amy Fitzgerald's voice speaking in the background.

Peters laughed. "Excuse me. What Amy found out."

Amy Fitzgerald had been Peters' physical therapist during the months he had been confined in Harborview Hospital. She was still his physical therapist as far as I knew, but by now she was also quite a bit more than that. Her off-duty hours seemed to revolve around Ron Peters' room.

"About Larry Martin?" I asked.

"That's right. A woman brought him in to Harborview Emergency Room on Saturday afternoon about one-thirty. He said he was a carpet installer and that one of his tools had fallen on him. They put twenty stitches in his face and head."

"Twenty stitches? That's some cut," I said. "It must have fallen from a long way up."

"Amy says there would have been a lot of blood. I guess facial cuts bleed like crazy."

"There was blood all right," I said. "What about the woman? Was she hurt?"

"She was covered with blood, too. One of the ER nurses said one eye was swollen shut, but she wouldn't give her name and refused to accept any treatment. The nurse figured it was a domestic quarrel of some kind, but the woman didn't want to let on for fear of having one or the other of them wind up in jail. She denied the man was her husband."

Peters was referring to a recent Washington State statute that requires law enforcement officers to attempt to ascertain who's the primary aggressor in domestic violence cases and to lock up the responsible party. It's a law that works a hell of a lot better on paper than it does in real life.

"She was telling the truth there," I said. "If that was LeAnn Nielsen, her husband's dead."

I stretched the kitchen phone cord across to the refrigerator and browsed for food. There wasn't much to be found. In addition to the sodas and ice cream, Tracie and Heather had cleaned me out of English muffins, crackers, peanut butter, and cheese slices. They had also raided the fruit bowl. One lone banana remained, so ripe that it was fermenting in the peel. Banana liqueur on the hoof.

"So what are you going to do now?" Peters asked impatiently. It had to be frustrating for him, lying there trapped in a hospital bed. He could help turn up the pieces of various puzzles but he was unable to manipulate them into place.

"I think maybe I've finally got a line on the wife," I told him. "I have a meeting at nine tomorrow morning. If that works out the way I hope it will, I'll be able to ask her some questions in person."

It wasn't much of an answer, but it was the best I could do under the circumstances. I told him I'd call him as soon as I knew anything more, and asked him to gather anything else he could. With that we signed off. I gave up searching for food in the kitchen and mixed myself a stiff drink instead, pouring the dregs of my last bottle of MacNaughton's over ice and adding a drop of water.

Taking my drink with me, I walked back into the living room and settled down on the window seat overlooking Elliott Bay. It was a cloudless, still evening, the long, late dusk of a Seattle summer. As the sun gradually faded behind the Olympic Mountains, the water came to life with lights, mirroring back the glow of the city on one side and West Seattle on the other. Ferries moved sedately back and forth across the water, their lights shimmering both above and on the water's surface. Behind them trailed inky black shadows where the chop erased all reflections from the glassy water.

The conversation with Peters had depressed me. Most of the time talking to him didn't bother me, but that particular night, it got me good, right in the gut. Oh sure, I was thankful it was him and not me who was slowly learning to walk again, to feed himself, and put on his own clothes. But I railed at the unfairness of it, at the injustice, of a man Peters' age, a man still with young children to raise, being locked up on the rehabilitation floor of a hospital for months so far.

If it had happened to me, it would have been different. At least my two kids were already grown, and I was financially set. But I was okay and Peters wasn't. I was still walking around on my own steam. Ron Peters had a broken neck.

He could be in a wheelchair for increasingly long periods of time now, and Amy assured us that one day, with the help of braces and canes, he would walk again. But for the time being, his only avenue of escape and self-determination was to talk on the handless speaker-phone my attorney, Ralph Ames, had given him as a gift. It was that and that alone that allowed Peters to feel he was still a part of life outside his hospital bed, not only with his daughters, but also with the department.

I slugged down the last of my drink, hoping to wash the guilt away, trying not to think about it anymore. The homecoming blasts from the *Princess Marguerite*'s ship's horn jolted me out of my reverie. Back from her daily excursion to Victoria, British Columbia, the ship was returning with a cargo of weary day-trippers. Flashbulbs winked from here and there on the deck as inexperienced photographers tried to use puny pinpricks of light to capture the approaching Seattle skyline. The *Marguerite* would dock at Pier 66, only a few blocks from where I live.

Glancing down at the street below, I saw a long line of cabs parked single file along Clay Street and turning onto Alaskan Way two blocks below. They would sit there and wait until the passengers cleared Customs and needed cabs. I wanted something to eat, and I wanted it fast, before hordes of *Princess Marguerite* tourists invaded the waterfront watering holes.

The strength of that one drink, combined with the fact that I hadn't eaten, ruled out any possibility of driving. From my window, I saw candles blinking in the bar at Girvan's Restaurant at First and Cedar, a block away. I had been inside it once when I was working a case, but I had never eaten there. It seemed as good a choice as any.

Pausing only long enough to put my jacket back on, I headed out to the elevator, rode down to the parking garage, and walked out through the side entrance on Clay.

The restaurant occupied the penthouse suite of the low-rise First and Cedar Building. I took the elevator up to the fifth floor and walked down a long hallway to the maître d's station. To my left was the dining room filled with quiet, late evening diners. On my right was a doorway. Through it I heard the raucous, comfortable din of a busy bar. That was far more to my liking than the sedate diners I could see in the restaurant. I waved aside the services of the maître d' and stepped into the bar.

It was busy, all right. Crowded even, for a Monday night. I zeroed in on the only vacant stool at the long bar. The bartender, a lady close to my own age, was a pint-sized brunette wearing a heavy squash-blossom silver-and-turquoise necklace over a long-sleeved blouse. She was there Johnny-on-the-spot before I was firmly settled on the stool.

"What'll you have?"

"Can a guy get something to eat in here?" I asked. "Or do I have to go into the dining room?"

"What'dya want? A sandwich?"

I nodded.

"Ever been in Butte, Montana?" she returned, looking at me with her head cocked to one side, a hand resting on her hip.

"No," I said. "I never have."

"You're not Jewish, are you?"

Now I was convinced I was losing my mind, but I shook my head. "Fallen-away Presbyterian," I told her.

She grinned then. "Boy, do I have a treat for you," she said. "Now, what'll you have to drink?"

"MacNaughton's and water," I said, "light on the water. But what the hell kind of sandwich am I getting?"

"Specialty of the house," she answered. "A pork chop sandwich just like they make 'em at Pork Chop John's back home in Butte."

The priorities were definitely on straight. She poured my drink and served it before she disappeared to place the order for my sandwich. I tested the drink. It was fine—strong enough to help me forget Detective Ron Peters and his broken neck.

While I sipped my drink, I looked around the room. I suspected most of the crowd was from some kind of impromptu office party that had started early and run late. Most of the people seemed to know one another, and they were all having a hell of a good time. It was beginning to wind down though. A few people filtered out of the bar.

The pork chop sandwich, when it came, was enough to make me wish I'd been born and raised in Butte, Montana. It was terrific. I plowed through it like I hadn't seen solid food in a week. When I pushed the plate away, the bartender was back.

"Did your mother always make you clean your plate like that?" she asked with a grin. "If you're still hungry, I can order you another one, or how about dessert?"

I shook my head. "One sandwich is enough, but I do want another drink."

"You new around here?" she asked when she brought the MacNaughton's. "I don't remember seeing you in here before."

"I just moved into the neighborhood," I said. I didn't offer any more specifics. I wasn't wild about making polite conversation. All I really wanted to do was savor my drink in peace.

Someone down the bar signaled for another drink and the bartender went to get it. Next to me a man got up and walked away. A newcomer, a woman, pounced on the vacant stool like her life depended on it. A man I took to be her escort planted himself firmly between the woman and me. He was tall and blubbery with a hairline that had receded almost as much as his chin. His companion was a frowzy, dated blonde whose skirt was about fifteen pounds too tight.

I don't usually object to tight skirts, but this one wrinkled and bunched where it should have been smooth. And I don't object to women getting older, either. The bartender was a prime example of someone who was comfortable with life in her forties. The dame next to me was dressed like she was fourteen and looked like a worn fifty.

She instantly endeared herself to me by hauling out a package of those long brown cigarettes, lighting one, and striking a fake glamour pose with the cigarette up in the air like a Statue of Liberty torch gone bad. Naturally the smoke blew directly into my face.

I would have moved down the bar, but by now the troops from the *Marguerite* had arrived and the place had filled back up. There was nowhere to go.

About that time my seatmate's companion, still standing between us, began shooting off his mouth. As soon as he started chipping his teeth, I knew he was smashed.

"I tell you, Mimi, when I was here in '80 you could see the Space Needle from right here. From right here where I'm standing, I swear to God. Where the hell do these goddamned developers get off putting up buildings like that god-awful pile of shit that ruins the view for everybody else?"

Gesturing with his drink, a Jack Daniel's and water, he pointed toward Belltown Terrace, my building. As he did so, the better part of his drink slopped out of the glass and ran down my trousers. He set his glass on the bar and grabbed a damp napkin, using it to mop halfheartedly at the wet trail running down my leg.

"Sorry about that, old buddy," he said. "Didn't mean to spill all over you."

"That's all right," I answered, gritting my teeth.

"But did you ever see such an ugly building? I mean, I come here all the way from Abilene. When I'm in Seattle, I want to be able to see the Space Needle. That's why we came here to have a drink, isn't it, Mimi. I told her I knew a place where we could have a drink and see the Space Needle all at the same time. Isn't that right?"

Mimi nodded. "That's right, Buster. That's what you said."

Buster straightened up and tossed the napkin on the counter. "Hey, barmaid. Fix this gentleman a drink, would you? I spilled my drink on his leg. The least I can do is buy him one. What're you having, fella?"

"MacNaughton's and water," I said.

He made a face. "That slop?" he demanded, shaking his head. "If you're going to drink Canadian, how about something decent, something with some class like Crown Royal or VO?"

"I happen to like MacNaughton's," I said, trying to stay reasonably civil.

Buster clicked his tongue. "No accounting for taste," he said. He turned to the lady behind the bar. "MacNaughton's for him and another Jack Daniel's for me. What about you, Mimi? You ready for another one?"

"Why not?"

Why not indeed? Buster paid for the drinks with a fifty and pocketed every last dime of the change. If there's one thing I can't stand, it's an obnoxious, overbearing, tightfisted drunk. When he had tucked his bulging wallet safely away, he turned back to me.

"Tell me, what do you think about that building?" he asked.

He could have pointed to any other building in Seattle and it wouldn't have mattered, but I happen to own a sizable chunk of Belltown Terrace at Second and Broad. Hoping to dodge some of Mimi's cigarette smoke, I had stood up. Now one of Buster's shoes came down hard on my toe.

"I like it," I said firmly, moving my foot away.

He stared at me in shocked disbelief. "You've got to be kidding! You actually like that place?" Buster's voice was rising in volume, and he was beginning to sway dangerously like a giant sequoia about to bite the dust. People turned curiously in our direction. "It's got no class. I mean architecturally speaking, it's a bunch of crap."

Carefully I set my drink on the bar. "I like it well enough to own one fifth of it," I said.

Most of the time I know better than to argue with a drunk, but by then I'd had several myself.

"Bullshit! You don't mean you actually own part of that god-awful piece of junk?"

"Don't knock it until you've tried it," I returned.

The bartender came back down to where we were. With one clean sweep she cleared all the glasses off the counter in front of us. It was a precautionary measure. A wise precautionary measure.

"Like hell you own it!" He turned toward me while still pointing a drunken finger in the bartender's face. "If you own that building, I suppose the little lady here owns this joint, too, right?"

"As a matter of fact, I do," she replied briskly.

He gazed at her blearily for a moment.

"Hey, wait a minute. You took my drink. I wasn't finished with it."

"You're finished with it all right," she said. "Cut off. Eighty-sixed." She turned and called over her shoulder, "Hey, Bob, call this gentleman a cab, would you? We'll pay."

The maître d', a burly young man who looked to be in his thirties, popped his head around the doorjamb. "Sure thing, Mom," he said.

Mom? Had he said, "Mom"? I glanced at the bartender in admiration. If that was true, she must have had him when she was twelve.

Moments later, the maître d' and two waiters showed up again to escort the protesting Mimi and Buster out of the place. The bar patrons got quiet long enough to watch the excitement, but the volume went back up as soon as the elevator door closed behind them.

"Sorry about that," the bartender said, setting another drink in front of me. "This one's on the house." She stood there waiting while I took the first sip. "What's your name?" she asked.

"Beaumont," I said. "J. P. Beaumont. What's yours?"

"Darlene," she answered. "Is it true what you told him, that you own part of that building?"

"That's right," I said. "What about you? Does this joint belong to you?"

"You'd better believe it," she said with a grin.

First liar doesn't stand a chance.

CHAPTER 9

Most people despise alarm clocks with abiding passions. I don't have to—I have a telephone. I also have a collection of early-bird friends who think that as long as they're up, everyone else should be, too.

The phone beside my bed jangled me awake, and I groped for it blindly.

"He did it again!" Peters announced when I finally fumbled the receiver to my ear. "That big bozo did it again."

People who've been up for hours always expect me to come up to speed instantly. "Who did what?" I mumbled.

"Your old friend Maxwell Cole. He's running off at the pen again or the word processor or whatever they use these days."

Maxwell Cole is no friend of mine. Never

has been. We met in college when we had the misfortune of being in the same fraternity at the University of Washington. He's been a thorn in my side ever since. Currently, he's a thrice weekly columnist for the local morning paper, the *Seattle Post-Intelligencer*. Because of our respective jobs, we frequently stumble into each other. When that happens, you can count on the two of us being on opposite sides of any given issue.

His crime column, "City Beat," burns me up every time I read it, so I don't read it. At least I *try* not to, but there are some people, like Peters for instance, who feel compelled to bring it to my attention anyway. I've learned to put up with it the same way I used to choke down my mother's occasional doses of castor oil when I was a kid.

I propped a pillow up behind me and peered at the clock. Seven-thirty. Plenty of time.

"What is it now?" I asked.

"The headline says, 'Murder Moves Uptown.' "

I was gradually coming to my senses. "Sounds catchy," I said. "Maybe somebody should set it to music."

"You won't think it's so funny when you hear what it's about," Peters growled. "How does Dr. Frederick Nielsen grab you?"

"Not by name! He didn't put the name in there, did he?"

"He sure as hell did. Want me to read it to you?"

"That asshole! That goddamned stupid son of a bitch!"

"Do you want me to read it to you or not?"

"You could just as well."

" 'A little over a year ago, area dentist Dr. Frederick Nielsen closed his Pioneer Square office and moved uptown. He told his old neighbors that he was sick and tired of his patients being hassled by drunks and panhandlers and petty criminals. He said he was moving his practice to a nicer neighborhood in the Denny Regrade.

" 'Dr. Nielsen's patients won't have to worry about petty crime anymore, because their dentist died Saturday afternoon, brutally murdered in his recently refurbished office on the ground floor of one of Seattle's newer high-rise condominiums.

" 'I can't help wondering why Seattle P.D. has been keeping such a tight lid on this case. Maybe they don't want people to know that it's possible to be murdered in broad daylight in one of Seattle's posher downtown settings. After all, letting word out could be bad for business. Certainly it's bad for developers and real estate magnates who are trying to sell the idea of downtown living to a largely indifferent suburban public.

" 'Those suburbanites have every right to be indifferent. Why should they leave relatively crime-free neighborhoods in the north end or on the east side and come downtown where murders are almost routine?

" 'For years the Seattle homicide toll has been about one a week. Fifty-two a year. It would be interesting to know exactly how many of those occur in the downtown core.

" 'Seattle P.D. does acknowledge that Dr. Nielsen's death is number thirty-one for this year. In case you don't want to do the math yourself, that means we're currently running five ahead of this time last year.

" 'If murders are up that much, it seems reasonable that the police department would be doing something definitive about it. Are they? Not as far as I can tell.

" 'A check with the Seattle P.D. media relations office revealed that only two homicide detectives are assigned to and actively working on the case of Dr. Frederick Nielsen. Those two, Detectives J. P. Beaumont and Allen Lindstrom, may be long-term homicide veterans, but they do not constitute the Seattle Police Department's mounting a major, concerted effort to solve this case. Arlo Hamilton, Seattle P.D. public information officer, stated that so far there are no leads in Dr. Nielsen's case. Not any. None.

" 'Remember, I'm not talking here about a couple of nameless, drug-crazed addicts duking it out in a darkened alley between Pike and Pine at one o'clock in the morning. This is the bloody midday slaughter of a Seattle businessman who died in his downtown office at one o'clock on a sunny Saturday afternoon.

" 'Broad daylight, folks.

" 'And there aren't any leads?

" 'Come, come now, Seattle P.D. Certainly you can do better than that. Certainly you can afford to put more manpower into this case than just two measly detectives.

" 'It's ironic that Dr. Nielsen moved out of Pioneer Square to escape petty crime. Obviously it didn't work. Crime—major, not petty—came right along with him, loaded into the moving van along with his office equipment and furniture.

" 'Dr. Nielsen tried a geographical cure for crime. Geographical cures usually don't work because they never deal with the underlying problem. In this case the bottom line is that crime is rampant in our city streets.

" 'I don't pretend to have all the answers, but I do have a suggestion or two. Maybe all the people who are planning to take a drive downtown to look at condominiums next weekend should call their real estate agents and cancel.

" 'After all, if the mayor and the city council and the police department can't make downtown Seattle safe to live in, if a law-abiding dentist can't work there in his own office on a Saturday afternoon without putting his life in jeopardy, then maybe it's time for people to vote with their feet, their moving vans, and their checkbooks.

" 'The mayor's office is busy promoting his In-Town-Living campaign. Maybe he should rename it. In-Town-Dying would be more to the point.' "

"That's it?" I asked, when Peters stopped reading.

"Isn't that enough? Why did he mention Nielsen by name? He claims to have talked to Arlo Hamilton. If that's the truth, you can bet Max knew good and well that no next of kin notification had been made."

"He did it to show off," I told Peters. "To prove to himself and to us that he could do it with or without our help. And because he's a first-class asshole."

"What if the wife sees this article before your appointment this morning? Will she still show up?"

"That remains to be seen." I didn't say that LeAnn Nielsen's appearance had never been a foregone conclusion. Now it was little more than a remote possibility.

"Speaking of which, I'd better hit the trail. Al doesn't know we have an appointment at nine o'clock over in Madrona. I'd better get on the horn and tell him. By the way, were you able to come up with anything else on that Martin guy?"

"No such luck. Amy says she's sorry but the name was all she could get."

"Too bad," I said, "but thanks for trying."

As soon as I said good-bye to Peters, I called Al Lindstrom's house in Ballard. Molly told me that Allen, as she calls him, was already on his way to the department, that I'd have to catch him there. So I hauled my tail out of bed, threw on some clothes, and headed for the Public Safety Building myself.

I didn't bother to eat anything for the very good reason that there still wasn't anything fit to eat in the house.

Al Lindstrom was on the phone when I came into our cubicle. His face was beet red. Veins stood out in a vivid blue pattern on his flushed forehead.

"What's going on?" I asked when he slammed the receiver down, throwing the telephone halfway across his desk in the process.

"That was the prosecutor's office. Remember that assault-with-intent case that was supposed to come up last week and never did?"

I nodded. "What about it?"

"It's come up now, first thing this morning. The prosecutor's office figures they'll need us right around ten, maybe a little after."

"What do you mean? We've got an appointment to meet with a lady from the shelter and possibly LeAnn Nielsen at nine o'clock. Where the hell do they get off not giving us any more warning than that?"

"Beats me. That's what I was saying just as you came in," Big Al said. "They said they tried to reach us yesterday, but I don't have any messages about it."

"We flat can't do it," I told him. "Our nine o'clock is at Thirty-fourth and Union. There's no way we can be back by ten."

Al snatched up the receiver and dialed. "This is Detective Lindstrom. I was talking with a Jeannie somebody about today's court schedule. Yeah, let me talk to her again. I'll wait."

He drummed his fingers impatiently on the table while he waited for Jeannie somebody to come back on the line. When she did, he explained our predicament and then sat there shaking his head while she droned on and on, giving him no opportunity to get a word in edgewise. Finally he slammed down the receiver once more.

"She said they'd settle for one of us—they don't care which—but somebody has to be at the courthouse at ten o'clock sharp or the guy is off the hook permanently. The judge will dismiss with prejudice."

One of the major frustrations of being a cop, any kind of cop, is the hours spent tied to a desk or a phone waiting to put in a court appearance that may or may not ever come off. It's like being hamstrung. You can't go anywhere or do anything for fear the prosecutor's office is going to call and tell you to show up in court on the double. If we happen to miss a court appearance, chances are the crook goes free.

Between the two of us, I don't know who hates sitting around waiting to go to court more, Big Al Lindstrom or J. P. Beaumont. We're pretty much neck and neck on that score.

"Wonderful," I said. "Okay, I'll flip you for it."

Al shook his head. "Nope, you'd better keep the appointment with LeAnn Nielsen. After all, you're the one who made it. Any ideas about what I should do while I'm locked up here? I'd at least like to make myself useful."

"Try going through the Department of Licensing and see if you can get a line on Larry Martin's VW. And check with both the crime lab and the medical examiner's office to see if they've come up with anything helpful. Those'll do for starters. By the way, did you happen to read the *P-I* this morning?"

"No. How come?"

"Maxwell Cole's up to his old tricks again. Plastered Dr. Nielsen's name all over his column."

Al shook his head in disgust. "Damn him! Did you ever wonder what makes guys like that tick?"

"Not me. I don't want to know. Finding out would scare the hell out of me."

Al was reaching for his telephone as I got up to leave.

It wasn't hard to find Thirty-fourth and Union, but I was a little dubious about the Hi-Spot Cafe. It seemed to be a small storefront in the middle of the block. A huge black spider, regally ensconced in a front window, was labeled CHARLOTTE in small, square letters. The spider evidently occupied the window undisturbed.

I opened the door and the yeasty smell of freshly baked cinnamon rolls rolled over me. They say that smells stay in your memory banks better than any of the other senses. Opening the door to the Hi-Spot Cafe made a believer out of me.

Instantly I was transported back to my

childhood. I couldn't have been more than five or six. My mother managed to scrape out a living for us in a tiny alterations shop just off Market Street over in Ballard. The shop next to Mother's was a bakery. The owner wasn't much better off than we were, but about closing time every day he always seemed to have a plate of leftover cinnamon rolls or doughnuts that he swore would go stale by the next morning if someone didn't give them a good home. I remember times when cinnamon rolls were *all* we had for supper.

The scent of those rolls dragged me into the Hi-Spot Cafe like a high-powered magnet. I couldn't have turned and walked away if my life had depended on it.

Once inside, I stopped to look around. It seemed to be more of a take-out place than a restaurant. There were several people lined up at the counter waiting to buy rolls from a huge tray that had just come out of an oven and were being sliced apart on a huge, flour-covered table in one corner of the shop.

I had my wits about me enough to remember I was supposed to ask to sit at the round table. The problem was, every table in the room was a round table.

It was a tiny place, and the eight or so visible tables were all of the round, postage-stamp cocktail-lounge variety. None of them were big enough for two people to eat a regular meal on, and they didn't look particularly private, either.

Just then a woman appeared at the top of a half flight of stairs at the back of the room. She looked down at me. "Are you here for breakfast?"

I nodded. "This way," she said, turning and disappearing up the stairs. "Do you smoke?" she asked over her shoulder.

"No," I answered.

I followed her. The stairway turned out to be an umbilical cord connecting the tiny storefront shop to an old-fashioned two-story house set behind it. The lower floor of the house was crammed with tables, although only five or six of them were actually occupied. At the back of the house, behind a shoulder-high pass-through window, I could see someone hustling around in a kitchen.

"How about right here, then?" the woman asked, holding out a chair at a small square table next to a window that looked out onto the street. "Or would you rather sit outside?"

I glanced around me. All the tables I could see were either square or rectangular. "I was told to ask for the round table," I said.

The woman shrugged. "You won't be alone, then?" she asked.

"I guess not."

She led me to another room, one just off the kitchen. From the looks of the place, it must have been the original dining room back in the old days when the house had been a home not a restaurant. The round table was there, an ancient oak pedestal one, tucked out of sight in a corner behind a door. There was no one at that table or at the gray Formica one on the other side of the room.

"Coffee while you wait?"

"Yes, please," I said. She brought me coffee in a mismatched cup and saucer. The dishes and silverware may not have been part of a set, but the coffee was strong and hot, just the way I like it. I was a few minutes early. While waiting, I sat there quietly sipping coffee and inhaling the enticing aroma.

Right at nine a woman stopped in the doorway of the small room. She looked straight at me. "Are you Detective Beaumont?" she asked.

Alice Fields was short and grandmotherly-looking, with narrow glasses, short white hair, and a buck-toothed smile that showed some evidence of gold spot-welding.

"Yes, I am." I stood up and held out my hand. She shook it firmly. "Mrs. Nielsen couldn't make it?" I asked, trying to conceal my disappointment.

Alice shook her head. "I don't know. I had

one of my volunteers drop a note off at her place last night, but it's up to her whether or not she comes."

"At her place?" I repeated.

"She's moved into her own apartment. Phoenix House is only a temporary shelter, Detective Beaumont. We encourage our clients to get into their own places as soon as possible."

We were making some progress. At least Alice Fields had dropped the phony pretense that she didn't know LeAnn Nielsen from a hole in the wall.

"I see," I responded.

"Do you?" Alice Fields asked, looking at me with sharp penetrating eyes. "The women we deal with have already been dreadfully victimized. I'm here to make sure she isn't further violated by you, the system, or anybody else. Is that clear?"

It was clear all right. I shifted uncomfortably under the leaden weight of her gaze. "So you didn't talk to her in person," I said, clearing my throat. "You didn't tell her what has happened?"

"No," Alice Fields said. "But I did see the article in the paper this morning. I hope and pray she didn't. It would be terrible if she found out that way."

A waitress appeared and placed another

mismatched cup and saucer in front of Alice. "Here's your coffee," she said. "Are you having breakfast this morning, or just coffee?"

"Coffee and a roll, please. How about you, Detective Beaumont? The rolls are delicious here."

"The same," I said.

The waitress started away. Alice Fields stopped her. "How's it going, Diane?"

Diane turned back to us. Looking for a name tag, I saw none and wondered how Alice Fields knew her.

"All right," Diane answered. "I'm plugging away." With that, she left us.

I must have looked puzzled. Alice Fields smiled. "One of our alumnae," she explained. "Our job is to help women get back on their feet. Many of them have never held jobs outside the home before, and they don't have any training. The owner here has been a big help in hiring some of our people and giving them a place to start."

Diane was back almost instantly, carrying two of the biggest, gooiest cinnamon rolls I had ever seen. They were still hot from the oven.

Miss Manners and Emily Post notwithstanding, there is only one way to eat a hot cinnamon roll properly—tear it apart, layer by layer, and butter each bite as you go. I was well into the process when a second woman stepped through the doorway and stopped beside Alice Fields.

She was thirty-five or so, with doelike eyes and fawn-colored hair. She was small and delicate and scared to death. There was a huge purple bruise under her left eye.

"Why, hello, LeAnn," Alice Fields said, ignoring the ugly bruise. "I'm glad you could come. This is Detective Beaumont, the person who needs to talk with you."

I stood up, attempting to wipe the sugary goo off my fingers. They were so sticky the paper napkin shredded completely. "I'm glad to meet you, Mrs. Nielsen, won't you sit down?"

LeAnn sat, but almost without seeing or acknowledging me. She was concentrating on Alice Fields.

"I got your note," LeAnn said. "Is something wrong?"

Alice glanced at me, one eyebrow arched in question. I nodded. It would be better if the words came from someone LeAnn knew rather than from a total stranger.

"Have you read the paper this morning?" Alice asked.

LeAnn shook her head. "No. Why?"

"Detective Beaumont has been trying to reach you since yesterday," Alice Fields said.

"Something terrible has happened, LeAnn. Your husband is dead."

For several long seconds we sat there quietly at the table with Alice Fields' words lingering in the air. The only sound was the clatter of dishes in the kitchen on the other side of the wall.

"You're kidding," LeAnn said at last.

Alice shook her head. "Ask Detective Beaumont," she said.

LeAnn Nielsen turned to me. "Is it true?" she asked.

"Yes, Mrs. Nielsen," I answered. "I'm afraid it is. He was murdered in his office sometime over the weekend."

LeAnn began shaking her head, moving it slowly from side to side. "It can't be. It can't be," she repeated over and over.

Tears sprang to her eyes. She put one hand to her mouth as if to stifle a sob, but the wail that escaped her lips wasn't a cry so much as it was a laugh, a strangled, hyenalike, hysterical laugh.

The very sound of it made my blood run cold.

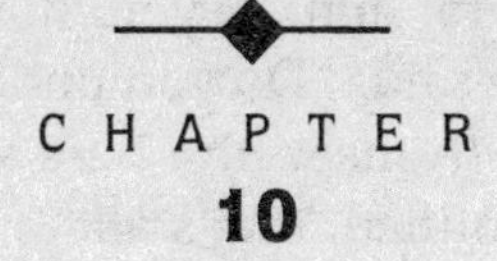

CHAPTER 10

LeAnn Nielsen's reaction was anything but typical. In all the years I'd been doing next-of-kin notifications, no one had ever laughed before. I waited, unsure of what to do or say, while Alice Fields took LeAnn in her arms and held her in a fiercely protective hug. She was there to backstop LeAnn every step of the way.

Gradually LeAnn's strange laughter evolved into something different, into something that approximated genuine weeping. At one point I started to say something, but Alice leveled a forbidding look in my direction and gave a slight shake of her head that told me to shut up, take a number, and get in line. I'd talk to LeAnn Nielsen when Alice Fields was damned good and ready and not a moment before.

Eventually LeAnn quieted some. Alice Fields patted her comfortingly. "You don't have to talk to him if you don't want to, LeAnn," Alice said. "Do you understand that? I wanted you to meet him here so you could be officially notified, that's all."

LeAnn Nielsen nodded numbly.

"And you don't have to answer any questions without having an attorney present, is that clear? You might say things that could be held against you later."

It wasn't exactly an official reading of LeAnn's rights, but it was as close as Alice Fields would let me get. If I had tried it, she probably would have packed LeAnn up right then and disappeared with her.

"Why would I need an attorney?" LeAnn asked. Since the question was addressed to Alice Fields, I let her answer it.

"Detective Beaumont told me on the phone that you're a possible suspect."

For the first time LeAnn seemed to be aware of my existence. Paling, she turned and looked at me, her brown eyes deep and unsettling. She swallowed hard before she spoke. "Is that true? Am I?" she asked.

I nodded briefly. There was no point in dancing around the issue. Alice Fields wouldn't have let me get away with that for one minute. "You are a possibility, Mrs. Nielsen. You have to understand, though, it's still very early in the investigation. We haven't ruled anyone out yet."

"A suspect," she said incredulously, as if saying the word aloud would somehow help her comprehend it. "I had no idea he was dead. How could . . ." Her voice faded away. She stopped talking and sat looking at her hands. She clenched them tightly and placed them in her lap.

There's a standard set of questions that relatives usually ask in this kind of situation: How did it happen? When? Where? LeAnn Nielsen asked none of the usual ones. She just sat there, silently staring at her hands. Alice Fields finally broke the long silence.

"What about your children?" she asked, butting in and changing the subject. "Where are they?"

I'm sure Alice Fields got to be executive director of Phoenix House because she was decisive and insightful. She seemed to grasp all the ramifications of what had happened and what would need to be done, but for my money, someone like her is the very last thing a homicide detective needs when he starts to question a suspect.

Alice Fields was the last thing I needed, but there was no way to get rid of her. She was there for the duration.

"I left the kids in a day-care center near the apartment," LeAnn answered quietly. "I'm supposed to go in this afternoon for a training session at Sea-Tac. I thought it would be good for them to stay at the center all day, to try it out and see how they like it."

"I'll call and cancel the training as soon as we finish here," Alice said firmly. "Then I'll take you down to pick up the children. You should have someone with you when you tell them."

LeAnn nodded gratefully, then she turned back to me, but still without asking any questions. The thought crossed my mind that maybe she didn't have to ask. Maybe she already knew.

"Do you want me to tell you what happened?" I asked.

"Yes."

I took a deep breath before launching into it. "Your husband died sometime early Saturday afternoon. He wasn't found until yesterday morning when his receptionist came in to work."

"That bitch!" LeAnn's two-word reaction was explosive, instantaneous, and totally at odds with her previously mild appearance.

"Who?" I asked.

"You know who! Debi Rush, that's who!"

"What about her?"

"She wasn't just a receptionist," LeAnn said bitterly.

I put one and two together and came up with a triangle. "You mean she was having an affair with your husband?"

LeAnn nodded. With that gesture, Debi Rush's uncontrollable grief, the heartbroken sobs we had heard at the crime scene, suddenly made a whole lot more sense. Receptionists don't necessarily fall apart when their bosses die. When lovers die? That's a different story.

Alice Fields interrupted again. "LeAnn, I'm not sure you should say anything more without having an attorney present."

LeAnn's dark eyes flashed with anger. "Why shouldn't I tell him? I've pretended long enough. Lived a lie long enough. It's time people knew the truth about Fred. It's time they heard the real story."

She dissolved in tears again. This time her whole body shook with wrenching sobs that bore absolutely no resemblance to her earlier eerie laughter. It was several long minutes before she grew quiet again, straightened up, and blew her nose into one of the paper napkins from the table.

She looked directly at me. "What do you want from me?" she asked.

"When did you last see your husband?"

LeAnn drew in a long, shuddering breath, the kind you take when you try to stop crying. Alice Fields reached out and took one of LeAnn's hands, lifted it to the surface of the table, and held it there. The older woman shook her head in silent warning, but LeAnn ignored it.

"No, it's all right, Alice. I'll tell him what he needs to know." LeAnn turned to me. "I saw him Saturday afternoon."

"Where?"

"At his office."

"When?"

"I got there right around one. We had an appointment."

"What for?"

She sighed. "She told me not to go."

"Who told you not to go?"

"My counselor from Phoenix House. She didn't say so in so many words, but we're not supposed to have any contact with the abuser."

"And you went anyway."

"I needed money for my apartment. I'd found a job on Friday, and I needed to get moved in and settled. Fred promised he'd give me the money if I'd just come by and see him. He said he was sorry for what he'd done. He begged me to come."

"And you agreed?"

"Because I *had* to have the money," she answered. "I had given the landlord a small deposit, but I had to have the rest of it that afternoon or I'd lose the deposit. I wouldn't have been able to move in over the weekend."

"He did give you the money, then," I continued. "I understand from Mrs. Fields here that you did get moved into your own place."

If she heard my comment, LeAnn didn't acknowledge it. She seemed distant. When she spoke, her mind was still locked on the money and her need of it.

"My counselor was right. Fred used the money for bait to get me to come to him. He had it there waiting for me in an envelope on his desk. When I reached for it, he pulled it away from me, pulled it closer to him. He said I'd have to pay to get it."

"Pay? What do you mean?"

"What do you think I mean?" She dropped her gaze. Her lower lip trembled. In the silence that followed, I could hear the clatter of silverware and the muted conversation of diners in the other room. Alice Fields had been right. The round table did provide some privacy. Some, but not enough.

When LeAnn spoke again, it was in a ragged, painful whisper. "He said being with me made him want me again, turned him on. He said I could have the money if I'd make love to him there in his office, on the couch."

"LeAnn, you don't have to do this," Alice said. "You shouldn't do this."

Their hands were still clenched in what seemed like a death grip. Both sets of knuckles were white.

"No," LeAnn insisted. "I have to tell him what happened. I told Fred no. It was the first time ever. I told him I wasn't his whore, that he couldn't pay me enough money to have sex with him." She paused and then continued. "That's when he hit me."

"On your face?"

She nodded, self-consciously touching the angry purple spot below her eye. "He hit me first and then he grabbed my arms and held me against the door. That's when he told me about her. I didn't want to listen, I didn't want to know about it, but he forced me to. I couldn't get away. He told me how nice it was to have a real woman for a change, one who knew her place and didn't mind doing things his way."

"Such as?" I asked.

"Like keeping his office immaculate and falling on her back whenever he snapped his fingers."

"He told you that?"

"Yes, he told me that," she hissed. "He wanted to rub my nose in it. He wanted me to understand that it was *my* problem, not his."

I felt like I was missing important pieces of the conversation. "*What* was his problem?"

"Sex. He wanted me to know that he could get it up with her even if he couldn't with me." She paused. "Except . . ." she added as an afterthought.

"Except what?" I asked.

"Except when he beat me up. He could do it then."

"Did he?"

She looked at me without flinching. "He tried. He let go of one of my arms to unfasten his pants. That's when I managed to get away. I grabbed the money and ran." She stopped.

"Go on," I urged. "What happened then?"

"There was a man standing right outside the door."

"A man? Who?"

"A carpet installer. I didn't know him, didn't know he was there. He was working in the other room and heard us. He said he heard me scream. Fred must have forgotten about him, too. Anyway, he told Fred to leave me alone, so Fred went after him."

"Where was this?"

"Out by Debi's desk. All I could think about was getting away, but I couldn't get past them.

They were wrestling there in front of the door. I tried going out the back way."

"Through the garage?"

She nodded. "But the lock had been changed. My key wouldn't work. Fred came charging into the room. He picked up something by the door, a tool of some kind, and came after me with it. I fell against a flowerpot and knocked it down. Just then the other guy came in. He got between us, and he and Fred struggled. Fred hit him with that tool, that thing in his hand, and he started bleeding. That's when I hit him."

"Hit who, Fred?"

"Yes, with a piece of the flowerpot. I remember picking it up with both hands and hitting him over the head with it."

"Where? On the back of his head? On the side?"

"Here," she said, pointing to a place just above and behind her left ear.

"And then what happened?"

She shook her head. "I don't remember."

"What do you mean?"

"I must have gone back to Phoenix House, but I don't remember it. Someone told me I had blood all over me . . ."

Alice Fields had become more and more agitated as LeAnn talked. At last she could restrain herself no longer. "That's enough,

LeAnn!" she ordered. "Don't say another word. We're going now, Detective Beaumont. You're not going to stop us."

She stood up and glared at me defiantly. She must have thought I'd whip out a pair of handcuffs and arrest LeAnn on the spot. I didn't.

"I'll need your address and telephone number," I said quietly to LeAnn. "Someone will need to come to the medical examiner's office and make a positive identification."

LeAnn started to answer me, but Alice Fields stopped her. "No more questions until she has legal counsel with her, Detective Beaumont."

"Of course," I said agreeably. I didn't want to press my luck with the executive director of Phoenix House.

"One of our attorneys will be in touch with you today or tomorrow," Alice declared firmly. "In the meantime, since you didn't read LeAnn her rights, I wouldn't count on using anything she said in a court of law."

With that, Alice Fields pulled LeAnn bodily to her feet and hustled her out of the room. She left me holding the ticket for both our cinnamon rolls.

LeAnn's story sounded on first hearing like a case of self-defense. Grabbing whatever weapon happens to be at hand—including a broken flowerpot or a dental pick—and using it to ward off an attacker doesn't imply premeditation. It's not in the same class as sitting in a room with a loaded gun in your hand waiting for some poor sucker to walk in the door so you can blow him away.

Besides, I'm opposed to rape, all kinds of rape. Including marital rape. As far as I was concerned, LeAnn Nielsen's story had played to a pretty sympathetic audience.

For a moment I considered trying to follow them in an effort to find out exactly where LeAnn lived, but that would only have provoked Alice Fields. It might have speeded the process some, to be able to question LeAnn at my convenience instead of at Alice Fields', but I could afford to wait until LeAnn showed up with her attorney. I hoped he'd be a good one.

About that time Diane came by with a coffeepot and offered a refill. While I waited for it to cool off enough to drink, I scribbled down some notes from what I remembered of LeAnn's story.

Reading back through it, I could see that most of it rang true. The part about using the money as bait and having LeAnn come over to his office to get it certainly squared with everything else I knew about the late, unlamented Frederick Nielsen.

Abusers are controllers. My years on the

force have taught me that much. They want the people in their lives to dance to their tune like puppets on strings. They want to call the shots, all of them. If he was true to type, Nielsen would have wanted LeAnn to grovel for the money, preferably to crawl around on her hands and knees and beg for it. Barring that, if that hadn't humiliated her enough, then forcibly taking what he regarded as his personal property and throwing Debi Rush in LeAnn's face should have done the trick.

But it hadn't worked. LeAnn hadn't knuckled under. She had caught a little of Alice Fields' contagious spunk during her stay at Phoenix House. She had fought her husband every step of the way, taken her money, and run.

And that's when Larry Martin showed up to save the day. Of course, I'd have to get Martin to corroborate LeAnn's story, but that seemed simple enough. It sounded like justifiable homicide to me.

Just then, though, the tiniest corner of doubt crept into my mind. I've been a cop too long. I'm becoming a cynic in my old age. Why had the story ended with the flowerpot? Had Alice Fields ended the narrative then, or had LeAnn broken off of her own accord, stopping just short of telling me about the dental pick? I couldn't remember.

Doubts are meant to be resolved. My job is to prove things beyond a shadow of a doubt. So I went over the whole interview again in my mind. While the coffee grew stale in my cup, LeAnn's story began to sour in my mind.

Had it really happened that way? Was it mere chance that Larry Martin had been there just when LeAnn needed help, or was there some other connection between Larry Martin and LeAnn Nielsen that I didn't know about? And what about LeAnn's reaction to the news of her husband's death? Had she heard it from me first? If so, why the laughter? Relief, grief, shock? It could have been any of those things. Or none of them.

If LeAnn had known about Frederick's death since Saturday, if she had been there when he died, maybe she was laughing with relief because she no longer had to carry the secret around alone. Or maybe she was really happy that Nielsen was dead, that he would never be able to beat her up again.

I tried to fathom what LeAnn Nielsen was feeling. I know what it's like to lose someone you love. That hurts. It hurts like hell, but it's simple. This was more complex. LeAnn had both loved and hated her husband, feared him and yet gone to him for help when she needed it. No wonder she didn't know whether to laugh or cry.

"Are you Detective Beaumont?" A sharp voice penetrated my reverie.

"Yes," I answered with a start.

The woman who had shown me to the table was speaking to me. "There's a call for you. Somebody named Al. Says he needs to talk to you right away. The phone's down by the cash register."

I hurried back down the stairway. A red wall phone with the receiver swinging loose was between the end of the counter and the huge table where yet another steaming tray of cinnamon rolls was coming out of the oven. A clock on the wall over the oven said five after ten.

When I picked up the dangling receiver it was covered with a thick coating of flour. "I thought you'd be in court by now," I said to Al.

"Now they say eleven," he replied. "It looks like I'm going to squander the whole damn day locked up here in the office. Did the wife show? I hope I'm not interrupting something important."

"She showed all right, but she's gone. What's up?"

"I just took a call from one of the LOLs, the one who ditched us."

"You mean Rachel?"

"Yeah, her. I couldn't remember her name.

It musta been a mental block. She called to say that her sister's at home now. We're welcome to come by and talk to her sometime today."

"Al, you're shitting me. You're bored, so you made up this story to see what I'd say, right? Why would she ditch us one day and invite us to drop by for a visit the next?"

"I swear to God, I didn't make this up, but I thought I'd tell you so you could go right over there from where you are. Figured it would save you some time."

"Like hell you did," I retorted. "You're telling me now so I'll go there while you're still stuck on a short leash with the prosecutor's office, while you aren't in any danger of going yourself. Did that parrot bother you *that* much, or was it the LOLs?"

There was no answer from Big Al's end of the line. I had him dead to rights.

"Rachel said it would be better if we talked to Dorothy this morning. She's just out of the hospital and evidently used to sleeping some in the afternoons."

The lady from the cash register came over and pointed to a three-by-five card taped above the phone. On it was a typed message that read, *This is a business phone. Please do not tie it up with personal calls.*

"I've got to get off the line here," I said. "I'll head on up to their apartment as soon as I can.

By the way, if you get a chance, call the medical examiner's office and find out if there was a bruise behind Frederick Nielsen's left ear."

"Right," Al said. "Will do."

I hung up the phone and went back to my table. Diane came by and offered me one last cup of coffee, which I reluctantly refused. The bill for two coffees and two rolls was something less than five dollars. I left a ten on the table.

If Diane was just out of Phoenix House and struggling to get back on her feet, I figured she needed a big tip way more than I needed an extra five-dollar bill in my wallet.

It wasn't charity, either. She had earned it.

CHAPTER 11

Rachel Miller was waiting for me when I got to the Edinburgh Arms at ten-thirty that morning. She was seated on a wooden bench in the garden, daintily drinking coffee from a Melmac cup. The fountain with its pissing cherub gurgled in the background.

Sitting there in the dappled morning shade, she was the perfect picture of a sweet, demure little old lady. I happened to know, however, that as far as she was concerned, appearances were deceiving.

Rachel Miller may have qualified for senior citizen discounts, and she may have been sweet, but she was also the same spry old dame who had given Big Al and me the slip the day before. I didn't trust her any farther than I could throw her.

"Over here," she called, waving to me as I got out of the car.

She was dressed in an exact duplicate of the khaki uniform and Maine hunting boots I had seen her sister wearing the day before. A straw pith helmet lay on the bench beside her. She moved the helmet to her lap and patted the bench, inviting me to sit down beside her.

"I trust you'll forgive me for yesterday," she said apologetically. "I had to go with my conscience and do what I thought was right."

"No problem," I said, unwilling to give her the satisfaction of saying anything else.

"I'm glad you got here before I had to leave for the zoo. I'm going in today. Daisy and I have to juggle our schedules now so one of us can be home with Dorothy round the clock. Otherwise, she would have had to go to a nursing home."

"She's here with you now?"

Rachel nodded. "We picked her up from the hospital just this morning. She's resting now." Rachel Miller grew thoughtful. "I told her," she said.

"About her son?"

"Yes. I couldn't bear the idea of somebody else telling her, some stranger. You can understand that, can't you?"

"Yes," I said.

"She took it real hard. I was afraid she

would. Fred was Dotty's only child, you know."

Rachel Miller lapsed into an uncharacteristic silence, leaving me ample opportunity for comment. I held off, waiting, saying nothing.

"Now that she knows, now that she's gotten a grip on herself, she wants to talk to you, Detective Beaumont, either you or your partner. She wants to know exactly what happened. She wants to see the killer brought to justice."

"So do we," I said.

"Did you find LeAnn?" Rachel asked suddenly.

"Just this morning," I answered. "The director of the shelter helped us locate her."

"Good. If you see her again, tell her to get in touch with us right away. Someone has to take charge of funeral arrangements. Dotty isn't in any condition for it. Daisy and I could, but it doesn't seem like our place. By the way, did you tell her about Dorothy?" Rachel Miller's eyes were brightly inquisitive behind the sparkling lenses of her glasses.

"Tell her what?"

"That Dorothy was . . ." She paused. "Sick," she added lamely.

I shook my head. "It never occurred to me. You're saying LeAnn didn't know her mother-in-law was in the hospital?"

"It happened after LeAnn and the children

left. There was no way for her to find out about it. We didn't know how to reach her." She shrugged. "Besides, I'm not sure she would have cared."

"They didn't get along?"

"It's hard for more than one woman to live in the same house. Daisy and I do fine, but even with us there are times when it's sticky. We call it cabin fever." Rachel paused again, then continued. "I'm sure LeAnn was shocked to hear about Fred, but she's lucky to be rid of him."

Rachel Miller had evidently overcome her previous day's reluctance to wash dirty family linen in public.

"You didn't like your nephew much, did you?"

"No," she answered.

"Did anybody?"

"His mother, but mothers are like that."

"Was he upset when LeAnn moved out?"

"*Upset* is hardly the word for it. He came raging over here, wondering if we knew where she'd gone, demanding to know whether or not we had helped her."

"Had you?"

"No, but I would have in a minute if she'd asked. I don't blame her one bit. I thought Fred was going to have a stroke on the spot. He swore up and down that he'd see to it she never got another penny out of him. He was such a skinflint, I doubt she got much more than that the whole time they were married anyway."

"He offered to give her money on Saturday, enough so she could move into her own apartment."

Rachel looked incredulous. "Really? He didn't actually give it to her, did he?"

"Evidently," I said.

"Amazing. He was a wholesale tightwad, that man was. Just like his father, if you ask me. The idea of having to split things up in a divorce settlement scared him pea green. Dotty told me he was afraid LeAnn would get into his office and try to lay hands on his financial records. That's why he changed the locks."

"He changed them?"

"All of them—the house, the office, even the cars."

"Cars?" I asked.

She nodded. "They had two cars. A new one and an older. One was his and the other was supposed to be LeAnn's."

"But you said he changed the locks on both of them."

"That's right."

"LeAnn didn't take a car when she left?"

"No. I don't know exactly why, either. I

would have if I'd been her. As I understand it, she left by bus. One of the neighbors saw her and the kids getting on a bus down on Green Lake Way. When Fred found out she was gone, he signed LeAnn's car over to Dorothy."

"That's not legal," I said. "LeAnn would have had to sign the title."

Rachel looked at me as though I was somewhat dense. "LeAnn's name wasn't on the title," she said. "Her name isn't on the deed to the house, either."

I could see that, community property laws notwithstanding, Dr. Frederick Nielsen had done his best to keep the deck stacked totally in his favor. LeAnn should have invested in a top-notch lawyer before she left the house.

"Where's the car now?" I asked.

"Out in our garage. Dorothy can't drive it now, not with her hip, of course. If I could figure out a way to give it back to LeAnn, though, I would."

Across the driveway the door to Rachel and Daisy's apartment opened and shut. Daisy came striding toward us, one hand shading her eyes.

"So you are here," she said to me, dropping her hand from her face as she walked up to the bench. "Why didn't you come in and let us know, Rachel? Dotty's been asking for him."

"She's awake then?"

"Has been for some time," Daisy replied. There was an undercurrent in the conversation that made me suspect that a serious case of sisterly cabin fever was brewing.

Rachel got up and placed her pith helmet over her silver hair. "All right then, take him in to talk with her. I'm going on over to the zoo. I'm almost late as it is."

I held open the door to the Buick while Rachel climbed inside. With George's help they must have managed to unload the U-Haul. It was nowhere in evidence.

When Rachel switched on the ignition, the old car coughed and sputtered and smoked, but gradually the engine caught and ran. Standing safely to one side, I watched the car lurch out of the driveway. She must have been using both the gas pedal and brake at the same time. It's ladies like Rachel Miller who give women drivers a bad name.

"Are you coming or not?" Daisy asked impatiently. She was standing at the top of the plywood wheelchair ramp, holding the door open for me to enter.

"I'm coming," I said, hurrying up to the door.

All the curtains on the lower floor had been

drawn, throwing the room into cool, dusky shadow. The living room was still much as it had appeared the day before, except that the hospital bed was made up and the frail figure of a woman lay in it. The dining room, however, was stacked high with boxes and furniture, including Dorothy Nielsen's rocking chair.

From somewhere behind the boxes I heard Buddy's now-familiar voice. "Freeze, sucker."

"My goodness," said Dorothy Nielsen from her bed. "Can't somebody shut that bird up? He's driving me crazy!"

Daisy set off, threading her way through the stacks of boxes. Moments later, she returned. "He's covered, Dotty. He'll be quiet now."

It sounded as though Buddy was in for some tough sledding with Dorothy Nielsen in the house. I don't think she liked him any better than Big Al Lindstrom did.

"Detective Beaumont is here now," Daisy said to her sister. "Would you like me to raise your bed so you can talk with him?"

"That would be fine," Dotty answered.

By the time she had been raised to a sitting position, I could see that Dorothy Nielsen was a paler, more delicate version of her two sisters. Her features, though similar, were finer, more patrician somehow. Her skin was smooth and unweathered. A box of tissue lay beside her on the bed. She groped for one as she sat up, daubing her eyes with it.

"I can't seem to stop crying," she said. "The tears just keep coming. I think they're finally gone, that I can't possibly cry any more. Then they start all over again."

"It's perfectly understandable, Mrs. Nielsen."

"You're the detective?"

"Yes, ma'am. Detective Beaumont."

"Are you going to catch my son's killer?"

"We can't make any promises, of course, but we're certainly going to try. We're working very hard."

She pointed to a newspaper at the foot of the bed. It was a copy of the *P.I.* folded open to Maxwell Cole's column. "That's not what they said in the paper this morning," she announced accusingly. "This man here said you weren't doing anything at all."

"The newspapers don't have access to everything we do," I said. I could have added "Thank God," but I didn't.

"So you *are* doing something, then?" she insisted.

"Yes, we are. You don't have to worry about that."

She shook her head. For several moments she seemed to drift away from me, lost in a maze of private, painful recollection. "He was such a good boy," she whimpered into a tissue. "Such a good boy. He never gave his father or me a moment's trouble. Grew up to be a professional man, just like his father. If only he hadn't married that woman."

"You mean LeAnn?"

Dorothy Nielsen nodded. "She wasn't good enough for him. She never was. He should have held out for something better."

"What do you mean, she wasn't good enough?"

"Dentists have to work very hard, you know," she declared, pausing long enough to blow her nose. "It's a very high-stress job. I should know, I was married to one. And when a man comes home from working that hard, he has a right to expect his house to be the way he wants it."

"And how was that?"

"Straightened up, for one thing. He hated to come in and find toys scattered all over the living room or the laundry not done and put away. And he wanted the children fed and asleep by the time he came home from work. He needed peace and quiet. I kept trying to tell LeAnn that she should pay more attention to those little things instead of doing all that running around."

"What running around?" I asked. Dorothy Nielsen was like her sister Rachel. It didn't take much to prime the pump and get her talking.

"LeAnn's a regular little joiner. Not things like the Junior League or something that would have helped Frederick, oh no. She worked on the P.T.A. used-book sale and insisted on being room mother, not just for little Freddy, but also for Cynthia's class. And then she signed them *both* up for Tee-Ball this year. Can you imagine? A girl in Little League! What's this world coming to, if they let girls do that!"

Tee-Ball and P.T.A. wasn't exactly the kind of running around I expected to hear about. I was hoping for something a little more wicked, something sinister that would add up to motive rather than motherhood and apple pie. What was the world coming to, indeed!

I tried approaching the subject from another angle. "You said if only your son had married someone else. Are you implying that LeAnn may somehow be responsible for his death?"

"It was terrible of her to leave him like that, just terrible. He was wild with grief. It hurt him so much, you can't imagine. He wasn't himself."

"But you didn't answer my question."

"Do I think she killed him? Probably not, but she didn't make him happy. That's what hurts me. If his life was going to be this short, she should have made him happy instead of running away, hiding from him, and breaking his heart."

"Why do you suppose she did that?"

We had been talking for some time, but Dorothy Nielsen hadn't been looking at me. She had been staring indifferently at a section of blank wall across from the foot of her bed, distancing herself from me the way invalids do when they're not firmly connected to whatever's going on around them. Now she turned and looked me square in the face.

"What do you mean?" she asked sharply.

"Do you have any idea why your daughter-in-law ran away?"

"None whatsoever."

"How long did you live with them?"

"Me live with them? They lived with me, young man. They moved into my home right after they were married. We remodeled the maid's quarters into a separate apartment for me. After all, there was no need for a maid anymore."

"How many years ago was that?"

"Eight or nine. It must be nine now. They got married the year Frederick opened his practice down in Pioneer Square. LeAnn worked in his office for a while, but she quit after little Freddy was born. Frederick insisted that his wife stay home with the children."

"Did the two of them ever quarrel?" I asked.

"Detective Beaumont," she answered indignantly, "all married couples quarrel on occasion, or haven't you noticed?"

"Did you ever see any signs of violence between them?"

"Violence?" she asked, mouthing the syllables as though the very word was foreign to her, offensive.

"Did you see any physical evidence of their quarreling?"

"Certainly not."

"What about with the children?"

She pulled herself up in bed, incensed that I should dare to suggest such a thing. "Are you asking if my son harmed my grandchildren? Is that what you're implying?"

"Did he?"

"Frederick believed that sparing the rod spoiled the child. Yes, he spanked them. Of course he spanked them."

"Were you aware that when LeAnn left she went to a shelter for abused women?"

"Frederick told me that, yes. It was the worst possible thing she could have done. If word had gotten out, it would have created a dreadful scandal, him being a dentist and all. Frederick couldn't believe she'd do such a disloyal, terrible, ungrateful thing. I couldn't either. LeAnn and I had our differences, but I thought she was a better woman than that, a better wife."

Again Dorothy Nielsen turned away from me. For a time she once more stared silently at the blank wall. "I'm tired," she said at last.

As far as Dotty was concerned, our interview was over. I was being dismissed, but I still had unanswered questions. Dorothy Nielsen's bedrock of denial fascinated me, made me wonder.

"How did you break your hip, Mrs. Nielsen?" I asked.

She shifted uncomfortably in the bed as though my mention of her injury had somehow reactivated the pain. She answered without looking at me. "I'm a stupid, clumsy old woman," she said. "I fell."

Before I could ask her anything else, she turned to Daisy. "I'm beginning to hurt again, Daze. Let the bed down and give me some of that pain medication. It's time for me to have it again."

Daisy moved quickly to Dotty's side and shook two small white pills into her outstretched hand. As Dotty raised the pills to her mouth, I noticed the hospital ID bracelet was still on her narrow wrist. Seeing it gave me an idea. While Dotty sipped water from a glass, Daisy went to the foot of the bed to lower it. She finished drinking, and I moved closer to her to take the glass and place it on a bedside table.

"I see you're still wearing your hospital ID bracelet," I said casually. "Would you like me to clip it off?"

Dotty looked up at me and nodded gratefully. "That would be nice," she said. "I hate those things."

She held out her wrist and I cut through the thin plastic band with my pocket knife. "How's that?" I asked.

"Thank you," Dorothy replied. "It makes me feel like I'm finally really out of that place."

Neither she nor Daisy noticed when I slipped the bracelet into my jacket pocket. I turned to go, then stopped. "Mrs. Nielsen, did your son have any enemies that you're aware of?"

She shook her head. "No. Why would he? He was a good, law-abiding, tax-paying citizen. He was a good son, a loving son. I still can't believe he's gone, though. It's such a waste, such a terrible, cruel waste."

I didn't argue the point with her, but I could have. Dr. Frederick Nielsen's death may have been a terrible tragedy to his mother, but I doubted it was much of a loss to the rest of the world.

From what I had been able to discover, it

seemed to me as though someone had done the human race a real favor in getting rid of him.

It was my job to find out who that person was.

CHAPTER 12

I asked Daisy if I could use the phone to check in with the department before I left the Edinburgh Arms. She obligingly led me to the kitchen. The receiver on the phone was dangling off the hook. "Is somebody using it?" I asked.

"No," Daisy answered. "We did that this morning as soon as we saw the article in the paper. Rachel said we didn't need people calling here. I know they mean well, sympathy calls and all that, but with Dotty just out of the hospital . . ." Her voice trailed away.

"Leaving it off the hook is probably a good idea," I told her.

When I dialed the department, Big Al wasn't in, so I asked to speak to Sergeant Watkins instead.

"Did the prosecutor finally put Al on the witness stand?" I asked.

Watty laughed. "Are you kidding? There's been another delay. He's at lunch now, but I've got a note that says they'll want him for sure at one. What's happening with you, Beau? I heard from Al that you've managed to reach Dr. Nielsen's next of kin. Arlo Hamilton has scheduled a press conference for twelve-thirty. Any objections?"

"None from me."

"How about leads?"

"It's coming together."

My answer was evasive. Watty knew it and called me on it. "So what are you finding out?" he asked.

"There's a witness up in Lake City," I replied. "Since I'm already halfway there, I think I'll go on up and see him. Once I talk to him, we'll know a whole lot more."

"That still doesn't sound like a straight answer to me. Come on. What gives?" Watty insisted, pushing me into a corner.

"This is all supposition, of course, but I'm leaning toward justifiable homicide."

"Justifiable! What makes you say that?"

"According to the wife, there was a fight. Nielsen tried to attack her and she fended him off, with the help of this other guy, a carpet installer named Larry Martin."

"The one you're going to talk to now?"

"Yeah."

"Are you going to arrest him?"

"No, I'm not going to arrest him. I already told you. I just want to ask him some questions. My guess is it'll probably boil down to self-defense."

Watty was silent, but only for a moment. "Tell me about the wife, Beau. Is she a looker? Your recent track record isn't so hot, you know. It wouldn't be the first time a pretty lady's turned your head."

"Go to hell, Watty," I snarled.

"By the way, Al says the medical examiner wants to know if you're psychic or what. He says there was a helluva bruise just behind Nielsen's left ear, a bruise and some pottery fragments."

"I'm psychic, all right," I told him. I hung up the phone long enough to cut the connection, then I dropped the receiver again, leaving it hanging loose the same way I had found it.

Behind me, Daisy came into the kitchen carrying a cardboard box. She opened it on the counter and carefully began removing and unwrapping the contents—a set of fine, bone china teacups and saucers. She held a delicate cup up to the window and examined it in the sunlight.

"Dotty wants us to use her things," she said. "I'm afraid we'll break them."

I could understand her concern. The china was as far from their worn Melmac as a shiny new Mercedes is from a broken down VW bus. Behind us the telephone squealed, letting us know it had not been hung up properly. We ignored it.

Daisy escorted me back through the living room. On the bed in the corner, Dorothy Nielsen appeared to be sound asleep.

"I couldn't help overhearing," Daisy said, once we were outside the apartment and well beyond Dorothy's earshot. "Did you say something about arresting someone?"

"Don't believe everything you hear," I told her. "That was my supervisor downtown. He's overeager. This is an important case. The department wants some action, especially after Maxwell Cole's piece in the paper this morning, but it's far too soon to arrest anybody."

"Do you have a suspect?" she persisted.

I didn't want to offend her, but I didn't want to spill my guts, either. "Look," I said kindly, "I can certainly understand your concern, but I can't answer that question without jeopardizing the investigation. You wouldn't want that, would you?"

She shook her head. I put one foot inside my car then pulled it back out. "By the way,

Sergeant Watkins did tell me that they've scheduled a press conference for twelve-thirty. That's when they'll release your nephew's name. I know word leaked out before, but this will be the first official announcement."

"All right," she said. "Thanks for telling me."

She seemed strangely subdued, far different from the angry woman I had seen the day before, one who had been pitching heavy boxes and furniture into a U-Haul trailer. Today she was less angry, more approachable. I decided to go ahead and ask her the question that had been bothering me ever since my conversation with Dorothy Nielsen. After all, if Daisy turned on me, the worst that could happen would be having the car door slam shut in my face.

"How did your sister break her hip?" I asked.

"You heard what she said," Daisy replied. It was an answer that avoided my question.

"I heard her say she was stupid, but stupidity doesn't usually break bones." Daisy turned her face away from me. Her eyes seemed to focus on a pair of squawking crows arguing noisily in a nearby tree. I tried another tack.

"What did you think of your nephew?" I asked.

She swung her face back toward me with

something of the previous day's fire snapping in her eyes. "He was a worthless little no-account, no matter what his mother says." With that, Daisy turned on her heel and marched into the house.

Her opinion of Dr. Frederick Nielsen tallied with everyone else's—everyone's but his mother's.

I drove back to I-5 on Forty-fifth and got on the freeway heading north. The Lake City Way exit is only two off-ramps above where I was. I cut across Seattle's north-end urban sprawl and through Lake City itself.

Someone in Lake City had recently invested a wad of money in a local neighborhood beautification program. Trees and shrubs had been set in the median along Lake City Way. The greenery was accompanied by some artwork that looked for all the world like baked potatoes with knives stuck in them. It's part of a program called Art in Public Places.

I call it Rocks in Public Places. For obvious reasons.

My notebook told me that Larry Martin's address was on Erickson Place N.E. I never would have found it without a map. It was a short street, not much over a block or two long, off to the right, north of Lake City proper. I spotted the address first, then the orange-and-black FOR RENT sign in the window.

The apartment fronted on an alley. It was a small frame walk-up built over the garage of a weathered house that faced the street. I climbed the steep stairs and knocked. There was no answer.

"You lookin' for a place to rent?" a voice called up to me.

I turned around and looked down. An old man in a faded blue plaid shirt sat in a wobbly deck chair on the back porch of the main house. The chair had been positioned to take advantage of the single patch of sunlight that wasn't shaded by a huge, overhanging alder.

"Actually, I'm looking for Larry Martin," I answered. "I understand he lives here."

"Used to live here," the old man corrected. "Lived here right up until this morning."

"What do you mean?" I climbed down the steps and crossed a tiny scrap of yard to where the old man sat. He was gnarled and wizened and totally bald. An old-fashioned hearing aid protruded from behind one ear. He leaned down and held out a misshapen paw of a hand.

"Name's John Caldwell," he said. "Larry came tearing in here in that little red bug of his just about an hour and a half ago. Looked like he'd been in a cat fight, if you ask me. He was cut up pretty bad, had stitches all over his face. Told me his mother was real sick. He said she was so bad off that he was going to have to move back home to help take care of her. He asked me if he could have his deposit back, but I told him no way, not without at least a month's notice in advance so we'd have half a chance to rent it to someone else."

"He moved out, just like that?"

"Yup. Lock, stock, and barrel. He left some boxes in storage in the garage. Said he'd be back for those later. I called Gertie, my wife. She still works downtown. I'm retired, you see. So while he was packing, I called Gertie and asked her what she thought. She said he'd been a real good tenant, been here the better part of five years, always paid his rent on time, always kept the place neat, never was any trouble whatsoever. He was a hard worker, too. Worked all day and went to school at night over to the university. He never said what he was studying.

"Anyway, Gertie says to me, you give him half his deposit today, since it sounds like he needs the money, and you tell him that we'll send the rest of it when we rent the place. So I did like she said. I gave him the hundred and fifty-three in cash, and he was real happy to have it. He must've been in a hurry. He went rushing off and didn't tell me where to send the stuff or when he'd be back for it."

My mind was racing. Why was Larry Martin in such a hurry to leave town? I could think of only one possible reason.

"What time did you say he got here?" I asked.

The old man shrugged. "Right around ten-thirty, thereabouts. No later than that. Maybe a little before, now that I get thinking about it."

I glanced at my watch. I had talked to LeAnn Nielsen between nine and ten. If she had known how to reach him, that would have given her time enough to warn Larry Martin that I was prowling around asking questions. Was it cause and effect?

I've been a cop far too long to think otherwise.

Playing it low key, I tried not to alarm the garrulous old man. I didn't want to shut off the flow of information.

"Did he happen to mention where home was?"

"Nope. If he did, I don't remember. Seems like he was from around these parts somewhere, but the details escape me. Gertie might know. She's good at remembering. Want me to call her and ask?"

"Sure," I said. "If it isn't too much trouble."

The old man helped himself up with the aid of a four-pronged cane that had been lurking beneath his chair. Once up, he paused long enough to straighten his shirt and snap his red suspenders.

"It's gonna be a scorcher by afternoon," he said, peering up at the cloudless blue sky overhead. "I don't like it when it gets too hot. Don't like it one bit."

He tottered into the house, leaning heavily on the cane. I paced impatiently back and forth in the tiny yard, waiting for him to return. At last he reappeared at the back door.

"Nope, Gertie don't remember either. She says she thinks he's from somewhere down around Raymond or Aberdeen maybe, but she can't say for certain. By the way, you didn't say what you wanted him for. He's not in any trouble, is he? I'd sure hate to think he was."

"So would I," I said.

Taking a piece of paper from my notebook, I jotted my home telephone number down and handed it to him. "If you hear from him, give me a call at this number, would you?"

"Sure thing. By the way, know somebody who's in the market for an apartment? We'd make 'em a good deal, I can tell you that."

"I can't think of anybody," I told him, edging toward my car. "But if I do, I'll have them stop by."

Once back in the car, I tried reaching Big Al by radio. I had a tough time getting through. All the dispatchers were busy with a major problem of some kind that seemed to center in the Fremont district. I waited my turn. Finally someone patched me through to Al.

"Beau, where the hell are you?"

"What do you mean, where am I? I'm coming back from Lake City just like I told Watty I would. Why? What's up?"

"Haven't you heard?"

"Heard what, damn it?"

"Larry Martin's holed up at the carpet store. He's gone berserk. He's barricaded himself in that room with Richard Damm. Nobody knows if he's armed or not. The secretary thinks so."

"How do you know it's Martin?"

"The secretary called 911. She said it was him. Watty came flying in here and wanted to know if that wasn't the name of the suspect in the Nielsen case. I told him yes. He's ready to pull you limb from limb. He tore out of here mumbling something about you and justifiable homicide. I'd watch my butt if I were you."

Grabbing my flasher, I stuck it on top of the car and jammed the gas pedal to the floorboard.

"So what else is new? Where is he?"

"Watty? He's en route to the scene. Probably there by now. He said to send you there on the double as soon as we heard from you."

"I'm on my way," I said. "What's the situation?"

"They've evacuated the building itself and some of the neighboring ones as well. They're deploying the Emergency Response Team right now. The Fremont Bridge is closed to all traffic. They're not letting anybody through. That whole area's tied up in knots."

"What's the best way to get there?" I asked. By then I was approaching the freeway on Lake City Way.

"Hang on," Big Al responded. He was off the radio for a moment, then he came back on. "Recommend taking Aurora southbound. Exit south of the bridge, then beat your way down the hill as best you can."

His directions came back just in time. I darted across I-5 and headed for Aurora.

"Who's in charge there?"

"Captain Logan," Al replied.

Dick Logan, the Emergency Response Team squad leader, is a tough, well-respected, longtime cop. I was relieved to hear his name. He's someone you can count on when the chips are down.

"What about you?" I asked.

"Me?" The word exploded in my ear as Big Al's voice shook with frustration. "Me? I'm stuck here waiting for the damn prosecutor! All I can say is, they'd better convict that crook. If they don't, I may just finish him off myself."

It wasn't the kind of calm, routine interdepartmental communication the brass likes to have broadcast over police band radios.

Fortunately, the brass, both collectively and individually, were far too preoccupied with the crisis at hand to pay any attention to Big Al's profaning of the airwaves.

Truth be known, I was probably the only one listening.

CHAPTER 13

Something that always amuses me whenever I watch television or movie police dramas is the Hollywood version of the car chase scene. They make it look so easy. Traffic melts out of the hero's way, letting him ride to the rescue just in time. Whatever doesn't move is either crashed through or jumped over.

In real life, traffic doesn't magically disappear, and municipalities frown on having their vehicles used in demolition derbies. That's just not the way it works in real life. And it's not the way it worked on Aurora Avenue that afternoon, either.

By the time I neared Green Lake, Aurora Avenue was stopped dead. One inattentive driver had rear-ended another, snarling the flow in both directions. So much for Big Al

Lindstrom's impromptu traffic advisory.

The City of Seattle is separated into sections by a string of interconnected lakes and channels—Lake Washington, the Montlake Cut, Lake Union, the Lake Washington Ship Canal, and Salmon Bay.

Damm Fine Carpets was on one side of the water. Naturally, I was on the other. With the Fremont Bridge closed to all traffic, I had no choice but to cut all the way across to Fifteenth in Ballard and cross the Ship Canal on the Ballard Bridge. Then I headed back toward Fremont on Nickerson.

And all the time I drove, my mind was racing. My justifiable homicide theory was pretty much out the window. Innocent people don't panic and take hostages. LeAnn Nielsen had warned Larry Martin, and he had snapped. That meant the two of them were in it together. I knew where Larry Martin was. All of Seattle knew where Larry Martin was, but what about LeAnn?

Damn. I had let her walk out of the Hi-Spot Cafe with Alice Fields without getting so much as an address or phone number. If Sergeant Watkins was pissed now, it would be worse when I gave him that bit of information.

Just past Seattle Pacific University I ran into a roadblock. A uniformed police officer told me that a command post had been set up at the top of the hill on Dexter, just above the intersection where Dexter, Westlake, Fremont, and Nickerson converge. Now I was on the wrong side of Damm Fine Carpets from the command post. Some days are like that.

The patrolman let me pass. I eased my vehicle through a crowd of dismayed people. Some of them were from small neighboring businesses, including the beer-drinking late-lunch crowd from the 318 Tavern across the street, who mingled with stunned evacuees from a service in progress at the funeral home half a block away. It was certain to be one of the most memorable memorial services any of those people ever attended.

I inched around on steep, North Queen Anne side streets, trying to reach the command post. Finally, I gave up on driving altogether, parked on Fulton, and walked the last few blocks. There was the usual collection of news media types and curiosity seekers. They stood congregated just outside yet another set of barricades. I dashed through the gauntlet as fast as I could, looking neither right nor left.

When I broke free of the crowd, I had a clear view of the garage entrance to Damm Fine Carpets. There, parked under the steaming cup of billboard coffee, tucked in among several other vehicles, sat a bright red VW bug.

The backseat was stacked to the gills with boxes. A heap of clothing occupied the rider's seat.

Larry Martin was there, all right.

Captain Dick Logan was speaking crisply into a hand-held microphone as I approached the command post vehicle. His barked orders were issued in a clipped but unperturbed manner.

"You've got everybody out of the funeral home now?" he asked into the mike.

"Affirmative on that. What next?"

"Hold tight until I verify that all the other buildings are empty. I'll get back to you," Dick said. He looked up then and saw me standing there. He raised one bushy black eyebrow. "It's about time you showed up, Detective Beaumont. I understand from Sergeant Watkins that this guy's a suspect of yours."

I nodded.

"What do you know about him?"

"Not much," I answered.

"Is he dangerous?"

"I don't know. I can't say. I thought he was pretty much an innocent bystander."

"Like hell!" said an angry voice behind me. I swung around. There was Watty, his face grim, his mouth a thin, taut line. "You sure know how to pick 'em, Beaumont."

I turned back to Logan. "Do you know if Martin's armed?" I asked.

"Not for sure. The secretary said that she thought he was, but she couldn't be positive."

"Have you made voice contact yet?"

Logan shook his head. "Not so far."

"What about the secretary? Where is she?"

Logan gestured with his head. "Over there, in one of the patrol cars. I had a detective take her statement."

"Let me talk to her," I said.

"Suit yourself," Logan replied while his radio crackled with another report.

As I walked from the command post to a cluster of other police vehicles, I was aware of the television cameras following me. I resent doing this job in the glare of television lights. It makes me feel like an insect on a slab of glass under a microscope. All I can do is squirm helplessly while my every movement is examined and recorded.

I wonder sometimes how reporters would like it if the tables were suddenly turned, if we cops took the cameras away and pointed them in the other direction for a change. Would they enjoy being scrutinized while they do their jobs? I doubt it.

Cindy, Richard Damm's secretary, was sitting in the backseat of a patrol car. It was hot, and the back door of the patrol car was wide open. I leaned down and looked inside. She was still blinking as much as ever, but the contacts were gone. In their place was a pair of incredibly thick-lensed glasses. She had evidently been crying. Both her nose and eyes were bright red.

"Hello, Cindy," I said. "Remember me?"

"Detective Beaumont," she wailed. "What's going on? No one will tell me anything."

"Why don't you tell me what you know first?"

"Larry called in around a quarter to twelve. He told me he was quitting and he needed his check. I talked to Mr. Damm. He said not to give Larry anything until we got word from Nick about the damage to the van and until Larry returned all his tools. When I gave him the message, he went crazy. He said he'd see about that, that he'd take his money out of Mr. Damm's hide if he had to. Fifteen minutes later, he showed up and barged into the office."

"Captain Logan told me you thought he was armed."

She nodded. "He was carrying something. It could have been a gun."

"Could have been? You don't know for sure?"

"No," she answered. "My vision's not that good."

"What happened then?"

"He went inside and I heard them arguing. I remembered that you had been looking for him. I was scared, especially when I heard breaking glass. I thought maybe Mr. Damm was in danger, so I tried opening the door. It was locked from the inside. Larry yelled at me. He said to go away and leave them alone."

"When you were there outside the door to the office, could you hear Mr. Damm at all?"

Cindy shook her head. "I'm not sure. I heard something about burning the place down. That's when I called the police. Did I do the right thing?"

"I'm sure you did," I reassured her.

"What if Mr. Damm is lying in there dead?" With that, she buried her face in her hands and burst into tears. There was no sense in trying to talk to her anymore, at least not right then.

"You stay here," I told her. "I'll come back and tell you just as soon as we know anything."

I straightened up and looked around. I wasn't looking for anyone in particular, but when I caught sight of Nick Wallace, I wanted to talk to him. He was standing by himself on a ragged patch of grass on the other side of Dexter, gazing longingly at the corrugated iron door on his precious garage. With hands resting on the hips of his blue coveralls and chin hanging dejectedly on his chest, he looked like someone who had just lost his best friend.

"Hey, Nick," I called to him as I approached. "How's it going?"

He turned and looked at me, shaking his head. "Not worth a shit," he said. "Three of my vans are inside. They wouldn't let me move 'em out. And all the tools too. I've got first-rate tools in there. It would take years to replace 'em. One of the cops told me he's threatening to burn the place down."

I could see that Nick was a whole lot more concerned about his vans and his tools than he was about his job. Who says pride in workmanship is dead?

"He won't burn it down," I said. "Not if we can help it."

I glanced across the street at Damm Fine Carpets, its grilled windows blindly reflecting back the noonday sun, making the building look like an impregnable fortress. Even close up, the small windows were far too high to give any hint of what was going on behind them.

Suddenly, I had an idea. "Is the inside door locked, the one from the garage into the warehouse?"

"Of course it's locked. What do you think I am, some kind of dummy?"

"Does Logan know that?"

"Who's he?"

"Captain Logan, the guy over there with the van. He's in charge of the Emergency Response Team."

"I don't know if anybody told him or not," Nick replied with a shrug. "Nobody asked me."

An idea was beginning to form in my head. "When you talk to Mr. Damm, how do you do it?"

Nick was incensed. "What do you think? I open my mouth and the words come out, just like I'm doing with you."

"No," I said. "You don't understand. Do you go to his office or what?"

"I call him on the intercom."

"You don't have to go through his secretary?"

"Hell no. You think I should have an appointment to tell him somebody's clutch went out?"

"Come with me, Nick. I need your help."

We hurried over to the van. Captain Logan had deployed his men. Now he stood with a bullhorn in hand, ready to establish voice contact.

"Wait a minute," I said. "Let me try something."

"What?"

"Give me a chance to go in there and talk to him."

"No way," Logan replied. "It's out of the question." He noticed Nick Wallace standing behind me. "Who's he? What's he doing here? Get him back on the other side of the barricades."

"He works in there," I said. "He runs the garage. He can let me in the back way. I can talk to Martin on his intercom."

"I told you no, Beaumont. I'm not endangering his life or yours."

"How many of your men have ever been inside this building?" I asked.

"None," Logan replied.

"Well, I have. I was in there yesterday afternoon, as a matter of fact. I happen to know there's an interior door between the warehouse and the garage. It's always locked from this side."

"Jesus Christ!" Logan exploded. "Why didn't someone tell me that before?"

"There's an intercom, too," I added. Logan was listening now, his heavy eyebrows knitted in concentration.

"An intercom connected to that room, the one he's in?" he asked.

"That's right. I've been in there too."

Logan looked at me for a long minute, then ducked his head into the van. "Hand me a couple of those bulletproof vests," he ordered.

He came back out of the van holding two vests. He handed one to me and gave the other to Nick. "Wear this if you're going to be here," he said to Wallace. Logan turned back to me. "What if he's had time to break through the door into the garage?" he asked.

"It's a risk I'm willing to take," I told him, shrugging my way into the vest.

Logan shook his head. "I hate to do it, but at least you know where to look. That's more than my guys do. You're not going in by yourself, though. I'll send Howell in with you. Howell and Perez."

"Fine," I said. "Let's do it."

"I can't go?" Nick asked, disappointed.

"No," I answered, "you can't, but give me your keys."

He pulled a long, heavy key chain out of his pocket and handed it to me. There must have been at least twenty-five keys on it. I gave it right back to him.

"Take off the two I need," I said. "One for the outside door and one for inside."

While Wallace struggled to extricate the keys, I looked back at the building. The yellow walls were blank and forbidding. Logan was right: there had been plenty of time for Martin to have broken into the garage if he wanted to. And if he had, we could be walking straight into a trap.

Don't think I wasn't scared. I was. Cops are human. They don't put their lives on the line without being scared. But if anyone was going to go into Damm Fine Carpets and talk to Larry Martin, I was the one to do it. I was the only officer at the scene who knew the first thing about the inside of that building. Besides, it was my erroneous presumption of Larry Martin's innocence that had gotten us into the mess in the first place.

Nick finally handed me two loose keys. I slipped the key to the inside door into my coat pocket and kept the outside one in my hand.

"Where's the intercom, Nick?" I asked.

"Over on the workbench, right beside the telephone."

"And how do I work it?"

"Just press down on the white button and call. He'll be able to hear you."

"And will I be able to hear him?"

"Only if he presses the button in his office."

By the time I turned back around with the keys, Officers Howell and Perez were lined up and ready to move out.

"No heroics, now, Beaumont," Logan cautioned. "Just get my guys close enough to that room so they can lay down a couple of tear-gas canisters. That's all you need to do. You got that?"

"Got it," I said.

With Nick Wallace's key in one hand and my .38 Smith and Wesson in the other, I couldn't cross my fingers.

I crossed my toes instead.

CHAPTER 14

You don't think about how noisy doors are until you try to open one quietly. When Nick Wallace's key clicked home in the lock of Damm Fine Carpets' back door, the sound crackled in the silent air like an exploding firecracker, and when I slowly pushed the door open, the hinges squawked and creaked with electrifying shrillness.

Holding my breath, I more than half expected a bullet to come smashing out through the open door. It didn't. I crouched there beside the doorway, peering into the shadowy gloom of the garage, waiting for my eyes to adjust to the light.

Three vans were parked inside. Larry Martin's was still in the same place with the doors still open. Another was raised up on a jack. A tire lay on the floor beside it. My guess was that the alarm had caught Nick in the middle of changing the tire. The third, with no identifiable ailment, was parked nearest the door.

Using the vans for cover, we worked our way into the room, creeping along, heads down, weapons ready. Howell and Perez were packing automatic Uzis. My trusty .38 didn't offer nearly the fire power, but I was glad to have it. It felt like an old friend.

Perez reached the interior door first. He tried the knob and found it locked, then motioned for Howell to join him. Meantime, I made my way over to the workbench and located the telephone. The telephone and the intercom.

If I'd had my druthers, I'd have pulled the intercom off the workbench and ducked down behind one of the vans while I attempted to talk to Larry Martin. Unfortunately, this was Nick Wallace's domain. Both the phone and the intercom had been permanently stationed, bolted firmly to the wall behind his workbench.

I knew that Perez and Howell were poised between me and Larry Martin, but I still felt incredibly vulnerable as I stood with my back to them and to the door and pressed the white button on the intercom.

"Larry? Larry, can you hear me?"

There was no answer.

"Larry, this is Detective Beaumont with the Seattle Police Department. Can you hear me?"

I waited, but still no response. "If you can hear me, press the button on the intercom."

An endless period of silence ensued. In it, I could hear the minute ticking of my watch and the muffled beat of my own heart thumping away in my chest. I wasn't scared. Not much.

"What do you want?" Larry Martin's voice spilled into the room like a splash of ice water. "Where are you?"

"I want to talk to you, Larry. Where's Richard Damm? Is he all right?"

"I'm okay, but he's crazy. You hear me? Help me. Get him out—" Damm's voice, recognizable but verging on hysterics, was cut off in midsentence. I hoped for Richard Damm's sake that Larry Martin had simply released the intercom button and turned off the sound. I waited, expecting to hear the report of a fired weapon. None came.

"Larry," I said. "You're making a terrible mistake. Release him. Let him walk out of the building."

"No."

"Larry, please. It'll be a lot worse for you if you don't."

Larry didn't answer. At the door, Perez was motioning for me to join them and bring the key. I ignored him. I was determined to try it my way first.

"Look," I pleaded. "You know the place is surrounded. You can't get away. Give it up, Larry. Let Damm come out first and then you follow." Automatically I fell back on my negotiation training. Use the suspect's first name as much as possible. Try to win his confidence.

"You'll have to kill me first."

Those are chilling words when you're in a standoff. The hairs on the back of my neck stood on end. A clutch of cold fear gripped my stomach. Those are words that tell you that negotiation isn't working, that the other guy has nothing left to lose, that he doesn't care if he lives or dies. When that happens, you're not playing by the same rules. The odds aren't even.

"Larry, we don't want to kill you. You got that? We don't want you to die."

"I won't go back."

I heard what he said, and I knew what he meant, but I forced him to repeat it. "You what?"

"I said I won't go back. I've been in the joint once. Once was enough!"

It grew quiet again as I wondered what to say next, searching desperately for some lifesaving words that would break the stalemate. Again, impatiently this time, Perez motioned for me to bring him the key. I shook my head and released the intercom button for a moment, cutting Larry off from what was said.

"Wait," I told Perez. "Not yet." Again I pushed the button. I wavered, but only momentarily. "Did you kill him?" I asked.

"What?"

"You heard me. Did you kill Dr. Nielsen?"

"I was only trying to help," Larry answered. 'I thought he was going to kill her. Then he came after me. I didn't think she hit him that hard."

A wave of gooseflesh covered my body. It was the same thing LeAnn had said, the exact same story. "What did she hit him with?" I asked.

"Jesus, I don't know. Something from the floor. A vase or something. I didn't know he was dead, for God's sake. I never thought he was dead." Martin's voice broke into something like a sob. A light came on in my head. I knew then and there he was telling the truth, and if he was, so was LeAnn Nielsen.

"Larry, I believe you. Let Richard Damm come out. Help me get to the bottom of this."

"No," he answered stubbornly. "It's a trick. You're lying. I'm sure of it. I'm not going to talk anymore."

"Larry?"

There was no answer, only oppressive silence.

"Larry, I'm sure you can still hear me. What happened after LeAnn hit him? What happened next?"

Perez strode over to me, his face thunderous. I let go of the intercom button so Larry wouldn't be able to hear.

"Will you give me the fucking key?" Perez demanded.

"No," I answered. "Not yet."

I turned the intercom back on. "Come on, Larry," I wheedled. "Tell me what happened. Did he fall?"

"I caught him and carried him over to the chair."

"The one there in the examining room?"

"Yes."

"And then what?"

"We left. There was so much blood in my eyes that I could barely see. She led me to my car and drove me to the hospital."

"And Nielsen was still alive when you left?"

"He was still breathing. His heart must have stopped."

"It stopped all right. It stopped because somebody shoved a dental pick in his throat."

I waited, letting my words sink home.

"What?"

"Somebody shoved a dental pick in his

throat after you left. He bled to death."

Perez was staring at me like I'd gone stark raving crazy, but I wasn't paying much attention to him. I was waiting to see what kind of impact my words would have on Larry Martin.

When he spoke again, he sounded stunned. "You mean he didn't die because she hit him over the head?"

"That's right."

"You mean somebody else . . ." He paused. "Wait a minute, is this the truth?"

"It's the truth, Larry, I swear to God. Let Richard Damm go."

His voice came back, almost a whisper. "It's too late."

My heart fell. Was Richard Damm dead then? Had Larry finished him off when he tried to talk to me? I tried to stay calm, focused.

"It's not too late, Larry. It's never too late."

"If I come out, they'll kill me. I know how SWAT teams work."

"Larry, listen to me. I'm not on the SWAT team. I'm just a detective, a plain old homicide detective. If you won't come out, let me come in. Trade me for Richard Damm. Is he still there? Is he all right?"

I could hear a muffled sound in the background, but I had no idea what it meant.

"If you didn't kill Dr. Nielsen, you've got nothing to worry about. It's all a mistake, Larry. Don't make it worse. Let Damm go."

"It's a trick. It's gotta be a trick."

I decided to go for broke. It was a gamble, but all of life is a gamble, and there are far worse ways of dying than attempting to save innocent lives.

"It isn't a trick, Larry. I'll prove it. We're in the garage right now. There are three of us."

"Beaumont!" Perez howled. "What are you trying to do?"

"We're in the garage," I repeated, plunging ahead. "I'm with two guys from the Emergency Response Team. I'm giving them my gun."

Perez stepped away from me. "What? Are you crazy?"

"Unlock the door. I'm coming in unarmed, Larry. Just me, do you understand? You won't be able to talk to me anymore. I'm turning off the intercom."

I put my .38 on the workbench beneath the telephone and started toward the door with the key to the inside door clenched tightly in my fingers. "Okay, guys, let me through."

Howell was standing in front of the door. "You can't do this. Logan will shit a brick."

"Let him," I said. "I've got to end this before it gets worse. You two stay here."

They could have stopped me, if they'd put their minds to it. After all, there were two of them and only one of me. They had guns; I didn't. But there's a certain understanding that's usually unspoken among cops, a mutual respect, that says when to back off. Howell and Perez knew that Larry Martin was mine. Grudgingly, Howell stepped aside to let me pass, holding out his hand for the key.

"You've got five minutes," he said tersely. "After that we come in with the tear gas."

"It's a deal," I said, giving him the second key.

I made my way through the warehouse and showroom. The place was well lit yet eerily silent except for the soft swish of my shoes on the thick carpeting. Standing outside the door to Richard Damm's private office, I whipped off my jacket, revealing the empty shoulder holster under my arm. I tried the doorknob. It was still locked.

"Let me in, Larry. It's Beaumont. Hurry. There's not much time."

After what seemed an eternity, the lock clicked. I turned the knob and opened the door a crack. The room was totally dark. I stopped and shut one eye, hoping to help ease the visual transition.

"Turn on the light so you can see I'm unarmed. I just want to talk to you."

"Come in first. Put your hands up."

Martin's voice came from behind the wall next to the door. With my knees shaking, I stepped into the room and stopped. Behind me the door swung shut. I was still holding my breath when the lights came on.

The room was a shambles. The fish tank had been smashed to bits. The carpeting was soaked and littered with shards of glass and pieces of decorative shells and plants that had once decorated the bottom of the tank. All the booze bottles had been shoved off the shelves of the bar and lay in a shattered, soggy heap on the floor. A huge hole had been beaten into the face of Richard Damm's big screen television set.

"Turn around slowly," Larry Martin ordered. "Keep your hands up."

I turned. The first thing I noticed was his face. Three separate lines of stitches fanned the length of his cheek from scalp to chin. He was lucky he hadn't lost an eye. He was standing there in a big league batter's stance with an old wooden baseball bat aimed at my head.

My initial reaction was to laugh. When you're expecting the muzzle of a rifle, a baseball bat is a welcome surprise. My relief was overwhelming. Cindy was nearsighted all right, so much so that the wooden bat must have looked like a gun to her. I canned the laughter, though, because the baseball bat was still a hell of a lot more weapon than I had, and Richard Damm's shattered haven gave mute testimony to Larry Martin's ability to use it.

"What do you want?" Larry asked.

"Where's Richard Damm?" I asked.

"Over there on the couch."

"Is he all right?"

"Sit up and show him, Dick," Larry ordered.

I glanced over my shoulder. Richard Damm sat up, his face peeking over the back of the couch. His skin was a pasty, unhealthy shade of gray.

"Are you okay?" I asked.

He nodded feebly.

"Can he go?"

"I guess," Larry said.

With no further prompting, Richard Damm scrambled to his feet and picked his way through the debris.

"Thank you," he whispered hoarsely to me on his way past. "Thank you so much."

"Don't thank me. Go out through the garage."

Richard Damm nodded and left. "Where's the intercom?" I asked. "Turn it on and tell them he's coming out."

"You go first," Larry Martin said. "It's over by the couch."

I led the way. A remote control for the intercom was on the coffee table. I leaned down and picked it up. "You tell them," Larry commanded.

He didn't have to say it twice. I sat down and punched the control button. "This is Beaumont," I announced. "Hostage coming out through the garage door. Acknowledge."

"We hear you," Perez answered.

"And I need more time. Make it ten from right now."

"Ten it is."

I looked up at Larry Martin. He was standing there staring at me like I had just stepped off another planet.

"A dental pick?" he asked. "You said a dental pick?"

I nodded.

"But where'd it come from? How did it happen?"

"You don't remember seeing one?"

"No."

"Tell me again what happened."

"She screamed once. I heard her and went looking. When she screamed the second time, I was right outside the door."

"The door to her husband's office?"

"That's right. She came running out with

him right behind her. I tried to stop him. We struggled there, in the hallway. She tried to go out the other door, the door in the room where I had been working. He broke away from me and went after her again. I got there just in time to see him grab up my kicker and start toward her. That's when he got me with it. He would have hurt me real good, if she hadn't hit him."

"You said she hit him with a vase?"

Martin nodded. "He started to fall. Toward me. We were over in the corner. The kicker fell out of his hand. It almost hit me again, but I ducked out of the way. I caught him before he fell."

"And you dragged him over to the chair?"

Martin nodded. "By then the blood was running in my eyes. I could barely see."

I remembered the unblemished whiteness of the carpet in Dr. Nielsen's hallway. No blood had dripped on that.

"How'd you get outside then?" I asked.

"We went out the back way, through the garage."

"But I thought LeAnn couldn't open that door. That's what she said."

"She found a key in the drawer by the door. She let us out that way. I wanted to stop and grab my tools, but she said we'd better get out of there before he came to, that we'd come back later and get the tools."

"How?"

"She kept the key."

"And did you go back?"

"We couldn't."

"Why not?"

"She forgot she didn't have a garage door opener. She said she'd left it in a car she doesn't have anymore."

I could relate to that. There's nothing quite so thoroughly closed as an electronic garage door when you're in the car and the garage door opener isn't.

Martin let the tip of the bat drop to the floor, then he sank wearily onto one arm of the couch.

"Larry, if you didn't kill him, why'd you do this?"

"LeAnn told me he was dead. I figured it happened when she hit him, and that you'd come looking for me. I tried to leave town, but Damm wouldn't give me my check. I came over here to get it. We got in a beef. Cindy must've panicked and called 911."

I nodded. "Go on."

"When I heard the sirens, I lost it. I figured I was going to jail for murder, either that or they'd shoot first and ask questions later."

"Beaumont?" Howell's voice came over the intercom. "Time's up."

I pressed down the control button. "I'm placing you under arrest, Larry," I said, loudly enough so Perez and Howell could hear. "Give me the bat."

"Not for Nielsen's murder? For this?"

"That's right, Larry. For this. Give me your bat."

He handed it to me. "It's not mine," he said.

"It's not?"

"It's Dick's."

I looked down at the bat in my hand and then back at Larry. "Where was it?"

"He pulled it out from under the couch when I came in the room. When I told him I wanted my money, he came after me with it. He said he'd burn the mother-fucking place down before he'd give me one thin dime. I wasn't about to just stand there and let him knock the shit out of me."

"If you didn't have the bat, what were you carrying when you came in? Cindy said she thought you were packing a gun. That's why she called 911."

"It was part of the kicker extender. She said he wouldn't let me have my check until I brought back all my tools. The extender's all I had left. Everything else was still locked up in

Nielsen's office. See? It's over there in the corner."

I looked where he pointed. A yard-long, chrome-plated, steel tube lay in front of the kitchen sink.

"There's one thing about it," I told him. "You sure as hell know how to be in the wrong place at the wrong time."

He nodded his head sadly. "It's the story of my life," he said.

I pressed down the button on the intercom. "All clear, guys," I announced to Howell and Perez. "You can come on in now."

CHAPTER 15

Howell and Perez were understandably wary as they entered the room, Uzis at the ready. With his eyes riveted on Larry Martin, Howell stumbled over a plastic garbage pail in the middle of the room. Water slopped over the top of it, splashing onto Howell's foot. He jumped back as though he'd been shot.

"The fish from the aquarium," Larry explained. "I saved as many of them as I could."

The poor bastard. Anyone who'd try to rescue dying goldfish sure as hell wasn't a candidate to shove a dental pick into somebody's throat. I was convinced, but I didn't bother to test the idea on Howell and Perez. They weren't buying.

Perez whipped out a pair of handcuffs and put them on Martin, while Howell handed me my Smith and Wesson. "Thought you might want this back eventually," he said.

I put my .38 back in its holster and went to the door to retrieve my discarded jacket. By the time I came back, Perez was reading Larry Martin his rights.

"I'll give Logan the all clear," Howell said.

When we walked out the door of Damm Fine Carpets a few minutes later, the street outside was wall-to-wall people—relieved police officers, eager reporters and television crew members, and a whole slew of just plain folks—all of them craning their necks to catch a glimpse of the crazed killer, Larry Martin—the guy who'd gone to the trouble of trying to save Richard Damm's worthless goldfish.

Larry walked beside me with his head bowed, his hands handcuffed behind his back. My heart went out to him. I knew how that felt from firsthand experience. Since I had helped get him into the mess, I figured I'd better do what I could to get him out.

While Perez locked Larry in the back of a patrol car, I went to find Captain Logan. "Look," I said. "I think we're making one hell of a mistake. Martin told me Damm attacked him with a baseball bat as soon as he walked into the office."

"Wouldn't you? He was carrying a gun."

"It wasn't a gun. He was carrying a carpet

kicker extender, one of his tools. That secretary's blind as a bat. She couldn't tell the difference. Where's Damm? Ask him."

"Medic One packed him off to Group Health in an ambulance. He was complaining of chest pains." Logan started to walk away from me, then he turned back, looking annoyed.

"Now, see here, Beaumont," he said. "Are you suggesting that after this joker threatened to burn down a building, after he held his boss hostage for an hour and a half and tied up the entire western half of Seattle in a gigantic traffic jam, after all that, are you trying to tell me I should let him walk away scot-free?"

"He's not a killer," I argued. "He even saved the damn goldfish in there."

Logan snorted. "Big fucking deal. I've got probable cause to arrest him on assault with a deadly weapon, minimum, and maybe kidnapping as well. You do what you want with the murder charge you're working on, but this one is mine. I'm locking him up. Understand?"

"How about taking him down to Harborview for psychiatric observation?"

Dick Logan shook his head. "What's the matter with you? Has everyone on the fifth floor gone soft on crime these days?"

"I'm telling you, Dick, that murder charge

isn't going to stick, and the assault one won't, either. Cover your butt. Send him to Harborview. Don't put him in jail."

For a long time Captain Logan stood there staring at me. Right up until he opened his mouth, I couldn't tell which way it was going to fall.

Perez came up to us a moment later. "We're ready to take him downtown," he said.

Logan answered Perez without taking his eyes off me. "Take him down to Harborview," he said. "Put a guard on him. Tell 'em he's there for psychiatric observation."

Perez's mouth dropped. He started to object, but Logan stifled him.

"That's an order," he snapped.

Perez beat a hasty retreat. I backed away, too. "I'll take my car and go there too."

"You do that," Logan said. "I think you're going to have some tall explaining to do if Sergeant Watkins ever catches up with you."

"I wouldn't be surprised," I answered.

Logan swung away from me, once more speaking into his mike. "Okay, you guys, let's see what we can do to get traffic moving again. It'll be rush hour before long."

I was in no hurry to run into Watty. I beat it up the hill to Fulton, grabbed my car, and headed for Harborview without bothering to tell anyone else where I was going.

Logan hadn't been kidding about the traffic. It was a mess. As I threaded my way through it, I had plenty of time for thinking, but only one question to work on.

If Larry Martin and LeAnn Nielsen hadn't killed Dr. Frederick Nielsen, who the hell had?

One question. Zero answers.

By the time I got to Harborview and found a parking place, Martin had already been admitted and placed in the psychiatric ward under a police guard. I was his first visitor. He was lying flat on the bed staring up at the ceiling when I walked into the room. He looked over at me.

"It's a hell of a lot better than jail," he said. "I thought that's where they were taking me."

"I talked them out of it for the moment."

He managed a small, grotesque grin as the lines of stitches wrinkled into a nightmare mask. "Thanks," he said. "I owe you."

"How about answering some questions about Saturday? You don't have to, of course, not without an attorney present."

"You believe me, don't you?"

I nodded.

"I don't need an attorney. I'll tell you whatever you need to know."

"Is there a chance LeAnn Nielsen went back to her husband's office alone, after you left her?"

Martin studied me for a long moment. I thought maybe he had changed his mind about answering. "I didn't leave her," he said finally.

"You didn't what?"

"We spent the weekend together. The first time we weren't together was this morning when she borrowed my car to come talk to you. I suppose that's going to look bad, isn't it?" he added.

"It could," I said.

"We didn't plan it like that. Things just worked out that way. She took me right from the office to the emergency room here at Harborview. She was so flustered that she ran the side of the van into a fire hydrant when she was trying to park. After they finished sewing me up, we went back to Cedar Heights for my tools, but we couldn't get in. I already told you that."

"What time was that?"

He shrugged. "I don't know. Three or three-thirty. I don't remember exactly. By then we were both hungry, so we stopped to have something to eat."

"Where?"

"Dag's Drive-In up on Aurora. We were on our way to the store to drop off the van. We were in no condition to go inside anywhere. And she was like, in shock, or something."

"Shock? What do you mean?"

"Like it was all too much for her. She was walking and talking and eating, but later she didn't remember anything about it. We dropped off the van and picked up my car. She was going to catch a bus, but I told her if she'd wait while I changed clothes, I'd give her a ride."

"And that's what happened?"

"Yes. On the way, she told me about her husband. He was a regular son of a bitch, wasn't he?"

"Exceptional, not regular," I corrected.

"Anyway," Larry continued. "She told me about going to see him to get the money for her apartment. She said she had to move out of the shelter that weekend, because they only let them stay for a month. Her time was up yesterday. She's a nice lady. I offered to help her move. She doesn't have a car."

"And she invited you to spend the night?"

"It didn't hurt anything. Her kids were still at the shelter that night. Besides, she needed the help. The shelter has a mini-warehouse with donated furniture and dishes and pots and pans. She rented a trailer and I helped her get her stuff moved."

"Where to?"

"A little apartment down in Tukwila. She got it pretty cheap. It's around the same area where the Green River Killer is supposed to be, that's probably why she got such a deal, but it's close to her job. I think she was scared to be there alone. The landlord told her she could put up wallpaper in the kids' rooms, so Sunday I helped her with that."

"I thought you were too cut up to work. That's what Richard Damm told me."

"I knew he'd give me all kinds of grief over the van and the tools. I just didn't want to have to put up with his comments about how I'd gotten scratched up. I didn't think he'd fire me over it, though."

"Tell me about what went on in Nielsen's office, from the beginning."

"It must have been about twelve when I got there. I was late. The first job that morning really held me up. There wasn't that much left to be done, though, just finish stretching the carpet in the one room, lay the carpet in the other, and put the molding back in place. Nielsen pitched a fit when I got there, but after he finished yelling at me, I went into the back and got started.

"I heard a funny bell a little later—you know, a sort of *ding-dong*. That must have been when LeAnn came in, but I didn't see her then. I was in the back with the door shut. When I heard her scream, that's the first I knew she was there."

"She screamed?"

"Yes. I thought it was an accident out on the street, somebody hit by a car or something. I came running out of the back room to see if I could help. That's when she screamed again. By then I could tell it was coming from inside his little office. I was about to open the door when she came out with him right behind her. She looked scared to death. He'd already hit her once. I swear to God, I think he would have raped her if I hadn't been there."

"I'm sure you're right," I said.

There was a knock on the door behind us. The uniformed guard poked his head inside. "Detective Beaumont?" he asked.

"Yes."

"There's somebody out here asking to see Martin. What do you want me to do?"

"Who is it?"

"She says her name's LeAnn something. She says you know her. My orders are not to let in any unauthorized people, but if you're willing to accept responsibility . . ."

"Have her wait," I said. "I'm not finished yet."

The guard disappeared with my message, but moments later LeAnn Nielsen bounded into the room. The guard was right behind her. "Hey, lady," he was saying. "I told you, you can't go in there."

The guard was followed by a young woman in a gray pin-striped suit with a brunette, Dutchboy haircut and huge dark-rimmed glasses.

"Mrs. Nielsen," the woman was saying, "I must warn you—"

LeAnn's face was desolate. She'd evidently cried until she couldn't cry anymore. She glanced briefly at Larry Martin on the bed, but she walked straight up to me.

"You can't do this," she said, grabbing my jacket by the lapels and shaking me. "He was only trying to help. Larry didn't hit Fred, I did. Don't you understand that?"

The guard reached out and took LeAnn by the arm, attempting to lead her from the room. At that, the second woman sprang into action. She grabbed his wrist. "You let her loose, you son of a bitch!"

The guard swept her hand away, and she cut loose with an impressive stream of profanity.

"Who's she?" I asked.

"She claims to be this one's attorney."

"Let them stay," I said. "It'll be all right."

"If you say so," the guard said doubtfully, but he seemed only too happy to leave the room. He beat a hasty retreat while the attorney, still cussing, turned on me.

"I don't know who the hell you think you

are. Are you trying to question my client without allowing me to be present?" She was a belligerent cat, puffed up and spitting and hissing.

"No, I'm not. Mrs. Nielsen came in here of her own accord," I said. "And I haven't asked her anything."

"You damned well better not, either!"

During this heated little exchange, LeAnn decided to let the attorney and me duke it out while she walked over to Larry Martin. "Are you all right?" she asked, leaning over the bed.

He nodded, patting her hand when she placed it next to him. "I'm fine," he said.

Satisfied, she came back to me. "You've got to let him go, Detective Beaumont. Don't you see? Larry didn't do anything. I'm the one who hit him. I just didn't know I hit him that hard."

LeAnn Nielsen had spent long enough thinking she was responsible for her husband's death. Alice Fields had pulled her out of the Hi-Spot Cafe before I ever got a chance to tell her that Dr. Frederick Nielsen had died with a dental pick stuck through his throat, not from a crack over the head with a broken flowerpot. It was time to set her straight.

"You didn't," I said.

"What did you say?"

"You didn't hit him that hard. The flowerpot isn't what killed him."

LeAnn stepped away from me, looking first from me, then to Larry, and then back to me. "What did then?" she asked.

"A dental pick. Somebody stabbed him with a dental pick while he was out cold in the chair."

By then LeAnn had backed far enough away from me that she was leaning against the edge of Larry Martin's bed. It's a good thing. If she hadn't been, she would have fallen flat on the floor.

"You mean I didn't kill him?" she asked. Her voice shook with disbelief. "You mean I really didn't do it?"

"No."

"Who did, then?"

"Beats the hell out of me."

"Why's Larry locked up like this, then?"

"That's a whole other problem. We'll have to work on that one later. This is the best I could do on short notice."

I turned to the attorney, who was standing, speechless, exactly where the guard had left her. "Any objections, Counselor?" I asked.

She shook her head and didn't say a word.

"Good," I told her, "because I'm going home. I'm off duty. It's been one hell of a day."

CHAPTER 16

I planned to go home. I meant to go home. I dropped the departmental vehicle off in the garage of the Public Safety Building, called upstairs to tell Margie I was gone for the day, and headed for Belltown Terrace with every intention of putting my feet up and settling down with a nice, cool drink.

There's a free bus zone in downtown Seattle, an area where people can hop on and off Metro buses without having to pay a fare. It's designed to help reduce automobile traffic in the downtown core, although I can't see it's made much difference. There still aren't any parking places when you need one.

That particular summer, they could just as well have posted Under Construction signs on the outskirts of downtown Seattle. Massive construction projects were everywhere, from the convention center rising over the freeway to the transit tunnel burrowing under the city. It was a noisy, dusty, crowded mess. What had once been a pleasant, straight-shot stroll from work back to my condominium now meandered through a maze of wooden walkways past buildings going up and holes going down. Dump trucks, some empty, some full, rumbled past while the jarring racket of jackhammers reverberated up and down the street.

With what I had been through that day, starting with Alice Fields and ending with Larry Martin, I didn't need to fight my way through an earsplitting obstacle course to get home. Bearing that in mind, I left the department and dashed down the hill to First Avenue where I climbed on board one of the free buses. I'm not cheap. Old habits die hard.

It was rush hour, so of course the bus was jammed, but I didn't mind standing for what should have been a seven- or eight-minute ride from James Street to Battery. Unfortunately the bus was not only free and crowded, it was also one of the kneeling ones, a vehicle that hydraulically lowers a wheelchair lift so disabled riders can board.

The bus stopped for someone in a wheelchair. Standing riders pressed farther back into the bus to make room for the chair. By the time the bus made two more stops, I was stuck between a reeling, reeking drunk who breathed noxious odors over my shoulder and a heavyset lady who kept both her purse and shopping bag jammed firmly into my ribs.

That did it. Walking past construction sites was preferable. I got off the bus at First and Stewart.

Coming down Second Avenue's slight incline toward Belltown Terrace, I had to walk directly past Cedar Heights. I looked up at it, and my mind shifted out of neutral and back into high gear.

Statistics say that if a homicide isn't solved within the first forty-eight hours, the chances of its ever being solved go down appreciably. Dr. Frederick Nielsen's case was well beyond that forty-eight-hour limit. We were a hell of a long way from figuring out who had killed him. Not that I personally gave a shit, but the Seattle Police Department frowns on unsolved homicides. No matter what I had come to think of the late Dr. Nielsen, his case file had my name on it—my name and my reputation.

Instead of walking straight past Cedar Heights, I paused briefly in front of the building and gazed at the glass door to Dr. Nielsen's office. There was a police padlock on the door with yellow CRIME SCENE NO TRESPASSING signs attached.

While I stood there staring, the earlier question I had been dealing with returned. If LeAnn Nielsen and Larry Martin hadn't killed Dr. Frederick Nielsen, who had? Who else had opportunity? And motive.

My memory did a free-fall through all the information Big Al and I had gathered, coming to rest on what the building resident manager had said about Debi Rush, how he had seen her hurrying into Dr. Nielsen's office at nine o'clock on Monday morning when she had told us she'd been there since eight.

It was a discrepancy we hadn't had time to check out yet, one that had considerably more weight to it in view of what LeAnn had told us about Debi Rush and Dr. Nielsen.

Lost in concentration, I focused momentarily on Debi Rush—the obliging dental assistant, the lying dental assistant, all puns intended. On the lady who had been only too willing to offer Dr. Frederick Nielsen the cleaning and conjugal services his wife had declined to provide. On Debi Rush, the lady with the gangly, nervous, dental-student, dumb-shit husband.

The answer I had been looking for came to me in a sudden flash. Cuckolded husbands have plenty of motive. I know something about that from the injured-party side of the fence. If I'd ever had a fair crack at him, I cheerfully would have murdered Karen's chicken ranching/egg conglomerate second husband. My heartbeat speeded up. Maybe I was on to something, but a voice interrupted my train of thought before the idea had a chance to jell.

"Hey, you can't go in there." It was the resident manager from Cedar Heights, still wearing his orange coveralls. He hurried out of the residential lobby next door, motioning for me to stay away. "The police told me not to let anyone go monkeying around here."

"I *am* the police," I said. "Detective Beaumont, remember?" Reaching out to shake his hand, I tried to recall the man's name, but it was gone, erased completely from my memory bank. Fortunately, he recognized me.

"Oh, I know you. You're the detective, aren't you? The one I talked to yesterday?"

"That's right. Has anyone else been snooping around here?"

The man shrugged. "Some reporters, I guess, and a few television people. That's about all."

I was impatient to get away, to follow up on my latest brainstorm, but I delayed long enough to make polite conversation with the overeager manager. It's called public relations.

"Have any of the tenants in your building reported anything unusual about last Saturday morning?" I asked.

He shook his head. "Not to me, they haven't, but then, I go for weeks without seeing some of the people who live here. They're in and out. Busy folks, you know."

"I'm sure they are," I agreed. "We need to talk to them, all the same. We should have done it today, but there was too much going on."

"I heard all about that. In fact, you were on TV just a few minutes ago. That was something else, wasn't it? They say the same guy's a suspect in this case, too."

I let it pass. Trying to explain otherwise about Larry Martin would have been too complicated, would have told too much.

"As I was saying, we should probably talk to the residents of the building and the commercial tenants as well. Would it be all right if my partner and I came around tomorrow morning to do that?"

The manager hedged a little. He was eager to help, but I could see he was torn. "I don't know. I suppose it would be all right as long as I was with you. This is a security building. The residents don't want a bunch of strangers wandering through the halls. They get real steamed up about that."

I nodded. "I can understand that. I live in a secured building myself. Detective Lindstrom and I will be here sometime tomorrow morning."

"Fine." The manager nodded. "We'll work it out. I'm on the reader-board in two places, under manager or under Calloway, either one. One of us will make the rounds with you, my wife or me."

I was grateful he had finally supplied me with his name. "Thanks, Mr. Calloway," I told him. "Is nine too early?" He shook his head.

As soon as Calloway walked away, I went back to Tom Rush. My mind lit on him like a vulture snagging a day-old road-kill. Why the hell hadn't I thought about him before?

I remembered how eager he had been to escape the confines of Dr. Nielsen's office while we were questioning Debi. He had been upset, shaken, hardly able to wait to get outside. I recalled that he had been tall, not necessarily strong, but that didn't matter. Shoving a dental pick into an unconscious man's throat doesn't require tremendous strength. And certainly that particular instrument would fall easily to hand if the hand happened to belong to a dental student. He'd also know how to run an autoclave.

Turning, I sprinted away from Cedar Heights. I ran the remaining block to Belltown

Terrace, dashed in the garage door, caught the elevator to P-4, and was in my Porsche heading out of the building less than a minute later.

I shouldn't have bothered to run. It was a case of hurry up and wait. Traffic on Broad wasn't slow, it was dead. Grid-locked. I had to wait through three complete stoplight cycles to get across the intersection at Second, and again at Denny. While I waited, I got out my notebook and checked on Debi Rush's address—2139 Eastlake Avenue East.

When I got there, the place turned out to be a rundown, clapboard, multiunit building. It gave the impression of being a onetime motel that had been converted into apartments. It was badly in need of another dose of rehabilitation.

Faded green paint was blistered and peeling. Wooden steps creaked under my feet. The thin, straggly grass had turned brown during the weeks of exceptional heat. In short, it was exactly the kind of apartment building impoverished students have lived in forever—cheap and old but relatively close to the university.

Through a sagging screen door, I saw that the inside door was wide open. A radio blared rock music somewhere in the background, bellowing incomprehensible words over the hum of a room-sized fan that stood near the doorway.

I knocked on the door and Debi Rush herself appeared. Barefoot, she wore a halter top and a pair of short shorts. She was far too well endowed both above and below the belt for the combination to be remotely appealing, but she was cordial enough.

"Hello, Debi," I said. "May I come in?"

She opened the door. "It's hot in here. I was just making some lemonade. Would you like some?"

"Sure."

She disappeared into the kitchen while I sat down on the ratty couch. Thankfully she switched off the music. Even with the fan, the room was unbearably hot and cluttered, too. Cluttered and dirty. The end table next to my elbow was gray with a thick layer of gritty dust. Evidently Debi's cleaning and polishing fetish ended at Dr. Nielsen's office door. The room was lined with bookcases of the classic brick-and-wooden-plank variety. One living room window had been covered with a vivid Mexican serape in a futile effort to block out the afternoon sun. These were definitely student quarters.

Debi came back into the living room carrying two tall glasses. "They say it's going to get all the way up to ninety-five today. It's a killer, isn't it?"

People in other parts of the world laugh

when Seattlites complain bitterly about ninety-five-degree weather, but ninety-five is no joke in a climate where very few buildings are air-conditioned. I mopped the sweat off my brow and wished I could take off my jacket.

Debi handed me a glass. "Of course, I don't suppose you came here to talk about the weather," she added.

She was right about that. I wasn't interested in idle chit-chat. "As a matter of fact, I didn't. Where's your husband?"

She looked puzzled. "He isn't here."

"Where is he?"

"Still down at the university, I suppose. He likes to do his lab work in the afternoons when it's too hot for him to study here."

I was relieved to know Tom Rush was out of the house. I'd make a lot more progress with Debi if I talked to her alone. I got straight to the heart of the matter.

"Where was he Saturday afternoon?" I asked.

"Tom?" she asked, setting her glass down on the armrest and shifting uneasily in her chair.

"Yes, Tom," I answered. "Do you have any idea where he was between noon and say two o'clock? Was he here?"

"I don't understand. Why are you asking me about him?"

I refused to pussyfoot around with her. "Debi, you neglected to mention to us that you and Dr. Nielsen were having an affair," I said.

She paled and swallowed hard. "I didn't think it was important," she responded after a long moment, her voice bleak and very small. At least she didn't try to deny it. I'll give her that much credit. "How did you find out?" she asked.

"Dr. Nielsen told his wife, that afternoon when he came to the office. He bragged to her about it."

I waited a moment, allowing my words to strike home. "Does hour husband know?" I continued.

She straightened suddenly in her chair. "No, he doesn't. Of course he doesn't. You're not going to tell him, are you?"

"What if somebody else already did?" I returned. "What if someone told him and he went down to Nielsen's office on Saturday afternoon to do something about it?"

A look of horror flashed across her face. She put her hands to her ears as if trying to shut out my words, my voice.

"He didn't," she whispered. "He couldn't. It isn't possible."

"Isn't it? Where was he, then? You still haven't told me."

"I don't know. He left that morning when I

did. He said he was going over to the U to study."

"Where at the U?" I demanded.

She shrugged. "I don't know. In one of the labs, I guess. He has a lot of lab work now. I don't go with him. I'm usually at work when he's there."

"And what time did he come home?"

"Late. Five o'clock or so."

"Did you notice anything unusual in his behavior that afternoon or evening?"

"No, nothing."

"Was he wearing the same clothes he had on when you saw him that morning?"

"I don't remember what he was wearing. I can't remember what *I* was wearing." Debi Rush was growing more and more agitated. I could see it in her face, hear it in the intensity of her voice. "He didn't do it. He couldn't have done it. He's a kind, gentle, nice boy."

"Is that why you were screwing around on him behind his back?"

"We needed the money," she said. "Dental school is very expensive."

"The money? What money?"

"Dr. Nielsen offered me a raise, a big raise. He said his wife didn't understand him. I know how that sounds, but he said that she wouldn't have sex with him anymore. He said if I'd sleep with him, it would be good for both of us."

I snorted. "That's right. Wages are deductible."

Two angry red spots appeared on both her pale cheeks, but she didn't continue. I finally broke the silence.

"Let me ask you another question, Debi. Why did you lie to us about yesterday morning?"

"What do you mean?"

"You know what I mean. You told us you got to the office on Monday morning at eight, that you were there right on time. But I have a witness who says he saw you come racing into the building at nine o'clock. What happened? Did you go inside and see something that made you think your husband might have been involved?"

"No. I didn't."

"You didn't what? You didn't come in then, or you didn't see something to link Tom with the murder? Which?"

"It wasn't like that at all. You don't understand."

"Explain it to me."

"When I saw Dr. Fred, like I told you, I was scared to death. I didn't know what to do. I couldn't think. I started to call the police right away, but then I remembered my diaphragm, the one I kept in the office. I was afraid if someone found it, they'd ask questions. So I got rid of it."

"How?"

"I took it out to the dumpster and threw it away."

"But the dumpsters are in the back alley. You were seen entering by the front door."

"I tried the back door, but I couldn't get out. Someone had taken the key to the dead bolt from the drawer. It wasn't where it was supposed to be."

Of course it wasn't there. LeAnn had taken it, but I didn't tell Debi that.

"And you don't have one?"

"No. I always used the one in the drawer."

"And was the dead-bolt lock changed when the other ones were?"

"Yes. I made the arrangements. I called the locksmith and set up the appointment. Dr. Fred asked me to."

"And how long ago were the locks changed?"

She shrugged. "A couple of weeks ago. I'm not sure of the exact date."

"After LeAnn Nielsen moved out?"

Debi nodded.

"What time will your husband be home?"

She glanced nervously at a clock on the wall. "Any time now," she said.

I got up to leave. "All right," I said. "I'm going. We'll be checking on your husband's movements on Saturday."

"Are you going to tell him?" Debi asked.

I searched her face. "What makes you think he hasn't already found out?" I asked. "And even if he hasn't, you must realize that he will by the time this investigation is over. You'd better be the one to tell him."

With that I turned away and left her sitting there. I didn't have enough evidence in hand to accuse Tom Rush of Nielsen's murder, and if the poor simple bastard really didn't know his wife was fucking around on him, I didn't much care to be there when she told him.

I don't like to see half-grown men cry.

Back home in Belltown Terrace, I settled into my recliner and sat there thinking about Tom Rush—wondering if he'd done it, hoping he hadn't.

The more I thought about it, the worse I felt. After all, I personally had walked several miles in Tom Rush's moccasins. I didn't want to have to arrest him for something I might well have done myself if I'd only had the opportunity.

I fell asleep with the sure knowledge that I was stuck between a rock and a hard place.

CHAPTER 17

I went to the Doghouse for breakfast the next morning and discovered J. P. Beaumont was suddenly a local media hero. "Saw you on the eleven o'clock news, last night," Wanda told me as she unloaded a platter of bacon and eggs in front of me. "Somebody else saw you on the five o'clock. They said you went in and talked that crazy guy into giving up."

"For once the news got something straight," I said.

"Weren't you scared? Looked to me like you were wearing one of those bulletproof vests."

"I was," I said. "What I really needed, though, more than a bulletproof vest, was a batting helmet."

Wanda stood there with her arms crossed, frowning. "What's that?"

"A batting helmet, like they use in baseball games. The guy didn't have a gun, he had a baseball bat."

Wanda grinned from ear to ear. "Really? They never told us that on TV."

"Why should they? It makes a better story if they imply the other guy had a gun."

"You don't mind if I tell the other girls, do you? They'll get a real bang out of it."

"Be my guest," I told her.

She hustled off toward the kitchen while I settled down to eat my breakfast.

Knowing I had deliberately avoided Sergeant Watkins the day before, I wasn't exactly looking forward to going into the office. My game plan was to go in, get Big Al, and get the hell back out ASAP. Watty must have read my mind. The sergeant was leaning against my desk waiting for me when I got to the cubicle.

"Got back too late to put in an appearance up here, did you?" he asked with a frown.

I nodded.

"You write me a report, Beaumont. We'll take it to Captain Powell together after I get a chance to look at it. He wants to know what the hell a suspected murderer is doing sitting in isolated splendor up at Harborview Hospital. Believe me, so do I."

I glanced across my desk. Big Al Lindstrom

was sitting there making himself as small as possible. When you weigh 220, that's no easy task. There was a definite twinkle in his eyes.

"I'll have a report on your desk in half an hour," I said.

"You'd better," Watty replied grimly.

He took off, and I turned to Al. "What the hell are you laughing at?" I demanded.

"For once it looks like the prosecutor did me a favor. At least my ass isn't in a sling."

"Don't count on it. What about that assault case? Are you done with it or not?"

"He plea-bargained down to simple assault late yesterday afternoon. I came by to tell you, but Margie said you'd already disappeared. What can I do to help?"

"Go check with the crime lab and the medical examiner's office and see if they've come up with anything while I get Watty's goddamned report out of my hair."

Twenty minutes later, I took my report into Watty's office. He read it through, then tossed it on his desk.

"I guess I owe you an apology," he said. "Margie was under the impression that you were on your way home. I didn't realize you still had someone else to see last night."

I didn't tell him that when I talked to Margie I *was* on my way home. I'm gradually wising up and learning when to keep my mouth shut.

"The captain isn't going to swallow this stuff about the wife and the carpet installer. It sounds fishy even to me, especially considering they spent the weekend together."

Watty certainly called that shot: Captain Powell wasn't impressed. He read my report with both Watty and me seated on chairs in his window-lined fishbowl. I felt like a kid stuck in a principal's office waiting to collect a swat. When Powell finished reading, he dropped the paper on his desk, glowering at me.

"I've already been on the horn with Logan," he fumed. "What do you mean talking him into committing Martin for psychiatric observation? What the hell kind of deal is that? For God's sake, man, that bastard held half of Seattle hostage yesterday afternoon."

"Have you talked to his boss yet to find out what really happened?" I asked.

"No one has talked to Richard Damm, if that's who you mean. He's in intensive care with a heart attack, and instead of putting his attacker in jail where he belongs, you've got him in a goddamned hospital. Beaumont, are you aware that Larry Martin's an ex-con who's already spent two years in the slammer?"

"Yes."

"Do you know that his fingerprints were found all over Nielsen's office?"

"I didn't know it for sure, but it makes sense. He was laying carpet there. Why wouldn't he leave fingerprints?"

"And now you're telling me that he spent the weekend shacked up with the grieving widow, but you still claim he had nothing to do with her husband's murder? Come on, Beaumont. Give me a break. I didn't just fall off a turnip truck yesterday, you know."

"Look," I said, "I've got a line on another suspect, the receptionist's husband. The good doctor and the receptionist were screwing around. If the husband knew about it, that certainly gives him motive. So far, we haven't been able to account for any of his movements on Saturday, from the time his wife left for work in the morning until he got back home about five o'clock in the afternoon."

"In other words, you'd rather go looking for another suspect altogether than track on the one we already have in custody."

"That's right. What's it going to hurt? It's no skin off your teeth. Martin's locked up tight, and it looks like he's going to stay that way for a while. In the meantime, I want to find the real killer."

Captain Powell shook his head in exasperation. "You are one stubborn son of a bitch,

Beaumont. I'll say that much for you."

I took that to mean I was dismissed, so I got the hell out of there and went looking for Big Al. I found him over by the coffeepot pouring himself a fresh cup.

"Seems like you made it out with a whole skin," he observed with a grin.

"Just barely," I answered. "Now, what did you find out?"

"They're in the process of running all the fingerprints through the computer. So far, Larry Martin's are the only ones that match."

"Tell me something I don't already know."

"Bill Foster says he got one real good footprint."

That got my attention. "No shit. Really?"

"Yes, from the carpet right in front of that back door. It's a distinctive tread of some kind. He'll let us know more as soon as he knows more."

"Good. Let's get out of here."

Al followed me, coffee slopping from his Styrofoam cup. "Where are we going, and why the big hurry?"

I glanced at my watch. "We're going to Cedar Heights. We're already fifteen minutes late."

"Late for what?"

"I made an appointment with Calloway, the resident manager, to take us through the building and find out if anybody saw anything."

"Good thinking," Al said. "We coulda done that yesterday, if I hadn't been tied up here in the office."

Henry Calloway was sitting in the lobby of Cedar Heights waiting for us, ready for his fleeting moment of glory. If helping us solve Dr. Frederick Nielsen's murder was going to be his only claim to fame, he was prepared to make the most of it.

He took us up to the nineteenth floor and we worked our way back down, knocking on every door as we went. He stood in the hallways with us and personally introduced us to every resident who answered the door. Of course, there were a lot of people who weren't home, and there were two units he skipped altogether because the residents were day sleepers who had given strict orders they were not to be disturbed.

All things considered, we could have saved ourselves the bother. Nothing came of it. The previous weekend had been one of perpetual sunlight. Everyone who had been able to do so had escaped to the mountains, the beach, anywhere but downtown Seattle.

By noon we had done Cedar Heights from top to bottom, and we'd checked up and down the block as well. To no avail. It was discouraging, but hardly surprising.

"What say we go try to track down Tom Rush?"

"Sounds good to me," Al replied.

We drove over to Eastlake. The wooden porch in front of the Rushes' apartment was littered with cardboard boxes, some empty, some full. I knocked on the door, and Debi Rush answered. She was crying.

"I hope you're satisfied, you son of a bitch!" she said, when she saw who it was.

"Why? What happened?"

"I told him and he told me to get out, just like that. He says he can't leave because it's only a month before the end of the term, so I have to."

"Where are you going?"

"Home to Yakima. My folks said I could come stay with them for a while."

She left me standing by the door while she went to the couch, got a tissue, and blew her nose. Then she picked up another box and carried it out to the porch.

"Did he know or not?" I asked.

She stopped and glared at me, the two angry spots I had seen before glowing bright crimson on her cheeks. "No, he didn't know. And he didn't *have* to know, either. I never would have told him if you hadn't made me."

"Where's your husband now?"

"Back at the U. He was up all night, throwing my things into boxes. He told me to pack my stuff, take the car, and be out of here by the time he gets home tonight." She started crying again. If it was a bid for sympathy, she was barking up the wrong tree.

"Do you know how we could find him?"

"Why the hell should I help you find him?" she demanded. "Oh, all right, the dean's office of the Dental School has his schedule. Now get out of here and leave me alone."

We got.

"That doesn't look so good for your theory, does it," Al observed once we were in the car.

"What do you mean?"

"If Rush was really the killer, wouldn't he be the one running away instead of sending his little woman packing."

Unfortunately, Big Al's question made a whole lot of sense.

The car sweltered in the noonday heat, and our little standard-issue departmental Dodge was without air-conditioning of any but the open-window variety. We peeled out of our jackets for as long as we were in the car, but we put them on again once we reached the university. Naturally, the only parking space available near the Health Sciences Complex was nowhere near any shade. Par for the course.

A receptionist directed us to the Dental School Dean's Office in D-Wing, and the dean's office passed us along to the student paging office on the fourth floor of B-Wing. We felt like a couple of rats lost in a maze, but surprisingly, the student paging system worked and worked well. Within ten minutes, we met Tom Rush on the grass outside the main hospital lobby.

"I didn't want to talk to you in there," he said, motioning over his shoulder toward the building. His face was flushed. His hands shook.

"I didn't do it," he rushed on, without waiting for us to ask. "Debi told me you thought I killed him, but I didn't, I swear to God. I might have if I'd known, but I didn't have the foggiest idea, not until last night. Why'd you make her tell me?"

"So we wouldn't have to," I told him.

He shoved his hands deep in his pockets and walked away from me. With his face averted, he spoke again. "At first I couldn't believe she'd done it again. I mean, it was just like the other time. We've only been married a year and a half."

"What do you mean 'the other time'?"

"She did the same thing with the other dentist she worked for. I made her quit that job when I found out, and then she went to work for Nielsen. What does she see in those old farts?"

He moved farther away from us across the grass. I heard the other part of his question, the unspoken part. The part that said, "What's the matter with me? Why aren't I good enough?" I knew those questions only too well. I had asked the same ones over and over after Karen took off.

I felt sorry for Tom Rush. I noticed he hadn't mentioned the money part, the raise Debi claimed to have gotten. I doubted she had lied to us about that. From their shabby apartment and threadbare clothes, I was sure it had taken every dime of that raise just to live and pay the bills. And I'm sure someone from the Equal Employment Opportunity Commission would have told me that this was a clear-cut case of sexual harassment and exploitation in the workplace. But still, I knew only too well what Tom was going through, and my heart went out to him.

Finally he got control of himself and came back to where Big Al and I were waiting.

"That's why you threw her out, then?" I asked. "Because it had happened before?"

Rush nodded. "I told her then that if it ever happened again, that was it. I would've left last night myself, but it's too close to the end of the term. I'll be damned if I'm going to blow dental school at this stage!"

He paused and looked away while a look of utter desolation passed over his face. "I'll probably take her back eventually," he said. "I did it before. I came here to school today because I didn't know what else to do. I've sat here the whole day, and I haven't done a thing. It's like my mind's paralyzed or something."

"I know this is tough," I told him. "But we need to ask you some questions about Saturday."

"You still think I did it?" Tom asked.

"Just answer the question," Big Al put in. "Unless you'd rather have an attorney present when you do."

"I was here," Rush answered quickly.

"Where, in one of the labs?"

"Yes. The same one where they paged me just now."

"Did anyone else see you?"

"Sure. There must have been five or six of us who were here all day."

"Are any of the others up there now? Could we talk to them?"

"Do you have to?" Tom Rush's pride was showing, but he didn't have any choice.

"With them you have an alibi," I said.

"Without them you're up shit creek."

Without another word, Tom Rush led us up to a small dental lab on the fourth floor of the building. There were probably ten people in the room altogether. We talked to all of them, one at a time. Six of them said they had been in the lab on Saturday, and all six confirmed that Tom Rush had been there with them. He had arrived before nine-thirty and hadn't left until after four. Three of them, including the instructor, had eaten lunch with him in the cafeteria.

When we finished talking to them, it was about three o'clock. We walked back out and got in the car. It was an oven. The steering wheel was too hot to touch.

"What do you think?" I asked, as we rolled down the windows and tried to breathe.

"Sounded like gospel to me," Al said. "Tom Rush isn't our man, period. You don't get that many people to lie off the tops of their heads and do that good a job of it."

"That's the way it sounded to me, too," I said.

"So where the hell does that leave us?"

"In this particular game," I told him, "I believe we're back to square one."

CHAPTER

18

That night after work I finally got myself up to Bailey's Foods on Queen Anne Hill to buy some groceries. I also made a foray across the street to the state liquor store to restock my depleted supply of MacNaughton's. Bailey's has installed one of those yuppie salad bars, so I treated myself to a huge taco salad—the kind my mother never used to make.

I went straight home and ate a medium-elegant dinner, served at my new glass-and-brass dining room table. I ate the salad from the chinette deli plate and drank my glass of chilled Vouvray from crystal stemware. It's no surprise that after dinner I ended up falling asleep in my recliner. I spend more time there than I do in my bed.

I have no idea what time I fell asleep, but I

know when I woke up—eleven. The phone on the table beside me was ringing its head off. I caught it just before the answering machine did.

"Hello," I mumbled.

"So it is you," a woman's voice announced. I'm not sure how she recognized my voice from that one-word grunted greeting. I sure as hell didn't know who *she* was, but I could hear the tiny telltale beeps that said she was calling from the security phone downstairs in the lobby.

"Who is this?" I asked.

"Darlene," she answered.

"Darlene who?" I couldn't recall anyone by that name. "I think maybe you've got the wrong apartment," I said.

"Darlene from across the street, remember?" she asked, sounding offended. "The one who brought you your pork chop sandwich the other night. Are you going to let me in or not?"

Darlene from across the street. It finally made sense—the bartender from Girvan's.

"I'll buzz you in," I said. I pressed the entry code on my phone, realizing as soon as I did so that I had failed to tell her what floor. As a security measure, Belltown Terrace has no listing of the tenants' names and apartment numbers either on the reader-board or in the lobby.

I was sure the phone would ring again, and I wasn't disappointed.

"Where the hell are you?" she demanded before I even had a chance to say hello.

"Twenty-fifth floor," I replied. "Turn left as you get off the elevator."

I pulled my jacket back on, straightened my collar, slipped shoes back on my feet, and went out to the hallway to meet her.

The twenty-fifth floor happens to be the penthouse floor. The interior design is slightly more upscale than the elevator lobbies on the other residential floors. It's supposed to make a statement. It evidently worked. Darlene Girvan popped her head out into the elevator lobby, looked around, and whistled.

"I'll be go-to-hell," she said.

"What's the matter?" I asked.

"You really *do* own a piece of this place, don't you! I thought the other night you were just bullshitting that creep from Texas." Unceremoniously, she shoved a brown paper bag in my direction. "I brought dinner," she said.

I didn't have the heart to tell her I'd already eaten. Besides, it seemed like a long time ago, hours I think.

"Thank you," I said. "How about a drink?"

"Thought you'd never ask," she replied.

"What do you like?"

"What have you got?"

"MacNaughton's," I answered.

"That'll do." With that she marched into my apartment and took over. She went straight to the kitchen, found two plates, and laid out two gigantic, pork chop sandwiches with their fat sesame-seed-dotted buns, one for her and one for me.

"Quite a place you have here," she commented over her shoulder as she prowled through my cupboards searching for glasses. I brought the MacNaughton's into the kitchen from the bar and set it on the counter.

"It'll do," I said.

She grinned at that. "You think you're cute, don't you."

"Hardly," I told her. "It's tough for cops to be cute. It goes against the image."

Darlene laughed aloud and handed me my drink. As she did so, her fingers brushed against mine in a way that couldn't have been accidental. I took a trial sip. MacNaughton's and water, just the way I like it—heavy on the booze, light on the water.

"Actually," she said, "that's really why I came here to talk to you."

I was still thinking about her fingers. My face must have been totally blank as I tried to sort out what she was really saying.

"Your job," she said, looking at me over the rim of the glass as she sipped her own drink.

"You are *that* Detective Beaumont, aren't you? The one who works for homicide? How can a cop afford to live in a place like this?"

Before I could answer she did an abrupt change of subject that left me standing with one foot in the air. "Can these plates go in the microwave? The sandwiches should probably be zapped for thirty seconds or so."

"Sure," I said.

I stood there stupidly, holding my drink, while she keyed in the microwave instructions. "Nice layout," she said. "A real slick layout."

The way she said it, she could have been talking about the kitchen, but I don't believe that's what she meant. There was another whole level to Darlene Girvan's conversation, one that had nothing to do with kitchens—or pork chop sandwiches either, for that matter. When the sandwiches came out of the microwave, she carried them to the table while I trailed along behind, carrying the drinks.

"You said you wanted to talk to me about homicide?" I asked after we were seated.

She took a bite out of her sandwich and nodded. "Sure," she said. "Henry told me you wanted to talk to me."

"Henry?"

She shook her head impatiently, making me feel like a first-class dummy. "Henry Calloway, the manager at Cedar Heights. That's where I live."

"Oh, him," I said. "So we're neighbors."

"That's right. Come on over and borrow a cup of sugar anytime."

If we were going to play double entendre, I was definitely out of my league. I went searching for solid ground.

"I don't remember seeing you when we went through the building."

"I work at night and sleep during the day. I'd have killed Calloway if he'd let you guys wake me up early."

"But he told you I wanted to talk to you?"

She nodded. "That's right. He said you wanted to talk to anyone who might have seen something out of the ordinary on Saturday afternoon. Here I am."

"I gave him my phone number at the department. How'd you find me here?"

She grinned. "Easy. When he told me your name, I remembered it from the other night. I wondered if maybe you two were related or something. I tried calling the department, but you weren't in. Then I tried looking you up in the phone book. You weren't listed. Nobody named Beaumont was. That's what made me figure you really were a cop. I mean, cops don't usually put their phone numbers out there in front of God and everybody. Maybe I should give up tending bar and become a detective. What do you think?"

"We'll take it under advisement," I said.

"So that's when I came over here looking for you," she continued. "I tried first this afternoon right after I woke up, but you weren't home."

"Tried what?"

"I came over here to talk to you. I called on the phone from downstairs, but you weren't home. When the answering machine came on, I hung up. I don't talk to answering machines. I hate answering machines. They piss me off."

"Wait a minute," I said, trying to pull the threads of her story into some understandable, cohesive whole. "Start over again from the beginning. Why did Calloway tell you to get in touch with me?"

"Because I asked him when he was going to get off his ass and post speed-limit signs in the parking garage like he's supposed to."

Maybe that answered my question for her, but it didn't help me at all.

"I don't understand what speed-limit signs and Henry Calloway have to do with me."

"Because he almost ran me down, goddammit."

"Who did?"

"Some little asshole wearing a brown hat almost ran me down in the parking garage about one-thirty Saturday afternoon. I mean, I almost died. I was carrying two bags of groceries. You know, bread and eggs and cigarettes, and I dropped one of the bags trying to get out of the way. Broke most of the eggs. Bruised my hip, too. Want me to show you?"

"No thanks. Later maybe."

I could feel the quick catch of excitement in my throat. It was the right time. And the Cedar Heights garage was the right place. "Go on," I urged.

"Anyway, he must have opened the garage door from the second or third level, because it was already open when he came around the corner. He didn't have to wait for it. Otherwise, I'd have caught up with that sucker, dragged him out of his fancy little car, and beaten the holy crap out of him."

"What kind of car?" I asked.

She shrugged. "Beats me. Some kind of foreign job. Not cheap, I don't think, but I can't say for sure. We never had any of those in Butte, Montana, when I was growing up, I can tell you that. I know Fords from Chevys from Buicks, but I can't tell one foreign car from another. Can you?"

"Sometimes," I said. "Did you get the license number?"

"Only the first three letters. KRE something.

That's all I could see. He knocked me flat on my ass."

"Three letters. Did you get any of the numbers?"

"Goddammit, I was sitting there on a pile of broken eggs, and you think I should have gotten the whole fucking license number? What do you think I am? You ready for another drink?"

Darlene got up abruptly and went to the kitchen, taking both our glasses with her. While she was gone, I managed to marshal my thoughts into some kind of reasonable order. I had asked Henry Calloway to report anything unusual. A hit-and-run in a private, secured garage right around the time of the murder was most unusual indeed. Calloway had been right-on-the-money to send Darlene Girvan in my direction.

"Did you recognize the car? Does it belong to one of the residents of the building, then?" I asked as she came back to the table.

"I wasn't on the residential side," she said. "What made you think I was there?"

"You live there, don't you? As I understand it, the residential parking lot is under the residential tower."

"I do live there, but we have an extra car. There aren't enough parking places in the residential garage, so we lease an extra space on the commercial side."

"Tell me exactly what happened," I said.

"I went up the hill to the store. When I came back, I stopped on P-1, the first level, to unload the stuff into a cart. It was Saturday afternoon. I figured I was probably the only person in the place, so I stopped right beside the elevator door.

"All of a sudden, I hear a crash and then this car comes screaming up from downstairs like a bat out of hell. I mean, he was moving! I heard him coming from down below, his tires were squealing like mad. I tried to get out of the way, but as he came around the corner, he skidded. He was coming so fast, I thought he was going to hit me or the wall. I had to jump straight up to get out of his way."

"You say it was a man wearing a hat?"

She nodded. "It's not very well lit in the garage on weekends, but it looked to me like maybe a state patrol hat."

"Are there any state patrol officers living or working in your building?"

Darlene shook her head. "Henry doesn't know of any. I already asked. So anyway, I figured, since whoever it was had a garage door opener, I'd be able to go down to the garage this week and find the car. I was going to leave a nasty note for the son of a bitch. But the car never showed up. I didn't think that much about it until today when I talked to Henry. He said maybe it had something to do with the murder."

"He could very well be right," I said. "You're sure you only remember the first three letters of the license number. KRE. Was it a Washington license?"

"I'm sure of that. Not one of the new ones. An old one, green and white."

"And the car. Can you remember anything at all about it?"

"It was dark colored. Maybe black or navy blue. I couldn't be sure. And like I told you, it was foreign. I prefer American cars myself."

"Was there anything at all distinctive about the car, anything that would help you identify it if you saw it again?"

"The back bumper looked like hell. He must have put it in the wrong gear when he took it out of park and smashed into the wall. That's all I saw."

"Can you remember anything about the man who was driving?"

"He wore glasses. I remember they caught the light as he came around the corner. That's it."

There was a short silence. I was trying to decide if there were any other questions I should ask. It was hard to concentrate, however. Darlene Girvan was looking at me speculatively.

"Henry's right, isn't he? The car does have something to do with the murder."

"Possibly," I answered. "And you can bet I'm going to get busy and check it out the first thing in the morning."

"What are you going to do between now and then?" she asked.

Instantly we were back into one of Darlene Girvan's multilayered conversations, and I was losing ground.

"Sleep," I said. "I'm going to sleep. I've had a hell of a day. As a matter of fact, I've had a hell of a week."

"And will you be sleeping by yourself?"

I still don't know quite how to navigate the shoals in this modern, Women's Lib world where women are free to ask for what they want. It catches me off guard whenever it happens.

"For the time being," I said.

"You're not interested?" she asked.

"I never said I wasn't interested. Wary's more like it. Once burned, twice shy."

"You've been burned?"

"On occasion."

"So I wasted my pork chop sandwich?"

"I wouldn't say wasted," I told her. "You've certainly got my attention."

She set her glass down in the middle of her plate. "I'm in the market for more than attention," she said, getting up. She took both our plates to the kitchen and put them in the sink.

"I'd better be going, then," she said. "They'll be looking for me." She walked to the door and paused there, with her hand on the knob.

"I don't seem to handle rejection very well," she said thoughtfully. "I'm not used to being turned down."

I'm sure she wasn't used to it. I wasn't used to doing it, either. I didn't want to hurt her feelings. "Don't worry about it," I told her. "I'm just basically shy when it comes to women."

"Not gay?"

"Definitely not gay. Shy," I repeated.

"So this isn't a permanent turndown?"

"No."

"Oh," she said. "Well, in that case, you know where to find me in case you get over it." She left then, quickly, closing the door behind her.

More stupid than shy, I thought, standing there in the entryway, staring at the closed door.

A hell of a lot more stupid.

CHAPTER 19

I didn't sleep. I spent the whole night, tossing and turning. I remembered when, over spring break, I had dragged Karen home from school to meet my mother. Karen had been from San Diego. My mother's comment was that I should look in my own backyard, try for the girl next door.

With our high rises just up the street from each other, Darlene Girvan was literally the girl next door, but hardly the kind my mother would have had in mind. She was bright, assertive, interesting, and available. So why the hell had I turned down her offer? What was the matter with me? Was I really getting *that* old? Or was I just plain old-fashioned?

I spent a long time chewing on the possibilities. I didn't much care for any of the answers that bubbled to the surface. Before I left the subject alone, however, I finally made one decision—that I'd spend some time hanging around Darlene's bar doing some in-depth research to see what, if anything, might come up.

Having disposed of the personal as best I could, I turned to the other part of the problem—Darlene Girvan's hit-and-run driver and what implications her story might hold for Dr. Frederick Nielsen's murder investigation.

Garage doors are implacable. You can't argue your way through one. They simply will not open for people without properly keyed openers. So whoever had almost run down Darlene Girvan had to be someone who belonged in Cedar Heights, someone who had a legitimate reason for being there, someone who had access to a garage door opener.

That boiled down to exactly two possibilities. Either the driver of the foreign car had something to do with Dr. Nielsen's murder or he didn't. That's my job, figuring out which is which.

I spent the rest of the night working the problem, but no answers were forthcoming. It was almost four in the morning the last time I rolled over and looked at the clock.

The phone rang at seven. "Rise and shine," Peters ordered cheerfully.

"Couldn't you let me sleep late for once?" I grumbled.

Peters was undeterred. "Nope, I called to ask for some advice."

"What kind of advice?"

"Romantic."

"Jesus Christ! What now?"

"I'm going to pop the question."

"To Amy?"

"Who else, asshole?"

"So why do you need advice from me?"

"I'm going to ask her tomorrow night, and I want to do it right. Where should I take her? Is there any place right around there close? If she says yes, I want to be able to come over and tell the girls, so they can feel like they're part of it."

Fortunately I had a ready answer to his question. "There's a place at First and Cedar," I said. "Girvan's. I was in there just the other night. They have a nice dining room overlooking the harbor."

"Candles?" Peters asked. "Atmosphere?"

"Affirmative," I answered.

"Good food?"

"I haven't had that much of it," I told him, "but what I had was good."

"What about wheelchair access?" he asked. "I can get a cab with a lift, but are there any stairs?"

"No stairs at all. There's an elevator. The restaurant's up on the fifth floor. Remember? We were there once on the bum-bashing case."

I could almost hear Peters nodding into the phone. "That's right. Now I remember. It was a nice place."

"It still is," I told him. "And I happen to know the owner. Want me to make a reservation for you?"

"Thanks, Beau. That would help. I want it to be a surprise, but that's not easy when Amy pops in and out of my room without any warning. So far I've managed to smuggle the ring in without her seeing it, but I don't want her to catch me calling a restaurant."

"What time?"

"Make it early, seven-thirty or so. The doctor says he'll give me a pass, but not to stay out too late."

"I'll take care of it," I said. "And by the way, congratulations. Amy's terrific."

"I think so, too," he said.

On that bright note, I got up and took a long, hot shower. By the time I'd chased the shower with a couple of cups of coffee, I was beginning to feel halfway human. After I was dressed and had put on my .38, I reached out to scoop my change off the dresser.

That was when I noticed Dorothy Nielsen's hospital identification bracelet. I had put it in my pocket the day before when I clipped it off her arm, then I had forgotten all about it. Completely. I hadn't even noticed it when I emptied it out of my pocket along with my usual fistful of change and miscellaneous crap.

I held the bracelet up to the light. The logo said it was from Swedish Hospital up on First Hill, Pill Hill as the locals call the hospital district. In addition to the hospital's name, the bracelet contained a few other relevant bits of information: Dorothy Nielsen's name, her patient ID number, her blood type, and another name, a Dr. W. Leonard.

As I stood there studying the bracelet, I couldn't help wondering. I recalled the ugly purple bruise on LeAnn Nielsen's face and remembered the determined way her mother-in-law had brushed aside my question about the origin of her injury. I still didn't know how Dorothy Nielsen had broken her hip.

I suppose it was mostly idle curiosity on my part, but a homicide detective needs to learn all he can about the people involved in any given case. That includes the deceased. And now I wanted to know, once and for all, whether or not the late Dr. Frederick Nielsen was responsible for his mother's injury. I knew for sure he was a wife beater. Was he also a mommy basher?

I picked up the phone book and located Dr.

W. Leonard's office number in the Arnold Medical Pavilion on Madison. It was only 7:30 A.M., but on a whim I dialed the office number. A tinny answering machine told me that the doctor's office was open 9:30 A.M. to 4:30 P.M. Monday through Friday. Unless it was an emergency, they requested that I call back during office hours.

This was no emergency. Dr. Nielsen was dead, and his mother had been released from the hospital. I put the bracelet back in my pocket along with a piece of paper on which I jotted Dr. W. Leonard's office number. Then I called Margie at the department, told her I had to stop off someplace on my way into the office, and set off for Cedar Heights to pay a call on Henry Calloway.

I found him outside, watering the parched street trees that were planted in the sidewalk around his building.

"They were looking a little sick to me," he said of the trees when I walked up. "They're not used to having to go this long without rain. I thought I'd help them along. What can I do for you, Detective Beaumont?"

"Darlene Girvan paid me a call last night. I wanted to thank you for putting her in touch with me."

"Happy to do it. You said to report anything unusual. That seemed pretty unusual to me."

"To me, too," I said. "From her description of the car, do you recognize it? Does it belong to someone in the building?"

"It may, but there's no way for me to tell. We've got more than a hundred cars in all, and it's hard to keep track of them. It seems like I'd remember one with its bumper all smashed in the way she said."

"What about the license number? Do you keep any kind of listing of those?"

"Nope. Too much trouble. People buy and sell cars all the time. We just keep track of the number of beepers we pass out to each tenant. They can move 'em around among cars to their heart's content."

It figured. It would have simplified my life too much if they had done it any other way.

"Have any openers been reported stolen lately?"

Henry Calloway shook his head. "Nope," he replied.

"Them's the breaks," I said, "but thanks just the same, Mr. Calloway."

"My pleasure," he said.

I left him to his hose and hurried on down to the department. Sergeant Watkins was waiting for me when I got to my desk.

"I understand from Al here that the other suspect you were telling us about yesterday didn't pan out, is that right?"

"That's correct."

"So where does that leave you?"

"Behind the eight ball," I told him.

Watty frowned. "Listen, Beau, the guys upstairs are getting antsy on this one. They want progress, real progress, and they want it now!"

"We're doing the best we can. I picked up another lead last night. We'll be checking that one out today."

"Get on with it, then. By the way, I never got a report from yesterday."

"I'll take care of it," I said. "What's the word on Martin?"

"Nothing that I know of," Watty replied.

"How long can they keep him up at Harborview?" I asked.

"Seventy-two hours is the maximum on an involuntary commitment. You can bet they won't cut him loose a minute before that."

"What about Damm? Has anybody talked to him yet?"

"Powell's assigning two other guys to handle that end of the investigation."

"How come? So he can squeeze us out of it?"

Watty shrugged in a way that told me my assumption was correct. Captain Powell didn't like my answers, so he was pulling rank, sending in reinforcements in hopes of finding answers he liked better. You can do that when you're the captain.

"Get out of here and let us go to work," I griped at Watty. "We're not accomplishing anything with you standing around here jawing."

As soon as Sergeant Watkins was out of the room, Big Al asked, "What's the lead?"

"One turned up on my doorstep last night at eleven: a lady who almost got run down by a car in the Cedar Heights commercial garage Saturday afternoon at one-thirty."

"No shit!"

"No shit," I repeated.

"So what are we doing about it?"

"We don't have that much to go on, first three letters on the license, dark, foreign make, bashed in rear bumper, that's it."

"It's a start. All we need to do is get Olympia to supply all one thousand registrations on a printout and start looking."

"Right," I agreed, "but first we're going to go talk to a doctor."

"What about? You feeling sick?"

"No, I'm not sick. About Dorothy Nielsen."

I picked up the phone and dialed Dr. Leonard's number. "Doctor's office," the receptionist said.

"I'd like to talk to Dr. Leonard, please."

"The doctor is busy seeing patients at the

moment. May I say who's calling?"

"My name's Beaumont. Detective J. P. Beaumont."

"Are you already a patient of Dr. Leonard's, Mr. Beaumont?"

"No, I'm not."

"The doctor isn't taking any new patients at this time."

"I don't want to become a patient. I'm a detective with the Seattle Police Department. I need to speak to the doctor regarding a case I'm working on."

"We'll have to schedule you for an appointment. The doctor doesn't see people without appointments. I could work you in on Monday. Would two-thirty be all right?"

The woman's voice was bright and cheerful enough, but I had a feeling I hadn't connected to her brain. If she had one.

"I don't believe you understand," I said. "I need to talk to the doctor for a few minutes regarding one of his patients."

"Her," the woman said.

"I beg your pardon?"

"One of *her* patients," the receptionist answered. "Dr. Leonard is a woman."

"Right," I said. "Fine." I was beginning to lose my cool. It was draining out the heels of my shoes. "As I said, I'm working a homicide case, and it's vital that I speak to Dr. Leonard regarding one of *her* patients."

"Well, she's leaving here in about ten minutes. I doubt you can catch her. She's scheduled for surgery in a little while. You can come by this afternoon and wait if you want to. Maybe I can work you in. She'll be back here by three at the latest."

"We'll be there at three," I said.

I put down the phone, shaking my head.

"We're not going to see the doctor, then?" Al asked.

"Not until three o'clock," I said.

Al picked up the phone and made the call to the Department of Licensing while I wrote up my report. People think that in this world of computers, the information police jurisdictions need is readily and instantly available. We should be able to feed minimal details into a machine and have the information back in a flash, right? Wrong.

The nature of bureaucracy is that things can only happen on schedule, and partial plate inquiries are printed only at night and mailed out the next day. Big Al finally made a deal so someone could at least come down to Olympia and pick the list up when it was ready. Then we'd be able to do the fun part, the physical labor of going through the list one at a time, by hand. Don't tell me about computers being labor saving devices. I'm not convinced.

We sorted our way through the maze of bureaucratic bullshit and afterward, on our way to lunch, took a side trip through the crime lab, where we picked up a facsimile of the shoe print Bill Foster had gotten from the crime scene. By two-thirty we were on our way to the Arnold Medical Pavilion. For a change, traffic was light. We walked into the good doctor's office right at three o'clock.

We were there. Dr. Leonard wasn't. As soon as I gave the receptionist my name, she started apologizing.

"I'm so sorry. I didn't have a number, so I couldn't get back to you. There's been an accident. Dr. Leonard is back in surgery. We canceled all her appointments for the afternoon, and I didn't know how to get ahold of you."

"What about tomorrow morning?" I asked.

"Tomorrow looks good," she said. "If you could be here by eight-thirty, I'll try to get you in before the first patient."

It was the best of a bad bargain.

We went back to the department and scrounged through what information we had, but nothing new turned up. After work, I went home and called the restaurant to make dinner reservations for Amy and Peters. I didn't ask to speak to Darlene—I wasn't up to that kind of mental sparring.

Once I was off the phone, I felt lonely, at loose ends. I finally went downstairs to see the girls. Tracie and Heather were already tucked in bed, but they weren't asleep. Mrs. Edwards was reading to them. She handed me the book, and I took over.

The book was *Little House on the Prairie*. The trials and tribulations of the Ingalls family were tame, pristine almost, when stacked up against the Nielsens and the Rushes of this world. Reading the story made me homesick for a saner, less sordid planet—one I've never lived on.

And never will.

CHAPTER

20

Nobody called me Friday morning, so naturally I overslept. It was already five to eight when I opened my eyes. I called the department and left word with Margie for Big Al to call me as soon as he got in, then I jumped into the shower.

My phone was ringing by the time I turned off the water. "You're late," Big Al groused when I answered.

"I noticed. Pick up a car and come get me," I said.

"What do you think I am, your personal chauffeur? Do you want I should bring the limo?"

"Come on, Al. Get off it. I overslept. Come get me so we don't miss our chance to see the lady doctor."

I went outside to wait for him and was surprised to find there had been a definite change in the weather. Summers in Seattle are like that—hot one day and chilly the next. What visitors don't understand is that too many days without rain, too many hours of uninterrupted sunshine, cause Seattlites to get crabby. They welcome the return of cool cloudy days. Several passersby smiled and nodded cheerful hellos as they walked by, bending into the chill wind tunnel that swirled around the base of my building.

Big Al picked me up in front of Belltown Terrace at 8:23, giving us just under seven minutes to drive through traffic and make it to the top of Madison for our appointment with Dr. W. Leonard. As he threaded his way through traffic, Al glanced in my direction.

"I'm just going to drop you off, if that's all right with you."

"Why?" I asked. "What are you up to?"

"Olympia," he answered. "The Department of Licensing has our printout ready. They're waiting for someone to come pick it up. I'm volunteering for the job."

I didn't object. Al had first dibs. He was the one who had checked out the car. He dropped me in front of the Arnold Medical Pavilion a few minutes late, but when I stepped off the elevator, the door to Dr. Leonard's office was still locked. I knocked. A latch clicked and the door opened.

A squat, stocky woman with short-cropped yellowish gray hair and a pugnacious nose opened the door. She looked to be in her late sixties or early seventies. She was vital and alert. "What can I do for you?" she asked curtly.

"I'm looking for Dr. Leonard."

"What do you want her for?"

"I need to discuss one of her patients." I had already gone over this ground with the air-headed receptionist and I resented having to do it again with someone who was probably a cleaning lady.

"Which one?" the woman asked.

"Look," I said, "couldn't I just speak with the doctor? It would save a lot of time."

"I *am* the doctor," she answered sharply. "Now, which one of my patients do you want to discuss?"

From the severity of her tone, I knew I'd been reprimanded. Dr. Leonard and I weren't exactly getting off on the right foot.

"I'm sorry, Dr. Leonard," I apologized. "The patient is a woman by the name of Dorothy Nielsen. Her only son was murdered last Saturday."

"Really!" she exclaimed, her shaggy eyebrows arching in surprise. With that, Dr. Wilhelmina Leonard swept open the door and motioned me into a waiting room. "My receptionist isn't here yet. Let's go back to my office, shall we?"

I followed her through a small suite of examining rooms and into a cramped, untidy office. Unlike Dr. Nielsen's compulsively clean quarters, this one looked as if it had been bombed. The desk was littered with a jumbled mound of papers, files, and open magazines. Had she sat behind the desk, I doubt she would have been able to see over the top of it. Several sweaters and jackets were strewn around the room, and on a hook behind the door hung at least three tired lab jackets.

Dr. Leonard walked in, cleared one side chair of clothing and general debris, and casually tossed the resulting armload into one corner of the room. "Won't you sit down?" she suggested, offering me the chair.

I sat. She perched on the front of the desk, while I worried about whether or not she would start an avalanche.

"Adele mentioned you to me yesterday. I seem to recall that she said something about you're being a police officer. Is that true?" she asked suspiciously.

I nodded and gave her my identification, which she examined with exaggerated care. When she finished, she handed it back to me with a flourish. Then she leaned back on the desk, folding her arms across an ample waist.

"All right, then," she said. "Now that I know you're a legitimate police officer, what can I do for you?"

"As I said, I'd like to talk with you about Dorothy Nielsen."

"First, maybe you'd better tell me about what happened to her son."

That seemed fair enough. "Dr. Frederick Nielsen was murdered in his downtown office on Saturday afternoon by person or persons unknown."

Dr. Leonard had sharp hazel eyes and a face that betrayed nothing of what was going on behind it. "How was he murdered?" she asked.

"Someone stabbed him with a dental pick. He bled to death."

She nodded. "I see," she said impassively. "If you're here because you think his mother may have had something to do with it, you'd better think again. I can tell you that she was in the hospital for four solid weeks before I dismissed her on Tuesday. It would have been impossible for her to have been involved."

"Dorothy Nielsen isn't under suspicion," I said quietly. "Actually, I'm a little surprised to hear you say she might be."

Dr. Leonard bristled at that. "I said no such

thing! Why are you here, then? Why did you want to talk to me?"

"How did Dorothy Nielsen break her hip?" I asked.

Dr. Leonard didn't reply immediately. When she did, her answer was subdued, controlled. "She said she fell down some stairs."

"Do you believe that?" I asked

Dr. Leonard gave me a long appraising glance. "Tell me once again: Mrs. Nielsen is in no way under suspicion?"

"No, she's not."

"In that case, I suppose I could go ahead and tell you what I think without betraying my doctor/patient relationship. Remember, this is only speculation on my part. I'm convinced she was pushed. She claimed she fell, of course, but I don't believe it. Her other injuries weren't consistent with a fall."

"What other injuries?"

"Bruises on her arms and shoulders. A cut on her face just below her eye. I asked her about it, but she denied it. She's always denied it."

"What do you mean, 'always'?"

Dr. Leonard smiled. "Dorothy Nielsen has been my patient for almost forty years now, Detective Beaumont, since before Freddy was born. In fact, she came to me with that first broken wrist while she was pregnant with him."

"She broke her wrist? How?"

The doctor shook her head. "I don't remember now exactly what she said, it's such a long time ago, but she's always claimed to be accident prone. It wasn't until much later that I began to have some inkling of what was really going on."

Slowly an important piece of Dr. Frederick Nielsen's background shifted into place. They say physical abuse runs in families, passed on from generation to generation like some genetically linked disease. "You mean her husband was abusive? He beat her?"

"From the very beginning, I would imagine, and probably Freddie too," Dr. Leonard replied. "I could never understand why a woman like Dorothy would stay with a man like that. It's possible that she felt she had married above her station, and she wanted to stay there—nice house, nice clothes, all the usual amenities. She often talked about how grateful she was to be married to a professional man. That's what she called him."

"Her husband?"

Dr. Leonard nodded. "She said the same thing about Freddie eventually, about how proud she was that he had followed in his father's footsteps and become a dentist, too."

"How many times did you treat her over the years?"

"For injuries? I don't remember. Numerous times. I could look up her records. I haven't seen very much of her in the last few years, though, not since Fred Senior died. I was surprised when she showed up in the emergency room a few weeks ago.

"Of course, awareness about this kind of abuse is much higher now. It's much more out in the open nowadays than it used to be," Dr. Leonard continued. "Even so, some women get mixed up with the same type of man over and over. I asked her that night in the emergency room if she had remarried, but she said no, that she lived with her son and daughter-in-law."

"Did she tell you that the daughter-in-law had just taken the two grandchildren and run away to a shelter, a domestic violence shelter?"

The bushy eyebrows waggled again. "No. Dorothy didn't tell me that, but one of her sisters did. We finally had managed to get Dorothy over a serious bladder infection, and I was trying to arrange for her release. I wanted her to go to a nursing home for a while rather than back into the same abusive environment with her son, but Dorothy was adamant. She wanted to return to her own home."

"Did you see her son while she was here in the hospital?"

"Freddie? Of course," Dr. Leonard answered. "He was very solicitous and accommodating the whole time his mother was hospitalized. He kept saying all the right words, that we should do whatever his mother needed to get well, that we should spare no expense. As far as he was concerned, money was no object. He'd pay the bill, no questions asked. He brought her flowers constantly and insisted that she have a private room. That kind of thing is standard, by the way."

"Private rooms?"

"No, no, no. That kind of behavior. Abusers do that, trying to get back in the victim's good graces. It usually works."

"You said you talked to Mrs. Nielsen's sister?"

"Both of them. When Dorothy absolutely refused to let me put her in a nursing home, I had to do something. I couldn't send her back home with her son. Another episode like that last one could very well kill her. This was bad enough."

"So you asked Dorothy's sisters if she could stay with them."

"That's right. I called and had them both come down to my office Saturday morning. I wanted to discuss my concerns with them.

That's when they told me about the wife. I'm sure that's what sparked the attack on Dorothy—anger and frustration that his wife had somehow managed to slip out of his clutches, that she was no longer under his complete control."

"Did you tell them what you thought had happened?" I asked.

"I certainly did."

"How did they take it?" I asked.

"They were shocked, of course," Dr. Leonard replied. "Very upset, both of them."

"How upset were they? What did they say?" I asked.

Dr. Leonard paused, her face caught in the startled expression of someone who has just remembered something they had forgotten. "Why, forevermore!" she exclaimed. "I blanked it out completely until just this minute when you asked."

"Blanked out what?"

"One of them swore about it. I was shocked. I'd never heard that kind of talk from any of them. She said he should be taken care of once and for all."

"Could what she said possibly be construed as a threat? Tell me what she said," I urged.

"You want me to repeat it exactly?" Dr. Leonard asked.

I nodded. "Word for word."

Dr. Leonard sighed. "Let me think a minute. I believe she said, 'Somebody should kill that mother-fucking son of a bitch!' "

Even as she spoke the words, Dr. Leonard seemed as surprised to hear them coming from her own lips as she had been when Rachel or Daisy had used them the first time. From the looks and sound of Dr. Leonard, I doubted she personally allowed herself anything stronger than an occasional *darn*.

"Which one of them said it?" I asked. "Rachel or Daisy?"

She shrugged. "I'm not sure. They look so much alike that I can never keep them straight. The one said it. The other one said, 'Don't be ridiculous.' "

"What happened next?"

"We talked for a while longer. They told me they'd see to it that Dorothy was taken care of, that they wouldn't let any more harm come to her. I told them I'd release her on Tuesday morning, if they could pick her up then. They needed that much time to build a wheelchair ramp, rent a bed, and get Dorothy's things moved into their house. After we finished making arrangements, they left."

"Were they still upset?"

Dr. Leonard nodded. "Yes indeed. I heard them arguing in the hallway outside my door while they waited for the elevator, but I didn't place any importance on it at the time."

She was quiet for a moment. "That's what you're thinking, isn't it," she added with a shrewd glance in my direction. "You think one of them may be . . . ?" She left the remainder of the question unspoken.

I nodded. "Or both."

"Oh, dear no. That would be dreadful. What in the world would happen to Dorothy?"

"Unfortunately, Dr. Leonard, that's not my concern," I said.

"It ought to be," she replied stiffly.

When I left Dr. Leonard's cluttered office a few minutes later, there were several patients waiting outside, waiting for their scheduled appointments.

Only when I stepped out of the Arnold Medical Pavilion into a gentle rain and the cool breeze did I remember that I was on foot. Big Al had taken the car to Olympia. I hopped across Madison and caught a Metro bus down the hill. On the way, I jotted down some notes on my meeting with Dr. Leonard.

Writing it down helped clarify my own thinking. Supposing Rachel and Daisy hadn't suspected the real source of Dorothy's broken hip until they learned about it from Dr. Leonard on Saturday morning. What if one or both of them had decided to take the law into their own hands and do something about it?

That sounded like motive to me.

The bus moved at a snail's pace, and I was suddenly in a tremendous hurry. I finally jumped ship at Fourth and Madison, with my mind running at full throttle. Big Al might very well bring back official confirmation from the Department of Licensing, but I had a better idea. In order to do it, I planned to dash into the departmental garage, grab a car without ever showing my face in the Public Safety Building, and go straight to the Edinburgh Arms.

Nice try, but no time. Captain Powell and Sergeant Watkins were also in the garage lobby waiting for a car.

"Hey, Beau, what's the hurry?" Sergeant Watkins asked as I rushed past them. "What's happening? I hear Detective Lindstrom's on his way to Olympia to pick up a partial license printout."

"Right," I answered.

"You seem to be in quite a hurry, Detective Beaumont," Captain Powell observed. "Are you two on to something?"

"Maybe," I said. "I just talked to Dorothy Nielsen's doctor."

"What for?"

"Look, Captain, I'm in a hurry. I need to check out a car. Can't we talk about this later?"

"We'll talk about it now," Captain Powell said. "I want to know what's going on."

"I've got one detail to verify, but I'm checking into his aunts."

Captain Powell shook his head in shocked disbelief. "His aunts? Those two nice ladies? Come now, Beaumont. I've had several dealings with Dr. Nielsen's aunts in the past few days. In fact, one of them called me just this morning about the memorial service on Saturday. She sounded reasonable enough to me. They both did. Neither one of them strikes me as a cold-blooded killer, someone capable of using a dental pick as a hole punch on somebody else's throat."

"Perfectly reasonable or not," I replied, "we're within a hair of having probable cause to arrest them."

"*Improbable cause* is a hell of a lot more like it," Powell returned derisively. "We've got a perfectly good ex-con in custody, but you'd rather pin the murder on a couple of sweet little old ladies. You're slipping, Beaumont. You are really slipping."

Their car arrived just then. The two of them got in and drove away, leaving me standing there in the garage with smoke pouring out both my ears. So far the evidence I had may have been strictly circumstantial, but I knew in my bones we were finally on the right track.

My car came eventually, and I drove straight to the Edinburgh Arms. Instead of entering the driveway, I went around to the back of the complex and parked on the street near the long row of neat, brick garages. The doors all had a thick coat of fresh cream-colored paint, and the windows at the top of each door were uniformly clean and polished.

There were no numbers on the garages, no identification of any kind to tell which garage belonged to which unit, and I sure as hell wasn't going to go ask.

I started at one end of the building and worked my way to the other, stopping at each door and standing on tiptoe to peer through the glass. I was about two-thirds down the row when I hit pay dirt.

Parked inside one of the garage stalls was an older model black BMW with a mangled rear bumper. The first two letters, the K and the R, were plainly visible, but the rest of the license plate was obscured by twisted chrome. No wonder Darlene could only remember the first three letters on the plate. That was all she could see.

I raced back to my car and headed downtown. As I drove, pieces of the puzzle swooped around and around in my head like airplanes waiting to land. The BMW had to be one of Dr. Nielsen's cars. Whoever was driving it would have had the garage door opener for sure and possibly access to the office as well. Office keys and car keys often share the same key ring. That would explain how the killer had unlocked the dead bolt to get inside.

But Darlene had said the driver of the foreign car was a man. What about that? Suddenly I remembered how Daisy and Rachel had looked once they donned their khaki Woodland Park Zoo docent uniforms. The matching pith helmets had totally concealed their hair. From a distance, especially if they had been seated in a fast-moving car, either one of them could have been mistaken for a man. For that matter, in the dim light of the garage, a pith helmet could have passed for a Washington State Patrol trooper's campaign hat.

After all, when the car had sped past her, Darlene Girvan was damn lucky just to be alive. I could hardly fault her powers of observation at a time like that.

I parked in the Public Safety Building garage and pushed my way into an already crowded elevator. I was headed for my cubicle, but Margie stopped me as I sprinted past her desk.

"Hey, have you heard the news?"

"What news?"

"Detective Lindstrom called in from Olympia. He was all excited. One of the license numbers belongs to Dr. Nielsen. He had stopped for coffee and spotted the name on the list while he was waiting for his food."

"I know," I said.

Margie's face fell. "Somebody already told you? I thought I'd get to you first."

I shook my head. "You did, but I'm a detective, remember? How long ago did you talk to him? Where is he now?"

"Only about fifteen minutes ago. I'm sure he's on his way back."

"All right. Get somebody to patch you back through to him. Tell him to get here on the double. I'll have the search warrant ready by the time he gets here."

The search warrant was signed and sitting on my desk long before Big Al showed his face. As I sat there waiting for him, I had some time to think. They weren't good thoughts.

Detectives usually get a real rush when they close a case. It's like an addictive drug, a high that we live for. But the rush was missing this time.

Every scrap of information we had gathered showed Dr. Frederick Nielsen to be something less than your basic, all-around nice guy. In fact, our victim was a wholesale son of a bitch who had learned what he knew about life at his father's knee. He had damaged and abused all those whose lives had touched his.

And now someone was going to have to track down his two LOL aunties, arrest them, and charge them with homicide.

It wasn't a task I relished.

CHAPTER 21

There's something almost un-American about reading someone their rights when they're wearing a red-checked gingham apron and kneading bread dough. Remembering Rachel's trick from the previous time, however, Al and I decided to cover both entrances to the Edinburgh Arms apartment. He went to the front door while I went around to the back.

Rachel was in the kitchen with her hands covered with flour. Tiny white specks dusted her eyebrows and eyelashes. Buddy was confined to a cage in one corner of the kitchen.

"Freeze, sucker," I heard through the screen door as soon as I knocked.

"Why, hello, Detective Beaumont," Rachel said, smiling in greeting and holding the door open to let me in. "How are you today? Cool weather like this always makes me want to bake, even in the summertime."

"This isn't a social visit, Rachel. Detective Lindstrom's at the front door." Through the dining room I heard Dorothy Nielsen call for Big Al to let himself in.

"Why, whatever is he doing there?" Rachel asked.

"What's your name? What's your name?" Buddy wanted to know.

I ignored him and focused all my attention on Rachel. "You gave us the slip the last time, remember? We're taking precautions."

Smiling again, she shrugged and returned to the counter, where she picked up a smooth round cushion of bread dough that had been sitting on a floured breadboard. "I explained all about that," she said. "I wanted to be the one to tell Dotty."

"I think it's time we stopped the charade, Rachel. We're here with a search warrant."

She stood there holding the dough, looking at me. "A search warrant?" she repeated, frowning. "What for?"

There were voices coming from the other room. Dorothy Nielsen had evidently captured Al and drawn him into conversation. Without waiting for him to show up in the kitchen, I pulled my plastic-covered copy of the Miranda warning from my pocket and began to recite it. After all these years I don't really need the cue card, but I keep it in my hand, just in case.

When I finished, Rachel was still holding the dough. She hadn't moved. "Why did you do that?"

"Because you and your sister are under investigation for the murder of your nephew."

The bread dough dropped unnoticed onto the breadboard.

"No!" she said.

"Yes," I responded. "Where were you on Saturday afternoon?"

"I was at the hospital, with Dotty."

"All afternoon?"

"From noon until four or so."

"Will anyone remember seeing you there?"

"I don't know. Dotty surely. I don't know about anybody else. The nurses perhaps."

Big Al appeared in the dining room doorway and was greeted by Buddy's usual salutation. Al made a face, but he spoke directly to Rachel. "Good afternoon, ma'am," he said. She didn't seem to notice him. Her eyes were glued on me.

"Tell us about your visit to Dr. Leonard's office that morning."

"What about it?"

"What happened?"

"She told us that Dotty refused to go into a

nursing home. She asked if we could have her here with us for a while."

For some reason, Rachel was still shying away from giving us totally straight answers. Verbally I forced her into a corner. "Why did she need a nursing home? Why couldn't she just go back home with her son?"

"She couldn't because he—" Rachel blurted, then she stopped.

"Because he what?"

She lifted the hem of the apron and wiped her hands with it. "He beat her," she said hopelessly, keeping her voice hushed and leveling a meaningful glance at the open doorway behind Big Al. "Freddie beat his own mother. I still can't believe it. The doctor said that's how her hip got broken."

"You never knew about it before Dr. Leonard told you?"

She shrugged. "We may have had our suspicions off and on over the years. I knew he ruled LeAnn with an iron fist, but I never thought he'd stoop to physical violence—not with LeAnn and certainly not with Dotty. She's his mother, for heaven's sake!"

"Is Saturday the first Daisy learned about it, too?"

"As far as I know. If Daze knew otherwise, she never mentioned it to me."

"Where was Daisy Saturday afternoon?" Big Al asked.

"The zoo, of course. Some of the time she works as an aide in animal health, but this week we've been busy getting ready for the Jungle Party. It's tonight, you know."

Al arched an eyebrow. "Animal health?" he asked. "Would she know how to run an autoclave?"

"Probably," Rachel said. "Why?"

"Never mind about that right now," I said. "What you're telling us is that Daisy wasn't with you at the hospital?"

"That's correct. She dropped me off on her way. I caught a bus home after visiting hours."

"Dr. Leonard told us you and Daisy were arguing as you left her office. What about?"

Rachel sighed. "It was something I said."

"What?"

"That Freddie was a worthless son of a bitch. That I wished he would die."

"Daisy disagreed with that?"

"She said someone needed to talk with him, to convince him that he needed help."

"Do you remember what Daisy was wearing that afternoon?"

"Her uniform. We had the appointment with Dr. Leonard, and then she had to get right over to the zoo. She had a tour scheduled for one o'clock. We all have to work a certain number of public contact hours, you see."

"So she was driving?"

Rachel nodded.

"Which car?"

"Freddie's. The one he gave Dotty. He told us we should drive it at least once a week to keep the battery charged."

"And what kind of car is it?"

"A nice one. A BMW. It's out in our garage. It's not that new, but it's a whole lot newer than our Buick. We thought we should try to keep it in out of the weather to protect the finish."

"Had it been in an accident the last time you saw it?"

Her eyes grew wide. "The BMW in an accident? No."

"It wasn't damaged when you saw it last?"

"Certainly not. It was fine. Daisy may drive fast on occasion, but she's not careless."

"Would you mind showing us the car."

"Of course not. Why would I mind?" She opened a drawer beside the kitchen door and removed a single key as well as another key ring; then she led us out to the garage. We went in by way of a door at the courtyard end of the garage.

"See there?" Rachel said triumphantly, pointing at the undamaged front end of the BMW. "What did I tell you?"

"You'd better take a look at the back," I said.

When she did, her jaw dropped. "When did this happen? It wasn't like this Saturday. Why didn't Daisy tell me about it?"

"Rachel," I said quietly, "would you mind doing us a favor?"

"What?" she asked.

"Is there any kind of check-in procedure at the zoo?"

"For docents, you mean?"

I nodded.

She looked at me for a long moment, then she nodded slowly. "So that's what you're thinking. That she didn't go to the zoo at all. We'll just see about that. I'll call and check. Once I do, you'll see you're making a terrible mistake." She turned and started briskly for the door.

"May I have the keys?" Al asked.

She whirled and glared back at us. "What for?"

"We have a search warrant to search your premises," I explained. "Including any vehicles."

I took the official document from my coat pocket and handed it to her. Without bothering to look at it, she flung the warrant and the keys on the floor of the garage and marched off toward the apartment with me on her heels.

We went back inside through the kitchen door. While Rachel dialed the zoo on the kitchen phone, Buddy tried desperately to draw me into conversation. "What's your name?" he whined plaintively. In his lonely kitchen exile, he was evidently quite miserable.

Rachel finally got through to the zoo and asked for someone to check the sign-in sheet. For several minutes she waited on hold, without speaking to me or acknowledging my presence. When the other person returned and began speaking, Rachel's head bobbed up and down in vigorous agreement.

"See there?" she said to me, holding the phone away from her mouth and covering the mouthpiece. "I told you she was there. Her signature is on the sheet right where it's supposed to be. In at twelve-thirty and out at three-thirty."

"How can that be? It doesn't make sense," I commented.

"Of course it makes sense," Rachel snapped. "I tried to tell you this was all a mistake."

"Did you say she was conducting tours?"

Rachel nodded.

"Who's in charge of them?"

"The tours? Madge," she answered. "She arranges the scheduling."

"Check with her and find out if Daisy actually appeared for her one o'clock tour."

Although Rachel clearly thought me unreasonable, she removed her hand from the receiver and asked to speak with Madge. It was a minute or so before she was connected.

"This is Rachel," she said into the phone. "Rachel Miller, Daisy's sister. I wanted to check on the tour Daze did on Saturday." There was a long pause and Rachel began to frown. "She didn't?" Her tone was incredulous. "You're sure?"

She listened to the answer, then hung up the phone. With a sigh she turned to face me. "Madge says Daisy never showed up. They held the tour for a while, but they finally had to send it out with somebody else. I don't understand. Why would she sign in and then not go on her tour?"

"Maybe she signed in and out later, hoping to give herself an alibi," I suggested.

Just then Al reappeared at the kitchen door. "You should come look at this, Beau." He nodded curtly in Rachel's direction. "You'd better come along, too."

"Rachel, what's happening in there?" Dorothy called from the living room. "I thought you were going to make us a pot of coffee."

"In a minute," Rachel replied. "I'm busy right now."

Big Al led the way back to the garage and around the car to the BMW's open trunk. "Look at that," he said.

A rumpled docent's uniform lay on the floor of the trunk. There had been some attempt to rinse the clothing out, but a splatter of brownish stains was still plainly evident on the material.

"That's Daisy's other uniform," Rachel said, "but what's that all over it? It looks like it's ruined."

"Try the shoes, Beau."

A pair of Maine waders lay at the front of the trunk. One was upright, but the other one had been knocked over on its side, revealing a distinctive chain-link pattern.

"It looks like the one Foster took from the scene," Al added, speaking guardedly.

"From the scene," Rachel echoed, looking back and forth between us. Suddenly everything we were saying seemed to coalesce in her mind. "You mean from my nephew's office? You're saying that's blood on Daisy's clothes?"

I nodded.

"Oh no," I heard her say. Without another word and in painfully slow motion, Rachel began slipping toward the floor. I caught her and pulled her to her feet, where she sagged in my arms like a limp rag doll. Still leaning heavily against me, she glanced once more toward the trunk, then turned away.

"It isn't true! It can't be true!"

"I'm afraid it is, Rachel. Where is your sister now?"

I expected a violent storm of tears. Instead, Rachel Miller shuddered visibly like a tree caught in a strong gale; then, with determined effort, she pulled away from me and drew herself erect.

"At the zoo," Rachel answered slowly, pronouncing each word slowly and carefully as though it belonged to some complex foreign language. "She's helping decorate for the party tonight. The guided tours don't start until five."

"What tours?"

"Behind-the-scenes tours, where people get to talk to the keepers and touch the animals. They put them on for the zoo patrons each year. Daisy's scheduled to work some of those."

"Will you help us find her?" I asked.

Rachel nodded in defeat. "Yes," she said, "but first let me call George. I'll see if he can come over and watch Dotty while we're gone. I can't leave her here all alone."

Following Rachel back into the house, we

waited while she talked to George. "He'll be over in half an hour," she said quietly when she put down the phone.

"Rachel," Dorothy demanded impatiently. "Isn't that coffee ready yet?"

With a sigh, Rachel turned to the cupboard and began making coffee. Al got on the phone and called Bill Foster.

"We need a crime-scene team out here right away," he said, giving Bill the address of the Edinburgh Arms and bringing him up to date. "I'll meet you out on the next street by the garages," he added. "There's no sense in your coming in here."

I dogged Rachel's heels while she made the coffee and set a tray with the special bone-china cups and saucers as well as a plate loaded with ancient Oreo cookies. She carried the tray into the living room and served her sister first, then she offered some to me.

It was a game gesture of hospitality, of carrying on with the niceties of life in the face of certain disaster. Out of respect for what she was doing, I accepted both the coffee and the cookie. I wasn't tough enough to turn her down.

While we waited for George to appear, Rachel carefully explained to Dorothy that she would have to be out for a while but that someone would be there in case anything was needed. It sounded like a mother explaining the presence of a baby-sitter to a willful child.

I didn't see Bill Foster arrive. The street was out of my range of vision, but Al came in a short time later and gave me a thumbs-up sign indicating the garage end of the situation was under control.

Rachel handed Al a cup of coffee, too, and there we sat, the four of us, all of us drinking coffee with three of us lying through our teeth. That's wrong. We were all four lying, come to think of it, but Dorothy Nielsen had been lying to herself and everybody else for so many years that she no longer knew the difference.

I could understand why Rachel wasn't ready to tell Dorothy the truth about what was going on. Big Al and I followed her lead. It was the least we could do.

When George finally showed up, Rachel met him outside. His initial grin at seeing her quickly faded as she talked to him, outlining the problem. He was somber but nodding in agreement as they came into the apartment.

"I'll be glad to stay just as long as you need me to, Rachel," he was saying.

Rachel smiled up at him gratefully, then she turned to me. "I should go upstairs and put on my uniform," she said. "It'll make it a whole lot easier for us to get around in the zoo."

Big Al and I exchanged wary glances. We'd been led down the primrose path on this kind of deal once before by the very same lady.

She read our reluctance correctly. "It's okay," she said. "There's no outside door up there."

"How about windows?" I asked.

"I told you I'd help," she answered.

In the end, we let her go upstairs to change. She was back downstairs in her uniform in less than five minutes.

"We'd better get started," she said, leading the way to the door. "The zoo's a big place. It'll be crowded."

It was one of the world's all-time understatements.

CHAPTER 22

On the way to the zoo, Big Al drove and I rode shotgun, while Rachel sat in the backseat. Big Al looked at me and nodded toward the radio. "Get dispatch and have them send us out some help," he suggested.

"What good would that do?" I returned. "Nobody else down there knows what she looks like."

"But if we try to do it all ourselves, it'll take forever. This place is huge. I brought my grandson here a couple of times. He walked both my legs off."

"It's only ninety-two acres," Rachel said reassuringly from the backseat.

"Ninety-two acres is a hell of a lot of territory for three of us to cover. Get us some help," Al insisted irritably.

"You know what comes with help," I argued. "Reporters, television cameras, the works."

"Please, no cameras," Rachel begged.

Her whole short course in media relations came from what had happened to her as a result of her nephew's murder. She may not have had my kind of longevity in the battle, but Rachel Miller and I were very much of the same mind when it came to the media. She didn't want her sister hunted down with nosy cameras recording the arrest.

In the end, Rachel's plea swung the vote. Al reluctantly conceded defeat, and that's how the three of us—two seasoned homicide detectives and a gray-haired little old lady—scrambled out of a departmental vehicle at the western entrance to the Woodland Park Zoo. We hurried inside with one single purpose: find Daisy Carmichael.

The Woodland Park Zoo got its start in 1903 when the City of Seattle purchased a pioneer family's estate and left a previously established herd of deer in residence. With the addition of various animals, the zoo evolved gradually over the years until the thirties when major development work was done by Frederick Olmsted, the same man who created Central Park in New York City.

Rachel had told us that the zoo covers ninety-two acres, and it's true.

If you happen to be a wheat farmer who lives in the vast rolling hills of Washington's Palouse, ninety-two acres probably doesn't sound like much. And ninety-two acres is small potatoes when compared to the eight hundred acres in Central Park. But on a rainy summer's day, with only three people searching for a fourth, ninety-two acres is plenty big enough.

Rachel Miller took off like a shot and led us into the zoo through a building marked ARC. That may sound like a cutesy reference to Noah, but it actually stands for Activities and Recreation Center. The place was bursting at the seams with dozens of children who streamed in and out of a room marked DISCOVERY. Echoes of laughter from a noisy slide show leaked out of the room into the lobby, where Rachel left us standing while she hurried off down a hallway marked EMPLOYEES ONLY.

"Something's bothering me," Big Al said after she left.

"What's that?"

"If Daisy took all that time and trouble to clean up the dental pick and rinse off her clothes, why the hell didn't she get rid of them before we found them?"

"Maybe she never got the chance," I suggested.

"From what Dr. Leonard said, they've been busy as hell getting ready to move Dorothy into the house. Or maybe Daisy figured she'd get caught eventually and that it wouldn't do her any good. Sometimes people want to get caught."

"Right up until they hear the iron door of the slammer," Big Al observed. "Then they chicken out."

I heard his words and felt the gut-wrenching pain I always feel when something reminds me of the past I keep trying to forget. Al had no way of knowing how his words affected me. He wasn't my partner then. We barely even knew each other. If he had heard about Anne Corley at all, it was only peripherally, but his casual comment there in the buzzing zoo lobby jarred me good.

Making a pretense of checking out the children's slide show, I walked away from him. I wandered into the Discovery Room and stood for a long time peering over the shoulder of a little girl who was engrossed in trying to reassemble the skeleton of a long-dead turtle. Eventually I got myself back under control and returned to the lobby just as Rachel hurried into the room. She was frowning, shaking her head.

"I don't understand it—Daisy isn't officially scheduled to be here working at all. I was sure she told me she was leading some of the behind-the-scenes tours. She always does that, but her name isn't on the list."

"What did I tell you?" Big Al muttered under his breath. "This whole thing is nothing but a wild-goose chase, if you ask me."

"I'm sure she's here," Rachel insisted. "Where else would she be?"

"Try Mexico, maybe," Big Al suggested dourly. His remark wasn't lost on Rachel, who gave him a withering look as she marched away, leaving us no choice but to tag along behind her.

She led us around to the back of the building where a waterproofed notebook hung by a chain from a peg in the wall. Rachel lifted it down. When she opened it, I could see that the notebook contained a volunteer sign in/sign-out sheet. Rachel made a notation after her own name, then scanned up the list until she located Daisy's.

"See there?" Rachel announced with a sharp glance in Al's direction. "She's here. I told you she was."

He shook his massive head. "All that means is she signed in. She could have done that any time—yesterday or the day before, for that matter. There's no time clock, no way to check it. And it doesn't mean she's still here, either."

"So where do we start?" I asked, wanting to begin the search before Big Al could think of another reason to call the whole thing off or bring in reinforcements.

"The north meadow," Rachel answered. "That's where the tents are. Maybe she's helping set up for the dinner or the auction."

Finding a lost person at the Woodland Park Zoo would be a tough assignment on any ordinary day, but on the day of the Jungle Party, it was a joke. The Jungle Party is an annual affair, the zoo's one big fling of a fundraiser. The place was a madhouse.

Rachel left the building and set off in a beeline for a huge white-and-yellow-striped tent that had been erected in a clearing northeast of the activities center. To one side of the main tent were two smaller ones.

"They're for the silent auction," Rachel explained as we passed the smaller tents. "The big one is for the dinner and the live auction."

The large tent must have been at least 150 feet long by 80 feet wide. One side and one end were open. A raised stage ran the length of the open side. On it auction items were being displayed. Behind the short closed end, a caterer's caravan of trucks was setting up shop.

Inside the carvernous tent itself a small

army of workers erected tables and covered them with brilliant wine red underskirting and plush white table linen. Tall stacks of wooden chairs with padded seats were scattered here and there around the area, waiting to be put in place once the tables were dressed. The end result looked far more like the huge dining room of a fine hotel rather than the interior of an outdoor tent.

Rachel beckoned for us to follow her as she threaded her way through various groups of workers. Now and then she stopped to ask someone if they had seen Daisy. The answer was always negative. We searched through all three tents to no avail.

"She must not be working on setup," Rachel admitted at last.

"So what now?" Al asked.

"Keep looking," I said. "Rachel, you lead the way."

Big Al grunted an objection, but he trudged along behind me as I followed Rachel out of the last tent. We moved north and east, leaving in our wake the three tents and all their feverish activity.

I have no idea how many people were at Woodland Park Zoo that afternoon. Hundreds for sure, maybe even thousands. It seemed like that many.

Aside from the people directly involved in

preparation for the banquet, the place was alive with Parks and Recreation personnel putting a spit-and-polish face-lift on the grounds for the mayor's annual obligatory visit. Add to that the regular zoo staff members plus a whole wad of uniformed docents. All told, it made quite a crowd before you got around to counting the ordinary zoo-viewing public.

The zoo-viewing public is a world unto itself.

By the middle of July, frantic mothers all over the city had finally realized just how long they had to hold out before being able to send their little darlings back to schools and teachers, where they belonged. Desperate to get their children out of the house, even at the cost of going out in the rain, mothers by the hundreds had flocked to the zoo with their broods that soggy afternoon.

The animals were locked up. Believe me, they should have been grateful. Hordes of children, very few on leashes or under voice control, were running loose and tearing the place apart. They were everywhere at once—in, over, under, around, up, and down—playing tag and war and screaming at the tops of their lungs.

Evidently, Big Al was thinking much the same thing. Two howling children darted between us and one of them landed squarely on his toe.

"These goddamned kids are the ones who ought to be in cages," he fumed. It was a private exchange, meant for my ears only, but Rachel picked up on it.

She glanced back over her shoulder. "We don't call them cages here," she chided. "They're exhibits."

If the situation hadn't been so serious, it might have been comical. I had to take my hat off to whoever was in charge of docent training. It was brain washing of the first water since Rachel's docent background was still fully alive and functioning on automatic, despite the grim circumstances.

It was four by the time Rachel led us past the bison, wolves, elk, and deer. As she walked, she continued to regale us with a running commentary on the animals and the zoo as well. Al was impatient and wanted to shut her up, but I understood and encouraged her with questions. The constant chatter was a reflex, a defense mechanism that allowed her to move through the process without thinking too much about exactly what we were doing. Or why we were doing it.

It started misting as we passed the snow leopards and the feline house, making me painfully aware that my lightweight summer jacket was neither water- nor weatherproof. The rain was falling harder by the time we got to the bear grotto, and it turned into a wholesale downpour before we reached the gorillas.

We were all soaked to the skin and Big Al was surly as hell by the time we reached the inside of the gorilla exhibit and huddled under the roofed-over part for shelter from the rain.

"This is stupid," Al muttered. "We've walked all over hell and gone and still no sign of her. Aren't you ready to give up yet?"

"No," Rachel insisted. "Please don't quit looking, not yet. I'm sure we'll find her."

Al shook his head in disgust while I kept my mouth shut. He had slipped off a shoe and was standing balanced on one foot while he massaged the sole of the other.

"What say we call in some troops now, Beau," he began. "That way we can at least get some coverage on the gates. Doing it this way doesn't make sense."

I walked over to the glass window of the exhibit. The gorillas didn't like rain any more than we did. They had come into their part of the shelter and were busily tossing loose hay around, making nests for themselves, and playing with a scatter of burlap bags left for casual games of tug-of-war.

One of them, a big male, looked up at me sadly, our eyes meeting through the steamy glass for several long seconds before he looked dispiritedly away. Al was right in principle. Bringing in more officers would ensure our finding Daisy Carmichael before she had a chance to slip through our fingers.

But calling for reserves would bring a pack of reporters in their wake as well. We'd be doing our job under much the same kind of scrutiny as that in which these gorillas did. I hated it—for the gorillas, for me, and, most of all, for Daisy Carmichael.

"No," I said, hearing the stubborn insistence in my own voice. "No reserves. We'll find her. Go home if you want to, Al, but I'm going to keep on looking. I'm going to look till I find her."

Big Al sighed. He wasn't a quitter, at least not yet. He put his shoe back on and straightened up. "All right, all right. Where to now?"

The rain let up finally and we set out walking again. Rachel seemed to be following some habitual route. By then it was after five. In addition to the families still lingering in the zoo we were beginning to see a few groups of evening-clad couples, people dressed in tuxedos and long dresses, the first arrivals eager to catch a behind-the-scenes tour.

One lady, a wildly red-haired one, wore a lush fur draped over one shoulder. Considering she was a visiting a zoo, that struck me as particularly tacky.

By six, Big Al was again ready to throw in the towel. We had made still another full circle of the grounds and were back by the zoo entrance when he stopped dead in his tracks.

"I'm not taking another fucking step," he whispered to me. "My feet are killing me."

"Go, then," I told him. "Take the car back to the department. I'll catch a bus home later."

Without realizing we were no longer following her, Rachel had walked on ahead. Now she returned. "What's the matter?" she asked.

"Detective Lindstrom has to leave," I said. "He's going to take the car and go back downtown. Why don't you call home and check with George to see if by any chance Daisy has shown up there?"

"That's the first sensible thing anybody has said for hours," Big Al grumbled. Rachel headed for the ARC to use the phone. "Are you sure you don't mind if I bail out on you?" Al asked.

"Not at all," I told him. "Go. Molly's probably waiting dinner. I've got nothing better to do."

Al was gone by the time Rachel returned.

"George says there's been no sign of her," Rachel said.

That didn't surprise me. Like Rachel, I was

still convinced that Daisy was somewhere on the grounds, but unlike Rachel, I didn't have a good feeling about it.

"Is there any animal here that's a particular favorite of hers?" I asked.

Rachel puzzled that one for a moment or two. "Daisy likes the giraffes," she answered. "The giraffes and the elephants both."

We had already visited both compounds several times, but what we had done so far wasn't working. "Tell you what," I said. "You've been walking all afternoon. Would you like to catch up with Al and have him give you a ride home?"

She stood there looking up at me for several moments, her eyes searching my face.

"What's going to happen to Daisy when we find her, Detective Beaumont? Will she have to go to prison?"

"I don't know, Rachel," I said, shaking my head. "Sorry. That's up to the courts. I'm a detective, not a judge. But she'll be a hell of a lot better off if you and I find her first, before the department issues an All Points Bulletin."

I let Rachel think that one over. Now that it was just the two of us searching, there was a fifty-fifty chance that she would be the one to find her. If that happened, if Rachel found Daisy first when I wasn't around, there was a good possibility she'd warn her, let her get away. Maybe that's really what I wanted. Maybe deep in the bottom of my subconscious that's what I hoped would happen.

Rachel Miller met my gaze without blinking or looking away. "What do you want me to do?" she asked simply. She was in for the duration and so was I.

"You go to the savanna and look for her there. I'll hang around the elephants. If you see her, come get me right away, understand?"

"All right," Rachel said. She hurried away.

Once she was gone, I straightened my shoulders and pulled in my gut. My feet hurt, too.

I was just too damn stubborn to admit it.

CHAPTER 23

I love stakeouts in the movies. They usually happen on fashionable streets, preferably ones with sidewalk cafes and lots of beautiful women. The hero sits comfortably at a table, casually pretending to read a newspaper and looking unobtrusive. Invisible, even. If no sidewalk cafe happens to be in the script, the hero still reads a newspaper, leaning against a nearby building.

This is unobtrusive? When's the last time you leaned against a building to read a newspaper?

The logistics of my finding Daisy Carmichael in the Woodland Park Zoo were a little more complicated than a Hollywood version of a stakeout. For one thing, we both knew each other on sight. If I recognized her, she would recognize me.

And was it better for me to stand in one place in hopes she would wander past, or should I mingle on the outskirts of the groups gathering for the Jungle Party? In the end, I did a combination of both.

I developed a pattern. After making a slow circle around the elephant enclosure and passing the prairie dog compound, I'd saunter over to the north meadow, past the pony rides, and into the tents. Booze flowed freely at the party. Everybody knows that tipsy auction attendees spend way more money than cold sober ones do. I'd make one pass through each of the tents, then wander back to the elephant enclosure again.

It was boring, lonesome, tedious work, especially since all those other people seemed to be having such a good time.

Not only that, I don't like zoos. Never have. Walking around and around it by myself that night did nothing to change my opinion.

When the kids were little, Karen thought taking Kelly and Scott to the zoo on a Saturday afternoon should have been top on my list of favorite fatherly pastimes. Except standing on one side of a set of iron bars looking at someone or something on the other side isn't my idea of a diversion. It reminds me too much of my job.

And zoos make me claustrophobic. They are built like mazes with no panoramic viewpoints where you can see from one end to the other. They're designed so each little piece of habitat is separated from all the others by a discreet hedge or a wall of trees or a curtain of bamboo shoots. It may be good for the animals' sense of privacy, but it sure as hell doesn't help when you're a police officer looking for a lady who isn't especially interested in being found.

By seven the rain had finally stopped, but the air was still moist and heavy, as though Mother Nature wasn't quite through with us yet. For probably the tenth time, I walked around to the back side of the elephant compound where a docent, not Daisy Carmichael, was giving a talk on elephants to a group of wide-eyed children.

They gasped and pointed with delight as one by one, four elephants came out of the barn into the moat-encircled compound. Two of the four were fully grown while the other two were obviously much younger. The smaller ones bounded into a round, elephant-sized swimming pool, playing and floating there briefly, while excess water splashed over the edges in foot-high waves.

One of the children broke away from the group and went scrambling toward the concrete fence. "I want to pet Dumbo," he called over his shoulder. "Here, Dumbo. Here, Dumbo."

The docent grabbed the kid by one arm and hauled him off the fence. "You mustn't do that! Ever! Elephants are very, very dangerous. This exhibit is their home. They don't like strangers coming into it."

"Dumbo wouldn't hurt me," the kid insisted tearfully. "I know he wouldn't. Anyway, if he tried to, I'd run."

"Elephants can run lots faster than people can," the docent explained.

"Even faster than grown-ups?" the little kid asked wonderingly.

"Faster than grown-ups," the docent replied, nodding.

Grasping the recalcitrant youngster by the hand, she led the group away, announcing firmly that it was time to go see the ponies.

"Way to go!" I said to her as she walked past me. "You handled that like a champ."

She smiled her thanks and kept on going, still holding tightly to the little boy's hand.

Time passed—how long, I'm not sure. Off and on I heard a distant rumble of thunder, a promise of more rain to come. Rain is common in Seattle. Thunder and lightning aren't. The elephants responded to each rumble by raising their heads, flapping their ears, and swinging their gigantic trunks from side to side. The biggest one, an African elephant, stood a good ten feet high and must have weighed nine thousand pounds. She ruled the roost in that compound. The younger ones, once they came out of the pool, were careful to stay at a respectful distance.

They moved with a peculiar, ponderous grace, the weight of their bodies landing on their toes as they walked. The smell of their bodies in the damp air was sharp and pungent.

Several groups of well-dressed visitors came through and were invited inside the glassed-in part of the elephant enclosure. Painted on the concrete floor inside was a yellow line marked DANGER. The visitors were careful to stand well back behind the yellow line with their backs to the windows while the handlers stood in what seemed to be nonchalant poses with their backs to their charges. Careful examination, however, revealed metal-and-wood elephant hooks tucked under the keepers' arms.

Each time a group came into the barn, the elephants would come in from outside, too, as if on command. It didn't take a Philadelphia lawyer to figure out why. At the end of each lecture, the keepers allowed the visitors to hand out carrots, passing them one at a time to the four eager, outstretched trunks that reached through the bars.

It was getting later, but still there was no sign of Daisy. And the smell of the food from the caterer's trucks was tantalizing. I hadn't eaten all day. On my next pass through the party area, I stopped at the door of the large tent where a sweet young thing in a bright blue dress was collecting invitations and marking off names on a sheet of paper. I waited in line to talk with her.

"Your invitation, please," she said, smiling up at me.

"I don't have one," I said, flashing my badge. "I'm working security."

"Oh," she said. "Okay. Go on in."

I did. I wandered in and out of the tent at will after that, always nodding pleasantly to the same ticket taker as I did so.

By now, most of the ordinary people had left the zoo. Only partygoers remained. At seven-thirty a gong sounded, signaling the end of the first silent auction. It was followed immediately by a clap of thunder. I was standing outside the elephant enclosure, watching. At the sound of the thunder, their heads and ears came up, their tails twitched. The pending storm made them nervous, agitated. As the rain started in earnest, they headed for the barn, and I followed suit, dashing for the main tent, not only to get in out of the rain, but also because I was starved.

By this time, the ticket taker knew me by sight.

"Any extra places?" I asked.

"Sure," she answered. "Help yourself."

Taking a blank check from my wallet, I filled it out and handed it to her. The amount was more than she expected.

"Sit anywhere you like," she said. "Anywhere at all."

Finding a table with one empty chair, I settled in.

I probably wasn't a very pleasant dinner companion. Unlike the others at my table, I hadn't consumed several drinks. They were well oiled and fully primed for the auction. I was only there to eat.

I must have been hungry. I gulped my salmon bisque, ignoring its close similarity to Rachel Miller's tomato soup. I mowed my way through a swordfish steak and a huge baked potato. I didn't bother to hang around for dessert, because by then the rain had stopped.

It was eight-thirty when I returned to the elephant compound for the last time. It was approaching dusk. As I left the tent, people were setting out sand-filled paper sacks with candles in them, lighting the luminaria as they went. Seeing them, I noticed that there was no interior lighting in the zoo.

As I neared the elephant barn, a large wooden gate next to it opened from the inside. A man I recognized as one of the keepers came out.

"Hello," he said. "Can I help you?"

"I'm looking for someone," I told him.

"There's no one here. The last of the tours ended over an hour ago. I stayed around because the elephants were so upset by the storm."

"You might know the person I'm looking for. She's one of the docents. Her name is Daisy."

"Oh, you mean Daisy Carmichael? She was here earlier, on the last tour I believe, now that you mention it. I remember seeing her here, but I don't recall seeing her leave."

"Jesus Christ!"

"What's wrong?" he demanded.

"What if she's still in there?"

"I told you, I'm the only one here."

I wheeled away from him and set off at a dead run, past the barn and around to the other side of the enclosure. I glanced in the window as I went past. Three of the elephants were still in the barn. I could see their dark separate bulks in the barn's shadowy interior.

But one of them, the biggest one, wasn't there.

When I came around the side of the barn, I saw a sight I'll never forget as long as I live. Even now, thinking about it brings an involuntary clutch of fear to my gut.

Daisy Carmichael was there, cowering against the wall of the moat, transfixed like a mouse hypnotized by a stalking cat. And that's precisely what the elephant was doing. The big African female was stalking her, moving imperceptibly, tiptoeing forward, ears up, head raised. Periodically she would stop and stand absolutely still with one foot lifted like a bird dog on point.

It was a moment frozen in time. I thought about Daisy. I thought about my Smith and Wesson. What good would a puny .38 do against a nine-thousand-pound elephant? And I thought about the mayor and his wife sitting at the head table in the banquet tent less than a hundred yards away.

I ran around the side of the moat, stopping just above her. "Daisy!" I screamed down at her. "Get out of there! Give me your hand!"

I bent over the side of the moat and reached out my hand. But she didn't move. Didn't seem to hear me or know I was there.

"Daisy!" I commanded. "Come on!"

She looked up at me then with sheer, uncomprehending terror written on her face. Still she didn't move.

The elephant took another step. She was almost on top of Daisy now. One more step and it would be too late. The .38 was in my hand. I was conscious of a fleeting thought about what would happen to me if I shot one of the mayor's goddamned elephants. But I couldn't just stand there and let it happen.

And that's when I jumped.

"*No!*" I roared. The instinctive word blasted out of me like a cannon shot.

My feet landed on something soft and mushy. I slipped in it and fell, but it broke the impact enough to keep me from smashing my ass. I struggled to my feet with the Smith and Wesson still clutched in my hand. Miraculously, the elephant had stopped moving.

Behind her the keeper appeared with a yard-long elephant hook in hand. "No!" he was shouting. "Back!"

And then, the elephant was moving back. One slow ponderous step at a time, but she was moving back.

"Stay there," the keeper bellowed over his shoulder. "Don't move until I have her in the barn."

He didn't have to say it twice. I glanced at Daisy. She was slumped against the wall, fainted dead away.

Once the four elephants were locked in the barn, the handler came back and helped me carry the unconscious woman into the keepers' office outside the enclosure.

"How the hell did she get in there?" he demanded. "She must have slipped through the bars when I wasn't looking."

We dialed 911 to get an aid car. She was coming around by then, but I wanted her checked out by a medic.

"You need one, too," the keeper said to me. "Your foot."

Up until he said that, I didn't know I was hurt, but once he pointed it out, my foot hurt like hell. It also stunk.

"What made the elephant stop?" I asked, still puzzling over the fact that the animal wasn't moving when I had scrambled to my feet.

"Elephants are dominant animals," he explained. "Man can't dominate them physically, so we do it mentally. You said one of the few words she happens to know, and you said it like you meant it. That's what stopped her."

"I'll be a son of a bitch," I muttered.

"A *lucky* son of a bitch," he added.

Daisy was fully conscious by then. "You shouldn't have," she said, averting her face. "I didn't want to be saved."

I moved over to where she was lying wrapped in a blanket on the floor.

"I saw you outside the barn. I knew then that you must have found out about me. Dorothy's still my little sister, you know. Fred shouldn't have done that. But I didn't want to go home and face her."

"There are worse things than that," I told her, although right that minute I was hard-pressed to think of any.

We sat there in silence, waiting for Medic One. It was over, I'd found the killer and she'd confessed. Why the hell did I feel so rotten? And then it dawned on me. I started to laugh.

"What's so funny?" the keeper asked. He must have thought I was going into shock.

By then I was laughing so hard, I could barely talk. "I forgot—" I managed, gasping for breath. "I forgot to read her her rights."

"That's funny?" he asked.

"Take my word for it," I said finally, pulling myself together. "It's a scream."

Unfortunately, the aid car came with full sirens blaring. It brought the curious flocking out of the tents and away from the volunteer potluck in the family farm. It also brought the news media—not the usual crime-scene slugs, but the ones who write for Seattle's society pages. There weren't that many faces I knew. The society page isn't my customary territory.

I didn't know them, and they didn't know me, either.

The medics checked Daisy, then one of them came over to me. "The lady's all right," he said. "What do you want us to do with her?"

"Take her up to Harborview," I said.

"The psycho ward?" he asked.

"You got it."

"There's another lady outside who claims to be her sister. Should we bring her along?"

I nodded.

"What about you?" he asked. "Somebody should X-ray that foot."

By the time I limped out to get in the ambulance, the mayor and his wife were standing right next to it. There was no way of getting in without walking directly past them.

"I understand you're a Seattle police officer?" the mayor asked.

I nodded wearily. "That's right," I said.

"What's your name?"

The jig was up. "Detective Beaumont," I said, wishing I could have thought of someone else's name. "Detective J. P. Beaumont."

"Nice going, Detective Beaumont," the mayor said. "I'll see that you get a commendation for this."

I wonder what he would have done if I had used the gun.

CHAPTER 24

I was still waiting for word on my X rays when Sergeant Watkins came striding into the emergency room. "You must like this place, Beaumont. Seems like you spend half your life here."

"Don't give me any crap, Watty. I'm not up to it."

"And another psychiatric observation case? What do you think, the department wants to fund a complete mental hospital?"

"Please."

"All right, all right," he relented. "But what have you got? Captain Powell dragged me out of bed and told me to get down here on the double."

Wordlessly, I handed him a letter Rachel had brought in to me. She had found it in

Daisy's jacket pocket. It was a signed suicide note that admitted the murder of Dr. Frederick Nielsen. It said that when she tried to talk to him, he was passed out. Drunk, she thought. She had attacked him without realizing what she was doing. The note went on to talk about wanting to dance with the elephants once before she died.

Watty read it over and handed it back to me with a shrug. "Maybe you're right. She sounds crazy to me."

"Incidentally," he added. "His Honor the Mayor called the chief and told him what you'd done. He says there's a movie company coming to town in the next few weeks to do some location filming on a murder thriller. He wants you to work with them as a special technical advisor."

"Jesus Christ, Watty! That's the last thing I want to do."

"The mayor thinks it's a reward. You'll do it and like it, Beau. That's an order."

We dropped the subject. "What about Larry Martin?" I asked.

"Richard Damm refuses to press charges. He says it was his own damn fault. With this letter, I suppose I'd better see about getting Martin released."

"Good," I said.

Just then the doctor came in carrying my X

rays. "I've got some good news for you, Detective Beaumont," he said. "Nothing's broken, but did you know you've got a bone spur?"

"A what?"

"A bone spur. It's an old injury that you've hurt again. Those things happen as we get older."

He was maybe thirty-five years old, and he said it with an engaging grin, but I wanted to punch his lights out all the same.

"Here's something that should help you get some sleep tonight, and an antiinflammatory prescription for later. You'll have to take these for a month or so. At least until the pain goes away."

"Fan-goddamn-tastic," I told him.

"The car's right outside, Beau," Watty said. "I'll give you a ride home."

Rachel's suitor, George, was just pulling up in the Buick as I hobbled out the emergency room door.

"Where is she?" he asked, hurrying up to me.

"Upstairs, with Daisy."

"Is Daisy all right?"

I nodded.

"And what about Rachel?"

"She's all right, too, but she's going to need all the help she can get," I said.

"What's going to happen to Daisy?" he asked.

I shrugged. "It's hard to say. Years ago, she would have gone to prison, no question. These days, things are different. It depends on premeditation, frame of mind, any number of things. It's up to the judge and jury."

"I see," he said. "Well, I'll go tell Rachel. I know she's worried about it."

When George walked away, Watty and I got into his car, the sergeant's own private car. "Dammit, Beau! Roll down your window, will you? Your shoes stink like hell!"

"You'd stink too if you'd been rolling around in elephant shit," I told him.

He dropped me in front of Belltown Terrace. It seemed like days had passed, maybe whole weeks, since Big Al Lindstrom had picked me up there that morning.

My idea was to slink into the building, sneak upstairs, and dive into my shower. Unfortunately, the elevator stopped on the eighteenth floor and the door opened. The first person I saw was Peters, sitting in a wheelchair.

"You girls shouldn't push both buttons at the same time," he was scolding. Just then he looked up and recognized me. "Hey, Beau, you missed the party. It was great, but now we've got to get back to the hospital before they send out a search party."

Laughing and joking, everybody piled into the elevator—Amy, pushing the wheelchair, Tracie, and Heather.

"Guess what, Unca Beau," Heather lisped, tugging at my shirt sleeve. "Tracie and I are going to get another mommie, and she's it." Heather pointed at Amy, who smiled and nodded in return.

"And we get to be in the wedding," Tracie added excitedly. "Amy says we can both have long dresses. Won't that be neat?"

"It'll be neat, all right," I said wearily.

The elevator door closed and we continued going up, all of us.

"How come you stink so bad?" Heather demanded wrinkling her nose.

"It's a long story," I said.

They all got off at my floor. Amy showed me her ring, and I gave the bride-to-be a careful peck on the cheek, making sure that neither my clothes nor shoes made physical contact.

"How was dinner?" I asked as I stepped away.

"Terrific," Amy said.

"Yeah," Peters added. "Tom even sent over a complimentary bottle of wine. Columbia White Zinfadel."

"Tom? Who's Tom?"

"Tom Girvan, the owner. I thought you said you knew him."

"The person I know is Darlene."

"She's his wife," Peters said. "We met her too. She's a real kick, isn't she? And did you know they're moving down to the waterfront? Better location, I guess." He turned back to his daughters. "Well, we'd better be going. The kids were just riding down to the lobby with us. Mrs. Edwards will be worried. Go ahead and press the button, Heather."

In a moment they were gone and I was alone in the elevator lobby. "His *wife*," I said to myself, repeating aloud the words Peters had spoken. "Tom Girvan's wife. I'm a son of a bitch."

Once in my apartment, I didn't bother to turn on any lights. Instead, I went straight to the deck, stripped off my smelly clothes, and left them outside in a heap. Then I went into the bathroom for a long hot shower followed by a longer, hotter Jacuzzi.

So Darlene, the purveyor of pork chop sandwiches, was actually a married lady.

Funny, she never mentioned that. On the other hand, to be fair, I had to admit that I had never asked.

It was probably just as well they were moving to the waterfront. It would help keep me out of trouble.